Copyright © 2024 by Adrian R. Hale

All rights reserved.

Cover design by Sarah Kill Creative Studio

https://www.SarahKillCreativeStudio.com

Edited by KC Enders

https://www.kcenderswrites.com

THE
BOURBON
Bride

ADRIAN R. HALE

Also by Adrian R. Hale

A Taste of Bliss
Drift Series
Drift Heat
Broken Drift
Southern Gods Series
The Bourbon Bride
The Bourbon Bargain
The Southern Thirst Trap
The Southern Submission

Playlist

You're On Your Own Kid — Taylor Swift
Whiskey — Devin Dawson
Take Your Time — Sam Hunt
Dark Side — Bishop Briggs
I Am Easy To Find — The National
Good Girl Gone Missin' — Morgan Wallen
Getaway Car — Taylor Swift
Welcome To Atlanta — Jermaine Dupri, Ludacris
Waiting Game — BANKS
All Of The Girls You Loved Before — Taylor Swift
Power Over Me — Dermot Kennedy
Dress — Taylor Swift
Don't Blame Me — Taylor Swift
Truly, Madly, Deeply — Yoke Lore
King Of My Heart — Taylor Swift
Weeping Willow — Warren Zeiders
Mastermind — Taylor Swift
Glory — Dermot Kennedy
I Did Something Bad — Taylor Swift
Lose Control - Strings Version — Teddy Swims
Bigger Than The Whole Sky — Taylor Swift

Content Warning

This story contains mention of attempted sexual assault, suggested marriage to an abuser, explicit sexual content, profanity, violence, and topics that may be sensitive to some readers. Your mental health matters. If these themes are triggering, this may not be the book for you. This story is best suited for readers 18+.

For anyone who has ever thought they weren't quite
enough — you are.

One

Paige

If being fed to the wolves will guarantee my freedom, I'll gladly offer myself up as a sacrifice every time. That's the only reason I am wearing a poofy white dress and standing on the threshold of an antiquated tradition to please the woman who dictates every stage of my life. It's always a possibility that *this* will be the last demand and I will finally have the control I so desperately crave for my own life. Or it could all be wishful thinking. It's a gamble I take for the potential reward, even when I more often than not end up disappointed.

"You ready, sweet pea?"

I look up into Daddy's lightly wrinkled face and give him a nervous smile.

Am I ready? Heck no. I just spent thirty minutes hyperventilating and trying not to get nervous sweat all over the bodice of this vintage Christian Dior dress.

I'm so not ready, I could easily slip out of Daddy's reach and pull a Homer Simpson becoming one with a hedge to disappear.

In fact, I would rather strip naked and swim in the fountain at Forsyth Park than walk down those stairs.

I sigh. I'm so far from ready, but this debutante ball is rolling and Mama will murder me, with a sugary sweet smile on her face while she does it, if I don't walk down these stairs into that party right on cue.

"Of course. Lead the way."

It's not that I'm worried about walking in heels or a giant dress; cotillion classes cured that in my teens. I'm also not worried about being in front of a large audience; Mama cured that issue by forcing me into a short-lived pageant career and untold volunteer hours leading history tours in period-correct clothing.

No. What I'm actually worried about is being the daughter my mama wishes I were. The perfectly poised, sweet as sugar, obedient little doll she can dress up, who's willing to follow every instruction to the letter. That's the daughter she has always wanted, and I've always been a little too quick to object or question her, a little too opinionated and desperate to find my own way.

"You look beautiful, my darling. Your mama and I are so proud. Thank you for doing this."

Daddy gives me a quick squeeze and holds out his arm for me to take. He understands my desire to not be here at The Abyss, making my debut to society like a proper Southern belle, yet we're both just pawns in Mama's society chess game and have no say in the matter.

I lift my chin and put on the expected demure smile. My white gown rustles with my steps as we descend the stairs into The Abyss and look out at the sea of black-tie and ball gowns.

I leveraged the unusual location for my debutante ball, insisting that it had to be here or nowhere if Mama was going to make this happen at all, and she finally gave in, which is a miracle in itself. It's the most exclusive nightclub in Savannah, at the very least, which seemed to pacify her indignation at not using our family's historic antebellum home-turned-boutique-hotel called The Mansion. That would have been her preference, as it would show me off along with our property which is the jewel of Savannah. Unlike the tarnished rhinestone I often feel like, given Mama's frequent criticisms.

Mine is the last ball of the season, Mama insisted. It's done up even more lavishly than the over-the-top affair Margot Declan, the mayor's eighteen-year-old daughter, put on last month. I declined to be a part of the International Debutante Ball in New York in January, so Mama made her one chance at showing me off count. It's a waste of money if you ask me, but there are some things I can't convince Mrs. Caroline Thackery Fairchild of, and my not debuting was one of them.

"Look at all the gaudy wealth in one room, Daddy," I whisper through my perfect smile like a ventriloquist. Fun fact: Mama made me study ventriloquism when she was pushing me to do pageants as a kid. I put my foot down with the dummies, but it didn't stop her from purchasing one anyway. I finally gave that creepy thing away to the granddaughter of my favorite doorman at The Mansion a few years back.

"You'd think they would have something better to do than gawk at the spinster deb on her entry to society."

Daddy chuckles next to me. "My darling, you are not a spinster. You're just stubborn and wanted to push your mama to her brink when it came to the timing of this event."

At twenty-one, I'm ancient in the debutante scene. Mama wanted me to be the epitome of a proper Southern belle and make my debut at eighteen, but I managed to push it off to the last possible year, using my time as a college student as my excuse. Even Daddy was willing to fight on my behalf against Mama's wishes for that outcome. It's true I wanted the best my education could give me, and attending charity functions or balls and parties every week would just distract me from my studies. Make no mistake, as soon as I graduated last May, she already had a planner filled with events, balls, and charity functions I was required to attend leading up to the fall debutante season.

"Presenting Miss Paige Kore Fairchild, escorted by Mr. William Edward Fairchild," the emcee announces as we hit the bottom of the stairs.

I curtsy and we take a stroll around the room, presenting me to those in attendance like a juicy morsel offered up for all. A ball of dread tightens in my stomach as I feel the scrutiny from the gathering of the Southern social elite. I'm a bit player in this game, shown off as a pretty possibility for some eligible bachelor under the guise of tradition. The band strikes up a waltz and Daddy leads me through the steps flawlessly. I've been in dance classes for over a decade to ensure I wouldn't embarrass Mama on just such an occasion. Faces blur as we whirl around the floor, but I still feel the stares and it makes my skin crawl. I tighten my smile, using it as my armor.

Necessary evils, I think to keep from bolting right out of the room. It's necessary to keep Mama pacified if I want to live a reasonably free life.

"Not so bad, right, sugar?" Daddy says through his own tight smile.

Like me, he prefers not to be in these very public showcases, but he's also at the mercy of Mama and proper Southern decorum. The waltz ends and we make it around the room and finally finish our promenade. He hugs me tight and kisses my cheek like the proud Southern papa he is.

"I'm going to find your mama and make sure she doesn't bother you the rest of the night." He kisses my cheek and beams proudly.

I smile back. "Now the hard part is over, so the real party can begin," I reply, accepting a champagne flute from a waiter. He shares a secret smile with me, kisses my cheek, and turns to go. I watch as he leaves and expertly cuts off Mama as she heads toward me. He redirects her to greet guests and I'm free from whatever critique she had for me from my trip around the ball-room. I probably missed a step or didn't smile brightly enough.

I sip my champagne, barely holding back from chugging the entire glass. Relief courses through me when the music volume increases and the people in attendance begin to lose interest as the free booze flows. Savannah high society has a minuscule attention span, and though I'm the heiress to a multimillion-dollar em-pire, I'm not exactly hot gossip or so very different from many others in the same position. My family name and combined assets keep them hanging around, always waiting for me to screw up royally, but I'm boring. I play by the rules, I make my parents proud—most of the time—and I would never so much as dare to taint the Fairchild family name. I know what would happen if I do, as some cousins twice removed have experienced. There's more than one reason I'm the sole heir to the family fortune despite having a large family tree.

"Paige, that dress is gorgeous! I thought you would have to wear something horrible your mama picked out ages ago." I turn to the familiar voice and smile at Alex, my best friend.

I smooth the poofy white satin skirt of the dress. "Mama may have a lot to say about my life, but she gave me the choice of three of her own picks, and this happened to not be one of them."

I stifle a giggle thinking of the fight we had at the dress shop when I insisted on the vintage gown rather than a brand-new cupcake gown she had in mind. The dress and the location were the only parts I insisted on, using the small amount of leverage I had with Mama to get them. Everything else, she picked out, despite dragging me through every planning meeting and pretending I had a say in anything.

"That tux really suits you," I say, hugging Alex. "The haircut is truly the cherry on top. Thank you for coming all the way from New York. I know you've been busy." I brush a lock of curly hair off Alex's forehead.

"Do you remember when we would play dress up in the attic at The Mansion, and I always went for the old suits and you picked the pretty dresses? It's like we've come full circle with that, but we actually fit in the clothes this time. Funny how no one figured me out sooner, right? I gave so many obvious signs that I was a dude, despite being in a lady's body."

Alex is my childhood best friend, the one ally I've always had, whether it was making mud pies and having tea parties in the garden of The Mansion or making it through the scathing social scene of our private school intact. Alex was the girl who I knew got me, who defended me, and who stood by me when my good name was dragged through the mud. But Alex has been transitioning over the last two years. He's dropped the feminine in search of the masculine he craves, beating back the righteously cruel and judgmental South to finally feel like his true self. While Alex has been supported in New York, the transgender lifestyle is still new to the upper crust of Savannah, as seen in the disapproving stares I catch from a group of people near us, who immediately begin whispering to each other. I turn Alex slightly so he can't see the looks he usually does his best to ignore.

"Did you see Liliana Bailey? I think she pilfered her grandma's entire jewelry box tonight with how much bling she's draped in." Alex nods in the direction of the aforementioned woman glittering with jewels.

You can take the woman out of the man, but you can't remove the urge to gossip from the Southerner.

"Hush. You know she likes to play dress-up. She's just never learned the art of subtlety." I look back at... well, she's not exactly my friend. She's more of a frenemy.

Besides Alex, I have a loose group of acquaintances I've grown up with due to our families all being in the same social circles. They flow from friends to enemies at any given moment depending on what gossip they want to share or believe. Liliana has always been on the other side of friendship, and she's one I watch out for due to her proclivities for viciousness.

Liliana is hanging on Garrison Daniels's arm like she wants to keep the bachelor locked in her clutches. I shake my head, glad I'm not having to fend off either of them tonight. Both have been incredibly cruel to me in the past. While Liliana likes to play nice to my face while stabbing me in the back, I only allowed Garrison to show me his true colors once, and he still gives me the creeps. I prefer to stay as far from him as I can, which has been easy with him away at school for the last seven years. Seeing him back here in Savannah makes me nervous.

I spent much of my high school years holding my head high when I was the center of vicious gossip and labeled first a prude, then a slut. Double standards were rampant in our social circle and apparently, I shouldn't have turned down popular senior Jason DeWitt, a notorious player, but then gone out with his friend, Garrison mere weeks later. I wouldn't sleep with Garrison, though he employed tactless and much unsexy prodding in his attempt to get me to change my mind. Despite my continued negative answers, he got impatient and gave me a bunch of drinks at a party and tried to have his way with me when I was stumbling drunk. It's not an unusual story, unfortunately, and it could have gone from bad to worse.

Thankfully, Alex thought to come looking for me when I was gone a little too long on a bathroom run. He opened the door just as Garrison was pushing down his pants and I was passed out on the bed. Later, I found out that Alex kicked Garrison's butt, literally, and knocked him over so he could help me out of that room. Thank goodness for a friend who actually cared about me, because I could have been another awful sexual assault statistic had he not.

Too bad my *friend* Liliana started a rumor that I was a sloppy drunk and she had heard me ask Garrison to go upstairs that night to *deflower* me. She spread the vicious rumor that I had brought it on myself all because she was mad he'd asked me out instead of her, I imagine. Garrison didn't think he had done anything wrong and never once shut down the gossip mill or explained he never had the opportunity to do the deflowering, which just kept the rumors circling that I'd lost my virginity while drunk at a party.

I was too embarrassed to tell anyone but my mama and Alex what had really happened. Alex wanted me to report Garrison to our private school, Savannah Prep, and then the police. Mama said nothing had technically happened, *"thank the Lord almighty,"* and I should just be glad to move on. She shushed me when I got more and more upset over the next few weeks as the rumors got worse, and finally demanded I never speak of it again.

So I didn't. Instead, I dealt with the stigma of being a sloppy drunk slut for the rest of high school. It didn't matter that I never went to another party or even considered dating, I remained the butt of their jokes and stories that began with *remember when Paige lost her virginity at a party freshman year*. If they only knew how far from the truth that was. I look again at Liliana and Garrison, who is pulling his arm away from her without much grace.

"They deserve each other," I say under my breath, but Alex hears me.

"You're a better person than I am, and a helluva lot more forgiving, too."

"I wouldn't say forgiving, exactly, but I am glad not to be in their crosshairs at the moment."

Alex takes a drink of champagne and swishes it around as if to wash his mouth out.

"I don't have the patience for the people who pretend to be friends only to gain access to privileged information, then sell you out faster than your mama's strawberry rhubarb pie at the Junior League charity bake sale." This is spoken from too-recent experience.

When Alex was still using she/her pronouns and only starting to transition to he/him, there were a few very unkind people, including Liliana, who decided to leak the story to the press in a mean-spirited attempt that hurt Alex's father. Judge Whitaker is on the supreme court for the state of Georgia, and the conservative majority of the state reacted strongly to the news that he had a transgender son that came out just as his six-year term was up for re-election. Thankfully, the small but mighty liberal voting population in his district helped him win his re-election despite the negative press. Alex had just been a tool Liliana and her like used to incite hate when the opportunity arose.

"That's why I have you," I say, squeezing Alex's hand. "You say what you mean and you do what you say, so I trust you implicitly. Also, I know you won't let anyone get one over on me if it seems the least bit suspicious."

I can't stop myself from looking over at Garrison Daniels as he moves toward my mama and daddy. Why is he being so friendly with them? His parents are friends with mine, but Garrison has been away at school, and I haven't had to deal with him for long enough that I question his chumminess with them now.

"Damn straight. I have less riding on my behavior than you do, so you know I'll whoop some ass if they go after you. Why not when I have a judge for a daddy, right?" Alex winks handsomely, his face so similar to the girl I grew up with, but even more perfect for who he is now.

"Shall we dance and give those old straitlaced biddies something to really talk about?" I offer my hand to Alex and meet his bright grin. It's better than questioning Garrison's motives and thinking about the past.

"I've been waiting all night for you to ask," he says, taking my hand and leading me to the dance floor.

Two

Hayes

I had meant to stay in my office, avoiding the gaudy revelry happening below in the nightclub, but my damn curiosity got the better of me.

I've been strategizing on how best to make my entrance into Savannah high society, but this is not how I want to do it. The type of people in attendance easily find they hate me for what I can do to them, even while they admire me for being so efficiently cruel.

I swirl the bourbon in my glass and look around at all the people who would normally shun this nightclub in favor of the local country clubs. I smirk at seeing them in *my* domain. I imagine this little party will work in my favor to put my exclusive club on their radar more so than I know it already was. The Southern Home and Garden feature of my rooftop garden would have seen to that, if my elusive presence wasn't enough.

Despite having a few business ventures, The Abyss is a soft spot and I gravitate toward the Gothic Revival nightclub in "Slowvanna" when other work should keep me in Atlanta with my brothers. There's something about the slow pace of the small city and the history of the only pre-civil war town in the South Sherman *didn't* burn that draws me to the squares and cobblestone streets here. That and a particularly uninterested potential business acquisition.

I survey the party from the gilded balcony above the dance floor, looking from one powerful man to another. These debutante balls really do draw a spectacular crowd, placing the richest families in Savannah, and maybe even the entire state of Georgia, in one room and letting them tear each other apart behind fake veneers. My own family is Southern and rich, but my brothers and I made it through without being expected to take part in the debutante scene that is securely anchored in high society.

Thank fuck for that.

After observing this group for a few hours, it's apparent I didn't miss much. It's what I would see at any other gala or charity event. The married women are unsatisfied in every way but don't want anyone to know. It's easy enough to spot how they put on a grand show of wealth to hide it, the diamonds getting bigger the more unhappy they are. The unmarried women are almost desperate gold diggers schmoozing their way through the crowd looking for any unattached man to sink their claws in to secure their futures. The men, both married and single, lazily eye fuck each woman who passes without regard, then return to their conversations about politics, golf games, and hedge funds. It's sickening, really.

Yet one woman keeps attracting my attention for all the wrong reasons. Glowing in her virginal white gown, she's hard to miss, even though she's the last fucking woman I should be fascinated with. Her daddy owns the hotels I've had my eyes on, and knowing I'd like to rip the family legacy out of their hands would make me persona non grata to her. However, it's always what is off-limits that captures my attention the most. My eyes track her movements like a wolf after a cute little bunny that has no idea it's going to be dinner.

I smile hungrily as I watch her politely greet and thank those in attendance in between dances with her companion. She politely accepts invitations to dance with the very few others who have asked but returns after each to the slight man with the floppy hair, and I wonder at her attachment to this person and the lack of people sweeping her around the dance floor. As the belle of the ball, her dance card should be full and she shouldn't have the opportunity to stand like a wallflower and chat with a friend. And friend he is, I decide. They don't appear romantic in the least, but she seems protective of him, angling him away from unapproving glares and distracting him as they share whispers and giggles. It's particularly interesting to watch her when the friend leaves to get a drink. I like the way she holds herself in perfect poise and refinement even though it's obvious to me in the way she shifts her eyes around that she's guarded. She knows the measure of the people who surround her but still gives into her joy on a dime when she thinks no one is looking.

Unfortunately for her, I'm always watching. Even when I shouldn't be.

I turn away from the party and make a stop at the bar to hook my fingers around the neck of a new bottle of bourbon. I push the button for the elevator that leads up to the greenhouse, knowing I need to leave before giving in to the urge to make myself feel better about not belonging in my own club with the Savannah elite by crushing their dreams in my hands. Normally, I would just make a call to my assistant to do some digging on their financial states in order to take advantage of any lapsed contracts or unused property I could covertly buy up just to spite them. Tonight, I feel morose about the situation and prefer to leave it behind me.

Once I'm in the moonlit and humid oasis of the glassed-in rooftop, surrounded by the scent of damp earth and tropical flowers, I relax. I pull a cigar from my suit pocket and flick a silver lighter, illuminating the rock wall next to me as a waterfall splashes down into a small koi pond that flows through this slice of the greenhouse. I refill my glass and set the bottle on the ground, survey-ing the extravagant garden that has only recently been finished after a two-year construction timeline.

The Elysium Garden, my extravagant rooftop green-house full of the most coveted plants, is as close to heaven as I think I'll ever get. I'm more of an underworld man, content influencing the life and death of companies that come into my corporation rather than schmoozing with pretentious pricks and their prissy wives, anyway.

I'm lost in thought when the French doors open, spilling the muffled party noise into my sanctuary for a moment before they softly close and return the silence. The spectral glow of a white dress floating into the dim space tells me who has entered my realm, and I'm not disappointed. From my shadowed spot against the rocks, I have the advantage of watching her walk through the lush greenery, one gloved arm extended at her side, fingers brushing the tall leaves and vines of flowers that spill out of every bed and hang from the industrial piping overhead while she delicately holds a flute of champagne in the other. She stops about ten feet from me, still unaware of my presence, and leans toward the low rock wall ringing the masterpiece of this garden.

"Careful, that one stinks like death," I say just loud enough to be heard over the splashing waterfall, hoping not to scare her too bad, but enjoying the possibility if I'm being honest.

She jumps, surprised by my voice, and spins to find the source.

I puff my cigar before blowing out a smoke ring, allowing her eyes to find the burning tip before I stub it out next to the bottle of bourbon. I like knowing she's watching me and take my time with it.

She says nothing, which surprises me. I would have expected her to demand to know what I'm doing here, even though it's my garden she's trespassing in. The party downstairs is strictly a first-floor affair. No guests were to come up here, despite the allure a rooftop greenhouse on an old historic building would attract.

Knowing I shouldn't, I take a few steps out of the shadows toward her, carrying my tumbler with me until we're both bathed in the moonlight that filters through palm fronds and glass windowpanes.

She watches me with rapt attention the whole time I move toward her, but fear never steals her composure. She finally drags her gaze up the length of my body to my face when we're only feet apart, curiosity fighting neutrality on her face.

"You don't look like the happy belle of the ball I was expecting," I offer in greeting.

"I beg your pardon?" A confused smile raises her deep red pout, the look on her face emphasizing her resemblance to a modern-day Scarlett O'Hara, even in the dim light. "As this is *my* debutante party, I would sure like to know what other belles you may have been expecting so I can lodge a complaint with the facility for double-booking events when we explicitly rented the entire club."

The entitlement of her statement shouldn't surprise me. She's likely used to getting what she wants, including going where she pleases, no matter the off-limits designation, given her high-profile social status and family wealth. What's surprising is that she shows no fear in the face of what could be considered a run-in with a dangerous stranger. Doesn't she have even a little of the natural instinct toward self-preservation? It's a damn good thing I mean her no physical harm because it would be too easy in this secluded setting.

A disjointed thought—I don't want to hurt her *or* see her harmed in any way— strikes me, and I check myself. Her safety isn't my priority, but I should play nice regardless.

"Oh, no one but you, my dear," I assure her with mock insistence. "I imagined you would spend the evening downstairs networking with all the powerful people in attendance, a big plastic smile pasted on your face as you played polite socialite. Instead, you've left the party to come up here and see a corpse flower that's thinking about blooming and smelling like a dead body to attract pollinators."

I offer her my tumbler of bourbon as I casually lean against the rock wall.

"Why would you offer me another drink when I have my own?" she asks, her white-gloved hand pushing the bourbon back toward me.

I shrug and lift the glass to my lips to drink. I swallow the burn of the liquor with the refusal of my offer.

"I've found that bourbon helps with social settings like the one you just came from. It gives a little more fire and fortitude than the bubbles of champagne." I nod at the half-empty flute in her hand.

She self-consciously sets the flute on the rock next to her and turns back to me. Her bright eyes catch the moonlight and I feel a breath stick unexpectedly in my chest. Fuck, she's beautiful. I knew this in an abstract way—I have eyes, after all, and my due diligence into the company I want pulled up all the information it could on the entire Fairchild family, including the squeaky clean and remarkably missing from social media, only daughter set to inherit. But a dossier on a debutante and the real thing right in front of me is like Heaven and Earth—you can only imagine what Heaven is like until you get to see it firsthand.

And this little one is positively angelic, so pure there is a part of me that wants to sully her innocence just to prove I can. Staying hands-off in my attempt to get what I want from her family may be harder than I anticipated.

She purses her lips and tilts her head inquisitively. "I'm sorry, I simply do not think I've had the pleasure of meeting you before, and I feel terribly rude not knowing your name now." She extends a graceful, gloved hand. "I'm—"

"Paige Fairchild, the debutante everyone in town is talking about tonight," I supply for her.

Surprise curves her lips in a grin that has me swallowing the lump in my throat and silently cursing myself for the loss of composure in her presence. This is... unusual. I hold tight control over myself at all times. Except in her presence, it would seem.

"And you are?" she asks, curiosity displacing the rote politeness she had first employed.

"Hayes Olsen. The pleasure is truly all mine, I assure you." I take her hand in mine for a brief moment before I let it go. I flex my hand as I lower it to my side again, feeling the warm ghost of her touch through satin even now and wanting to feel it against my body again. What would that soft tough feel like on more sensitive skin, and how can I entice her to leave the gloves on should I have the chance? I push the salacious thoughts from my head. She's not meant for me. Not now, not ever.

A radiant smile bursts across her face and I shake my head at the immediate gut-check reaction I get from it. She's not what I was expecting. Something about her is radically different, which could both help and hinder my goal. Right now, it's throwing me off the carefully cultivated cool I've mastered and depend on for every business transaction in my career. I must remind myself that she is simply that, a business transaction that requires my full attention.

"No way, you can't be!" she says, her tender age, despite appearing more mature, coming through in her exclamation. "Hayes Olsen, the mysterious nightclub proprietor who brought gothic nightlife to sleepy Savannah? Sir, it is very good to meet you."

She's heard of me? And she called me sir. While the logical part of me knows she meant it as a polite term, the deluded part of my brain that is fascinated with her thinks it sounded a little too sexy and wants to hear her repeat it. From her knees.

"Thank you for allowing my parents to throw this god-awful party in your club. I know events of this kind aren't typical for The Abyss, but it was my only request, macabre as it might be, to my slightly neurotic mother while she was scheming. Between you and me"—she abruptly lowers her voice and I lean in to catch each word that rushes out in her beautiful genteel drawl—"everyone has been talking about you. It seems you have made it difficult for some of the families in town to get in here, which made them all want to be at my party even more. I had hoped I could meet you but was uncertain if you would be in residence tonight. I'm so glad to have found you."

My chest puffs at the admission. She gives me a conspiratorial smile and I find my own smile tugging at the set of my lips before I can school my features.

I hadn't expected her to know about me in the slightest. I have indeed made it difficult for entitled bastards to use the club but allowed the Fairchilds the option because of my desire to own a piece of their souls. It seems she does her homework nearly as well as I do. I may need to revise how I want to go about this if that's the case, as a surprise really is a better tactic for what I have planned. I should take her back to the party and stop the part of me that wants to steal her away and see if she'll end up on her knees like I fantasized a moment ago. She's far too innocent, wholesome even, for what I would want from her now.

"The Abyss is at your disposal, now and in the future, should you need anything. It really was a pleasure." I extend my hand again. "I can escort you back to your party if you'd like."

Paige doesn't lift a hand to meet mine as expected, instead, she freezes me in place with a frown I'd like to wipe off her beautiful face.

"I'm disappointed in you, Mr. Olsen. You were the first person at this party who made conversation with me that didn't revolve around a potential marriage or a business deal. Instead, you offer me a drink in my respite from the banality of high society and then tell me to go back to it? You can't say things like that to a woman."

If only she knew. And Mr. Olsen? Hearing her address me so formally now drives home our large age gap, making her appeal that of forbidden fruit. I want to look *and* taste, but I shouldn't do either. She's practically a child, and, well, I'm old enough to know better. The coy smile she gives me is pure sugar and I instantly know not to underestimate the Southern wiles that are bred into her.

"Please, call me Hayes." I pause and consider her for a moment. I find myself curious about her and want to keep her with me longer than I had intended, maybe because of her appeal, but also because she intrigues me. "What had you so bored with the party downstairs that you decided to escape up here?" I ask, looking away from her hopeful face to the green space around us.

"The Elysium Garden," she says, gesturing around at the plants, "is why I wanted my debutante party at The Abyss. I begged the planner to allow us to have the party up here, but she said it would be too cramped around the plants."

Paige stops talking long enough to take the bourbon from my hand and tips back a large gulp. She coughs after she swallows and I'm reconsidering my offer of the drink. She's too young for bourbon.

"That was good!" She licks her full red lips with a pink tongue I can vividly imagine licking *me*. "What is it?"

I stifle the groan of longing that shudders through me, clearing my throat instead.

"Underworld Spirits bourbon. It's made especially for The Abyss. You can't buy it anywhere else, yet." I don't tell her that Underworld Spirits is another busi-ness of mine, so I have full control over all of its produc-tion and distribution.

"So exclusive."

She smirks and takes a smaller sip, her red lips leaving a print on the glass rim that makes me want to see the color ringing my dick. The visual is very appealing, indeed. I push the thought out of my head. There's no way I'll be able to concentrate on getting what I really want if I'm focused on the short-term goal of fucking her mouth.

"How bad was it?" I say instead.

"The bourbon?" she asks, looking down at the glass.

"Not the bourbon," I correct. "You left your own party. It must have been bad."

Her head tilts down. "This party... it wasn't really for me, if you must know. My mama insisted, so it was for her. I had hoped she would have flat-out refused my insistence to have the party at The Abyss instead of The Mansion and I could have skipped this antiquated madness altogether."

Ah, yes, The Mansion. The very hotel right here in town I crave to have as my own. It's like she's offering me enticing morsels on purpose and I'm the damn dog salivating at the thought. It's nearly Pavlovian how quickly I'm conditioned to respond.

"So, you didn't want to have your party here at all?" I feign horror, my hand splayed on my chest, and she smirks at me again.

"I didn't want to have *this party* at all. I used the unusual location request as a ploy to make her give up the whole thing. But Mama doesn't give up; she strategically gives in just enough to make me do what she wants."

"Do you always do everything your mama wants?"

I shake the empty tumbler at Paige as she considers the question. I push off the short wall and walk the few steps back to the waterfall for the bottle. I bring the whole thing back to the *titan arum* display where she waits patiently and accepts the filled glass when I offer.

"Mostly, yes. It's expected, and it usually doesn't cost me much to swallow my pride to do whatever trifling thing she wants. There's also plenty she doesn't know about and that's fine by me." She punctuates the last statement by saluting me with the tumbler before drinking.

"Rebel red runs through your veins, I see." The affection in my tone surprises me. I swallow it down with the sip of bourbon I take from the glass she hands back, marked with her lipstick on the opposite side.

She laughs. "I must have had too much to drink if you're thinking I'm at all rebellious."

Her eyes grow soft, and a small smile plays on her mouth as she sways back and forth, looking around the greenhouse. Her eyes sharpen and her body stills.

"Is that a pomegranate tree?"

I turn to follow her gaze and see the heavy red orbs nestled in the bright green leaves of a tree near the glass wall of the greenhouse. I stretch my arm out in the direction of the tree.

"My garden is your garden. Go have a look." I follow behind her, enjoying the quickness of her steps as she eagerly moves through the plants to investigate.

"It is! I love them. They're so hard to eat and make a huge mess, so Mama never brought any home. I don't think I've ever seen an actual real tree like this, though. This is beautiful."

I reach into the branches and select a ripe pomegranate, plucking it with a tug. I pull out a small knife and flick it open, puncturing the fruit to remove the bottom and finish cracking the fruit in half in my hands. Juice spills onto my palm as I hold out half for Paige.

"Getting messy is the best way to eat." I push out a few arils with my thumb. "Open your mouth, I'll give you a taste." My balls tighten with the innocent words that conjure what else this conversation could lead to, and I force my dick to calm the fuck down. She is absolutely off-limits. So not something I should tamper with. Definitely too young. And sweet. And innocent. And perfectly pliable. *Fuck*.

Paige bends forward at her waist, pushing the poofy skirt of her dress back, opening her mouth for me to push the pomegranate seeds onto her tongue. I bite my lip as her eyes close and she moans in pleasure. She has no idea the effect she has on me, watching her savor the taste.

She reaches up to brush the juice from her lips only to realize belatedly that she's just pressed a lipstick mark to her gloved fingers. "Oh, shoot! Mama's gonna kill me if I don't get this out." She starts plucking at the material, but her fingers are stuck and she makes a frustrated sound.

I drop the broken pomegranate and pull out a handkerchief to wipe my hands. "Let me."

Her fingers still their frantic motion and she looks up at me expectantly, her hand hovering between us in acceptance. So willing.

I pull each finger of the glove until I've worked it free from her hand and slowly slide it off her arm. Seeing her skin revealed inch by inch gives me thoughts of revealing what is under her dress, and I repress a shudder of desire. She gives me her other hand as the French doors once again open and carry party noises into the still garden.

"Paige Fairchild, you better be in here somewhere or so help me!" a shrill, disembodied voice calls out into the darkness.

Paige jumps and instantly moves behind me, her hands going to my arms as she uses me as a shield.

"Mama," she whispers. "She's going to kill me for running out of the party. If she catches us, she'll give me an earful, and you'll probably get a dressing down, too."

"I have a quick escape, if you need one," I say over my shoulder with nonchalance.

The thought that I wouldn't mind more time with her buzzes around my conscious with the threads of personal gain woven through. I could use a favor owed to me by this intriguing young woman. And I would love to keep her close a little longer.

She looks up at me with relief softening her stricken features. "Please, I'll do anything to avoid this lecture." She blinks big eyes at me reverently, the color washed out in the moonlight and alluding my knowledge. She has far too much trust, but I'm shameless enough to take it.

I grab Paige's hand and pull her farther into the greenhouse and out of sight. She grips my arm with her other hand and follows trustingly. We wind through the lush botanicals, ferns tickling our legs and flowers perfuming the air until I've found the discreet door set into the stone wall of the building. I fish out a keycard and unlock the door. It opens on silent hinges, thanks to a meticulous maintenance crew. I hold the door for Paige and follow her into the dark beyond.

Who knew my night would end with the heiress of the very empire I want to take down running right into my arms?

Three

Paige

I rush through the doorway into darkness and fall back against the door once Hayes shuts it. I'm breathing heavily and the absurdity of the situation bubbles in my chest until giggles are spilling from my throat and I clap a hand over my mouth, which is still tingling from the bourbon I've been sharing with Hayes.

Oh lordy, have I ever made a mess of things. I ditched my own debutante ball to hang out in a garden with a stranger who makes my belly tighten and butterflies take flight with a simple look. Now I'm running from Mama with Nanny Fairchild's stained opera gloves clutched in my hands. If I return the gloves to my Nanny in this state, she will give me the dressing down I rightly deserve for my careless act. I'm a mess in more ways than one. Who am I tonight, to go against Mama's wishes so brazenly and act as recklessly as I have? I rather like this version of myself, messy and all.

When Alex left, I couldn't take the scrutiny and having to be perfectly polite to people I know don't even care about me. I needed to get away from the fake and find something real. Elysium was calling me, and I couldn't resist the chance to see the renowned garden for myself, even if I had to sneak in when I knew it was entirely off-limits. Every garden club in town has spent the last season knocking down the door to get access to the greenhouse and all the tropical plants inside after everyone's favorite magazine, Southern Home And Garden, did a spread on the urban oasis right under our noses, and the intriguing man who made it happen. I never expected to see anyone in the out-of-bounds greenhouse, let alone discover I prefer his quiet company to anything that was going on downstairs.

Meeting Hayes, the brilliant mind behind the garden and the exclusive club that manages to stay discreet, though whispered about frequently, is the cherry on top of escaping my obligations and the party. *Mmm, cherries.* I'd like to pop him in my mouth and tie his stem in knots, but that's some real wishful thinking.

First of all, he's a *man*, not some boy my age who would want to mingle with a stupid deb, which is another reason debuting was dumb.

Second, I don't know the first thing about tying a man in knots in any capacity other than the fantasies that take shadowy shape in my champagne and bourbon-drenched brain.

Third, well, I don't recall much about the third point I'm trying to make on my own behalf, on account of that delicious Underworld Spirits bourbon.

Hayes is right, it was much more fortifying than the champagne I have been sipping all evening.

A light hanging on a chain above us clicks on to illuminate a short, nondescript hallway with several doors behind the tall, solidly built man who blocks the way. I blink rapidly as my eyes adjust to the bright light after my time in the dark garden.

Hayes faces me, his hand lowering slowly from the chain as I stare up at him. Good Lord, he's handsome. His dark hair is short on the sides, long and brushed back on top. His tan skin is smooth save for the rough brush of stubble along his jaw and the hint of thin lines perched at the corners of his eyes. He wears his expensive black suit and crisp white shirt like it was made for him, which it probably was, and boy does it look good on his body.

I sigh, not even able to stop the sound from escaping my lips. He's so far out of my league I might as well sit my butt back on the bench.

"I like hearing you laugh." He looks away, clearing his throat as if the admission was accidental and he can't recall how it slipped out.

"Silly debutantes have nothing better to do than laugh," I joke.

"Don't do that," he says, his eyes flashing with flecks of gold as the light finally allows me to see they're such a deep green I'd mistake them for brown from another foot away.

"Make jokes?" I cross my arms and stare at him, wondering if he's judging me for my faux pas now. So much of our interaction has been effortless, comfortable, and if I just messed that up, I'll die of embarrassment.

"Discredit yourself. You're hardly a silly debutante despite the reasons you're here tonight. You've got a brain and a purpose beyond being beautiful and rich, so don't make jokes at your own expense."

"You think I'm beautiful?" I choke out a laugh as the words that were supposed to stay in my head come out of my mouth and embarrassment creeps into my cheeks. *Great. Now I'm spilling secrets right along with him.*

"Your beauty is obvious," he evades. "What you do with it is more important."

I feel my lips twitch into a smile. "Did you get that from a motivational quote? People don't really talk like that with strangers."

He sighs deeply, his eyes closing as he tips his head to the ceiling.

I'm probably annoying him to the point he wants to get rid of me. How sad to know I can't even keep a man like him captivated when I actually want to. I really like watching his Adam's apple move as he swallows and will be quite disappointed when he asks me to go away again.

He's already offered to take me back to the party, so I'm probably on his last nerve at this point.

He surprises me by gesturing across the hall. "Come with me," he says instead of telling me to get lost. Hope floats to my awareness. He's letting me stay.

He pulls open a door and flicks a light switch as I follow him into a gorgeous office. The lights of Savannah and a sliver of the river can be seen through the large window across from us. A cognac-colored leather Chesterfield sofa and two club chairs are situated in a corner, making an enticing bid at my attention as I imagine curling up with one of the books from the wall of industrial pipe and rustic wood bookshelves. A large mahogany desk and chair take up a portion of the remaining space. The faint hint of cigar smoke lingers without staleness, and I wonder about the quality of the cigars and the ventilation system involved in making that happen. The cigars Daddy smokes can sometimes grow stagnant in his library and Mama threatens to leave him each time she catches a stubbed-out stogie in a crystal ashtray inside the house.

"Is this your office?" I ask to break the silence that stretches with my inspection of the office.

He settles onto the sofa, his elbows resting on his thighs with hands clasped between his knees casually. His eyes meet mine and I suck in a breath at the intensity. They are deep jungle green and smolder with his attention.

"The one I keep in Savannah, yes." His voice is a deep purr that washes over me with his gaze. I shiver and look away from the intensity.

I walk around the office, looking at the books on his shelves and running my fingertips along the shiny desk to give myself something to do that hides my fascination. "Where do you live? No one seems to know where you stay when you're in town."

He smiles, his features softening with the movement, and my stomach dips like I've gone down a rollercoaster. Good gracious, he is handsome.

"You're quite curious about me, aren't you?"

I pretend to be interested in a cut crystal bowl filled with tarnished silver coins that look ancient so I can avoid his gaze in my embarrassment. I pick up a coin, turning it to see barely discernible profiles and raised designs. They could be Greek obols, but I'm not familiar enough to know that for sure. I set the coin back into the bowl.

"You're just an enigma, I guess. It's rare someone shows up and has no desire to play nice with the people who run this town. I like that you didn't try to worm your way into society or toe the line the way they were expecting." My crush on Hayes is becoming more apparent as I willingly admit I'm curious about him just like that. *Do better, dang it!*

He nods. "A word of unsolicited advice. Don't do what's expected. And never let them make you feel less than."

I lift my chin at him and stay silent. I hope he doesn't question how often I've done just that. It wouldn't be pretty to admit that's what I default to.

He motions me closer, and I eagerly take a seat on the sofa near him.

"This floor of the building is my apartment. It's smaller than the other floors because the greenhouse takes up nearly all the space, but it works. I spend most of my time in Atlanta for business, so I don't need much."

"What exactly is your business? I heard The Abyss is owned by a subsidiary company that can't be tracked to its holding corporation."

Now I'm being nosy, but I can't stop myself from asking. Daddy sent me to business school so I could take over our family hotel business, the Xenios Group, at some point in the future, so it's both nature and nurture for me to be curious about how others do business.

"Have you heard of Olympus International?"

My eyes widen. "Of course. They own half of the South and have businesses all over the world. Is that you?"

If it is, he's far more powerful and influential than I imagined. Olympus is known for swallowing up failing businesses and turning them around with a Midas touch or picking them down to bare bones and selling them off as crushed remnants. They're business jugger-nauts, to put it nicely, and rich as sin because of ruth-less deals that greatly benefit them.

"Me and my brothers, yes. We took a family endeav-or and combined it with other assets into a conglomer-ate of sorts years ago. It's been profitable," he finishes carefully, but I know exactly what he means.

I turn my body and tuck my legs under myself, crumpling my dress terribly, but I don't care. "I knew there was something that had to have brought you here to Savannah. This building was for sale for years, and real estate development and nightclubs are not usual for Olympus, so there must be something in town you have your eye on. Tell me who's failing," I demand.

He looks at me curiously. "Why are you so inter-ested? Will it help you find a proper husband if you know your prospects will have a fortune intact in a few months?"

I smack his knee with the gloves I'm still clutching in my hand. "I'm not marrying anyone in this godfor-saken town, and if I were, it wouldn't be for money."

I have plenty of my own, but I keep that thought to myself. He tips his head at me in acknowledgment. Now I feel like I have to explain myself.

"I'm just curious. I mean, if my favorite ice cream shop were to suddenly be bought out and changed into something unrecognizable, I might have a problem. That's probably thinking too small for you, though." I look at him as I contemplate the possibilities while he gives me nothing but a look to go on.

"Definitely think bigger," he offers with a hint of a grin, like I'm entertaining him. Glad he's finally enjoying himself.

"There are a few types of industries in Savannah. Maybe shipping, agriculture, or manufacturing? The Daniels and the Baileys seem to be doing just fine." I absently name the two families who control much of those industries in the area and wonder if he would consider something in the tourism sector. Maybe the hotels on the way to Tybee Island or a bed and breakfast? There are plenty of national chains that wouldn't necessarily interest him, but there are a few one-offs here and there that may be worth his time.

"That big brain of yours working away on a puzzle is much sexier than the silly debutante you assume yourself to be," he murmurs.

I catch his dark gaze when I look up. I can feel it like a caress on my skin, despite the dress I wear. A hot blush spreads up my face until it's flaming.

"There's not much about me that's sexy." I look away and twist the gloves in my hands.

I've made sure of that because of my history with the awful rumors that ruined my high school years. I've gone above and beyond to be unassuming and plain to avoid enticing Liliana and her friends to come up with more. I stay off social media because it's nothing but a cesspool for mean people to bully and demean others. Keeping a low profile— unsexy, for all intents— has become a habit for me. Now I wish I were one of those girls who can take a compliment for what it is, but I trip all over myself to insist they must be wrong because I don't want the attention. Except, I don't feel the least bit of the creeps when the attention is from Hayes. I actually like his gaze on me, just like I enjoy knowing he's thinking about me and even calling me both beautiful and sexy in the same conversation.

"You underestimate yourself, darlin'." He angles himself toward me, his thick finger warm against my skin as he tips my chin up until I meet his eyes. "Don't shy away from who you are and what that means. You're powerful. Embrace it. I think it will suit you far better than this debutante thing you let your mama talk you into." His thumb softly brushes just below my bottom lip, and I feel it quiver in response to his proximity and touch.

It's impossible to look away from him when he speaks with an authority that zings down my spine and raises goose bumps on my bare arms. A strange urge to lunge across the sofa and kiss him grips me nearly as tight as the gloves I hold in my white-knuckled fist. There's no way he would want to kiss me back, though, so I find the tiniest sliver of restraint to keep me planted firmly in place. What's worse than impulsivity? The abject misery of rejection.

He drops his hand from my chin and rubs it across his face. Seeing him touch his own face after mine sends a shiver of longing through me. There is something so appealing about that thought that I lean toward him like I'm drawn to a magnet.

"I think it's time I got you back to your ball. If I'm going by her screech in the greenhouse earlier, your mama will murder me if I keep you any longer. Come on." He takes my hand in his and pulls me to my feet. My heart sinks into my stomach, but I stand with him.

"Please let me stay a little longer, I really don't want to go back." Ew. I sound like a petulant child. "I'm so over that crowd and the expectations that come with it." That's not quite mature enough to save the refined image I'd like him to see, but it was worth a shot.

Hayes turns and takes both of my hands in his, and I grip his fingers tightly like the lifeline they could be if he lets me stay.

"Sometimes we have to do things we don't like so we can get the outcome we want. Like it or not, your responsibility tonight is to be the center of attention and make important connections with influential people. You never know what opportunities may present themselves if you're in the right place at the right time."

"Like meeting you." My eyelashes flutter of their own accord and I hope he doesn't think I'm flirting. I probably am, but I couldn't help myself. He's just so smooth, and he smells delightful, and he's in the right place at the right time for me to fall over myself to keep him with me.

"I'm sure I'm the least exciting part of your evening, but you certainly made it more enjoyable for me. Thank you for the pleasure of your company, Miss Fairchild." His low voice is smooth and satisfying, pacifying my urge to fight the impending exit. He pulls my hands up to his lips and presses a lingering kiss against my knuckles that I feel deep in my body.

Warmth creeps through my belly and works its way lower until my thighs are clenching together at the unfamiliar feeling. I want to rub against him like a cat, cover myself in his manly scent, and mark him with the floral of my perfume so he'll remember me long after I've gone. How am I supposed to leave him speechless and enamored with me when I don't even know how to flirt properly?

When he releases my hands, I go with my instincts to wrap my arms around his waist and flatten myself against him. I bury my nose against the crisp, white dress shirt covering his hard chest and hope my red lipstick has faded enough to not leave a mark as I breathe in deeply and fortify my spirit. I may never see him again, so I might as well draw this out and get my fill right now.

His arms tentatively circle my bare shoulders and hold me close. A bulge below his belt presses against my lower belly and I inhale sharply. Could he want me? I'm certain at least a part of him does. His fingers slide up my back and thread through the hair at my nape, massaging my scalp until I purr out a contented sigh directly into his chest and feel him grow harder against my belly.

"You should go," he grits out, barely loosening his hold. "I'm not accustomed to denying myself what I want, but I'm not about to tarnish your exquisite innocence." The words are formal, but the gravelly tone of his voice speaks to my soul, wanting him to make good on that hint of a threat. Or promise.

But he's right. I should go. I'm in way over my head with a man like him and wouldn't know the first thing about pleasing him, even if he could easily steal my innocence and have me wrapped around his every whim. I swallow hard and force myself to let him go in a rush, like pulling off a bandage.

His arms slide down my back and linger on my hips a moment before he steps back and his touch is gone.

The world is bitter cold after having felt the dark inferno of him against me.

Four

Paige

Hayes shows me the private elevator from his apartment to the club below and without so much as a polite kiss on my cheek, he presses the button and allows the doors to close between us. The magic of the hour or so I just spent with him dissipates when the elevator doors open back into my reality. I wander into the foyer of the club, finding my bag and refreshing my lipstick in a mirror before I gather the courage to face the party, and Mama, once again.

"Where have you been?" Mama hisses when she spots me re-entering the party.

"I needed a breather; I was feeling a little warm and overwhelmed."

Her eyes narrow and I bet she can smell the hint of cigar and man on me. I raise my chin defiantly, not wanting her to know or shame me for discovering a dark indulgence I was unaware I need so badly in my life. She would forbid me to ever see him again if she knew where

I was. Not that I'll ever actually have the opportunity to spend time with Hayes again, but she would rule it out anyway.

"Well, it's about time you got back. There are plenty of people who want to talk to you and I've been making excuses for your untimely absence. Don't do it again," she warns, her hand grasping my arm. She looks down. "Child, where are your gloves?" she chastises and I feel every bit the little girl she invokes.

"It was warm, so I put them in my bag," I say, the half-truth easily sliding out in reply. I've learned it's often easier to give Mama a little white lie than the whole truth. She doesn't want to hear it, anyway.

She clicks her tongue at me and straightens up as we begin moving into the crowd. "No debutante should be without gloves, but I guess this will have to do," she says under her breath.

My heart hammers as she pulls me from one self-important person to another, forcing me to make small talk and keep a polite smile on my face as they congratulate me on entering society.

"Ah, there she is! This is quite the party. Welcome to society my dear," Mayor Declan says, pulling me into a hug that's a little too tight. He's obviously enjoyed the champagne and free-flowing liquor.

I fight the urge to roll my eyes and smile at him prettily instead. This party really doesn't signify a life change the way he insists. Maybe it would have in the 1800s when a young woman had to be presented as marriage material, but in the twenty-first century, we hardly need this antiquated tradition.

"Thank you for attending," I reply, my spine ramrod straight and my face smooth and pleasant. "I don't think we could touch the beautiful event you threw for Margot last month. It was simply stunning." It was a very nice event, though Mama ensured we would upstage even that one tonight.

"Oh, Mayor, my apologies, I simply must keep Paige moving. It was such a pleasure to have you join us tonight. We are honored," Mama coos.

"Of course, of course. There's no end to your duties tonight, right ladies?" he says, laughing at his own comment.

"We will have you and Catherine over for dinner soon. It really has been too long," Mama says as she once again takes me by the elbow to steer me away, the right people to talk to already mapped in her calculating little brain to make up for my missing hour.

We are nearly to the Prestons, some of Mama and Daddy's friends from the country club, when we're stopped by a voice I was hoping to avoid for the entirety of this evening.

"There she is, the belle of the hour. About time you made your rounds after your little disappearing act."

I stiffen and wipe every trace of emotion from my expression before Mama turns me to face Garrison

Daniels. It's been years since I've had to talk to him or be within a few feet of him. Up close he's just as cruelly handsome as he was in high school, though he looks worse for wear, bloated and tired.

It's like I'm transported back to my freshman year anytime I have to really look at him. Back when he had first shown me interest, I was thrilled. How had I, a lowly freshman, caught the attention of the hot senior? It wasn't until that stupid party that I realized his motives were self-serving and toxic and I wasn't special at all. I learned a hard lesson at his hands, and I vowed never to make that same mistake again. For seven years I have avoided boys and dating so I wouldn't be a victim to someone just like Garrison Daniels.

"It's been a long time. You're looking real good, sugar."

I cringe at the smarmy pet name he has no right to call me.

"You look"—I pause, surveying the slight paunch pushing the buttons of his tuxedo jacket to their brink—"like life has been full of decadence." I carefully tuck double meaning into my words like a true Southerner. We're born with the ability to simultaneously compliment and critique with a smile on our faces. Just take the phrase *bless your heart*. It means you're a sweet idiot but sounds so cute, no one can fault you for it.

I feel Mama's hand tighten on my elbow and know she's not happy with me.

"Garrison, we've missed you around Savannah. It's so nice to have you home where you belong. I'm sure your parents are so happy. Did I hear your daddy saying you went to law school?" Mama likely knows every answer to any question she could ask him, as she enjoys gossiping with the other parents in her social circle.

He turns to Mama, indulging her. "I just passed the bar, actually. I have a job with Dupree, Athena, and Fisk that I'm starting in the new year."

He probably let his daddy pull strings and call in connections to get him the job. He never worked for anything when I knew him, letting others do his homework and taking credit he wasn't due. I can't imagine he would have changed much if he didn't have to.

"It really is so good to be home." He leers at me a moment too long and I swallow hard. "I can't wait to pick up right where I left off when I went away for college."

"Wouldn't that be, hmm, I don't know, too immature? I'm sure you must have grown and developed enough as a person to not want to revert back to your old ways." I don't believe a word of that about him but know Mama will shake me if I say anything more cutting.

Garrison just chuckles, which doesn't bode well for any sort of maturity on his part. His eyes gleam as he slowly looks me over from head to toe.

Nope. Not me in his sights again. That will not happen. I know better this time around and know just what he's capable of. The only silver lining to having been a target of Garrison's misspent youth is that I do not have a list of heartbreaks, doled out by selfish boys, that would have crushed me. Instead, he helped me realize none of the boys in high school would be worthy of my time, only full of promises they never intended to keep just so they could get the outcome they wanted. That was enough to make me avoid the hook-up culture that is pervasive in my generation.

My thoughts wander to Hayes, wondering what it would be like to hook up with him, and my cheeks heat. I guess I avoided it all too well because now I have a whole new problem of not knowing the first thing about getting what I want when I finally have a man I'm interested in. I swear I can still smell Hayes's warm skin and the clean linen of his shirt on my skin. I bring my wandering mind back to the party and the jerk, who is the opposite of what I want, smiling at me now.

"You should come around more, sugar. I haven't seen you in ages. Why don't you hang out at the club or any of the other spots where our group spends time?"

"You could call it tactfully avoiding certain people." I allow a small smile to soften the words I very much mean. I stay five miles away from anywhere I could possibly run into Garrison or his group.

"Paige, we do not avoid anyone. Be nice, he deserves your respect," Mama says, a nervous laugh following the squeeze she gives my arm.

I turn to give her a quick glare. "Well, *I* like to avoid people who have shown me their true colors." My voice is low, but I wouldn't mind Garrison hearing my comment.

Does she not remember what he did to me? Everything that happened at that stupid party and the months after when I was tormented by lies?

Likely not. Even then, she had taken his side when I told her what he had tried, but failed to achieve, thanks to the divine intervention that was Alex stumbling on us. Mama insisted we didn't want to ruin *his bright future* when *nothing had actually happened*. Sure, physically I survived intact, but emotionally he had ripped an innocence from me before I was ready. The sheet had been torn and I began to see there were people who would take advantage of any situation. It was a violation despite not ending the way he had hoped.

Mama cuts in before I can come up with another snide remark. "Garrison just bought a condo downtown. Isn't that nice?" There's that Southernism again. *Isn't that nice* is her code for *you better compliment and congratulate him or I'll shake you.* "I can imagine he needs to be close to work since he will be so busy putting his new law degree to use."

"It's so nice of you to grace us with your brilliant lawyer presence for my little debut. There are so many other people here that I just have to thank, so we won't keep you. Bye-bye." The sarcasm drips like honey, but Mama can't do anything because I'm technically being polite. I glance at her and smile as I feel her frustration tremble through her hand into my arm. I learned from the best.

"Garrison, I do hope you'll join us for dinner tomorrow night. It's already set with your mama and daddy. Supper's at seven."

A burn creeps up my neck as fury rings through me. She invited the Daniels family to Sunday dinner without even telling me? And to ask Garrison to attend as well? This woman knows no bounds.

"I didn't know we were hosting a big dinner tomorrow, Mama," I say through clenched teeth. "Don't you think this weekend is busy enough?"

Family dinner is a tradition I can't get out of, no matter how hard I try or what else is going on around it. It's the only day of the week Mama actually does the cooking and most weeks my septuagenarian grandmother, Nanny Fairchild, joins us, badgering Mama about something or other just to get a rise out of her. Occasionally Mama turns it into a bigger deal by inviting a family friend or two, but she saves the big dinner parties for their own occasion, so at least I don't have to deal with a social event weekly.

"Your daddy and I want to take advantage of having so many of our old friends in town. Besides, it's just a little dinner." She turns back to Garrison and smiles sweetly. "I'll make that roast chicken I remember you were so fond of in high school."

I turn my head and cover my mouth as I gag.

Ugh, the roast chicken. Garrison had dinner with us before we went to that fateful party. Mama served her specialty chicken, and when I was violently ill that night after all the alcohol Garrison had forced on me, along with nausea from the thwarted assault, it was chicken that came up and it has haunted me ever since.

"Excuse me, I think I've had too much champagne."

I untangle my arm from Mama's hands and hurry away as she fusses at me. I look around for an escape and spot the alcove to the elevator that leads back up to Hayes. No, I can't run back to him. Besides, there was a pad for a special keycard to get the elevator to go back up, so I'd likely just be stuck if I tried. As much as I want to run away, what he said about responsibilities echoes in my head and slows my steps.

Well, shoot. I guess I have to pull up my big girl panties and tough out the rest of this party after all.

Five

Paige

"You should have given me a heads-up." I pick up a brush to scrub the potatoes Mama drops in the sink as I once again bring up the Daniels joining us for dinner.

"For the last time, I can invite whomever I want to my Sunday dinner, and you will be on your best behavior with them."

"What he did—"

"Is ancient history, Paige," she cuts in. "Nothing happened. You should be over this by now." When I try to butt in, she raises a hand in my face. "God help me, if you so much as bring it up again I'm cutting off your trust for a month."

I silently seethe next to her. She always uses this tactic to keep me in line. The trust is how both the Fairchild inheritance and the Thackery fortune trickle down until I'm married and gain full access to it. As long as Mama is alive and I'm unwed, she will be the executor with the power to make it flow or shut it off completely. It's an outdated tradition that has carried over from generations past in which women didn't inherit the legacy of the family business and required a sizeable dowry to ensure a good marriage. The trust is a selling point for any potential husband to marry a Fairchild daughter or a way to assure a good marriage for a spare son.

I'm a special case as I'm an only child and a female, so I not only stand to inherit the trust but also the legacy of the business. Even Daddy has less power over the way the trust works than she does. It's arranged so the trust is controlled by the mother in the hopes that she will be a bit more scrupulous in marrying off her brood of children who aren't inheriting the big-ticket item of the legacy.

Things became a bit more complicated because Mama and Daddy's marriage was arranged by their well-meaning parents much like a business deal. While not uncommon to have wealthy families promising their children in marriage to strengthen alliances and increase status, it became far more profitable to merge the two powerful families. They saw a way to funnel the Thackery agriculture money into the depleted Fairchild hotel business and in return, the hotel notoriety would come back to bolster the agriculture business, so they set their kids up and told them to play nice in order to build something even better.

That money saved The Mansion here in Savannah. It also allowed Daddy to take over and grow it into the Xenios Group which now has luxury boutique hotels in every major city and revered coastal town along the Eastern Seaboard. Once the hotel business was booming, the agricultural side of things got the boost it needed and expanded across the South as well. Daddy may have grown their empire and increased their fortunes, but it was because of Mama's money that he could make it happen. She's always had the upper hand in their relationship because of it.

"It's always about money with you," I grumble under my breath, but leave it at that. It doesn't pay to argue with Mama. She'll figure out a way to shut me up or resort to threatening my trust when she's lacking the high ground. She makes me even more dependent on her when she's my only source of income, which she loves, because then I have to do exactly as she says.

I can't exactly live a penniless existence right now. I took some time off after graduation to get through this debutante season. Not working means I don't have money outside of the trust. A business degree is good in theory, but without practice, it won't serve me well while unemployed. My internships during college were at major hotels in New York and Chicago, both of which offered me positions after graduation, but Mama wants me to stay here in Savannah where she can keep an eye on me. Besides, Daddy has always insisted I would run the Fairchild side of the business at The Mansion, where it all started, so I'm pretty deeply rooted in Savannah.

The Mansion has been in the family for generations and has an incredible, albeit often painful, history. My great-great-great-grandparents sold off much of their farming land and turned their antebellum home into a hotel after the Civil War when the idea of maintaining a plantation became abhorrent. Later, my great-grand-mother managed to keep her entire staff employed and even housed a few of their families during the Great Depression, a staggering feat for a single hotel run by a widow in the thirties. My grandparents helped draft the petition that turned the area that grew up around The Mansion into Savannah's historic district in the 1960s as their hotel business began to wither. Now Daddy has a whole host of gorgeous properties under his direction and wants me running The Mansion before I take over the Xenios Group. Someday, that is. Daddy is happily working on his empire, and I don't have the experience to take over, yet. I'll start in a management position at The Mansion in the New Year and will begin working toward my legacy that way.

"You scrub those potatoes any harder and we won't have anything to eat with this chicken," Mama says, opening the oven to put a tray inside to roast.

"I was just thinking about great-granny Fairchild housing the staff during the Great Depression. She was really something."

"Your granny knew she needed workers to keep the hotel running but couldn't afford to pay them with so few people able to travel or pay for a hotel stay. She let them work for room and board." Mama bumps my hip with hers to move me out of the way so she can wash her hands in the sink.

"She came up with a creative solution to a widespread problem. I admire her. I hope I can leave a lasting mark on the legacy like she did."

Mama shuts off the tap and purses her lips. "My grandparents donated cotton to the U.S. Army to make uniforms for both World Wars. What do you think about them?" she asks, wiping her hands on a dishtowel.

"Admirable as well." I put all the potatoes in a pot of water and pass them over to her to boil. A thought strikes me.

"Why didn't the Thackerys ever get into the processing business for their cotton and crops? They always dealt with the raw materials and sold them off for the rest of the process."

My mind spins with possibilities. I don't have much say in how the Thackery Agriculture endeavors are run, as that passed primarily to Mama's brother and my cousins after him. But she maintains a seat on the board, has a stake in the company, and has plenty of pull that will one day pass to me, and I have lots of ideas that could be beneficial for everyone.

"If they owned the processing and manufacturing plants to turn the materials into textiles, they could have increased revenue streams. Upward vertical integration."

"Hmm," Mama says absently, either not listening or not caring about what I have to say. "That's all I need help with now," she says with a wave. "Go change into something a little nicer."

I look down at my green silk blouse, tweed wide-leg pants, and dark brown booties with a stacked heel. "What's wrong with this? The entire outfit is designer and I know I look good. Besides, I didn't bring anything else with me." I chose the top because it's the same color as Hayes's eyes and that gave me a little strength to get through an unpleasant dinner.

"Just put on a dress, Paige. I have one picked out for you in my closet. Shoes, too. They're under the dress."

I scowl at her. This woman has no boundaries. I turn on my heel and march out of the kitchen, but not to get changed. She'll have to deal with my perfectly fine attire whether she likes it or not.

My attire is not fine.

Apparently, Mama shared the fancy dress memo with the Daniels and I'm the only one dressed down at the table. Mama had to hide her anger because I didn't come downstairs again until the company had arrived and it was too late. Had it been anyone else, I'm pretty sure she would have told me to march my behind right back up the stairs and change anyway. Something about the Daniels family makes her hold her tongue.

Dinner is an uncomfortable affair from the start. I'm seated across from Garrison and have to avoid his leering gaze. His feet keep feeling around for my legs like he wants to play footsie. That's a no-go for me. The one good thing about wearing unrestrictive pants to a fancy dinner is I can sit in my chair with my legs crossed on the seat and avoid his giant searching foot altogether.

Mama sets down a green salad at my place, knowing I won't eat the chicken. "You're looking a little *puffy*, Paige. Maybe you should avoid heavy foods for a while. I used a fat-free vinaigrette as dressing. Put your feet on the floor," she finishes on a hiss.

That's just her code for *you're gaining weight and I can't have a fat daughter*. And also, I'm embarrassing her.

I glare at her as she takes her place next to Daddy and uncross my legs to drop them to the floor, only to wrap my ankles around the chair legs to keep away from any more of Garrison's antics. I'll admit I've put on a little weight since graduating college. I blame the lack of a schedule other than volunteering opportunities and social events that all center around food. It doesn't make me feel any better about this dinner to be self-conscious about my body in addition to being irritated by Mama's meddling.

I'm quickly reminded that my parents are not the only ones who are meddling and obsessive.

"Garrison was in the top ten percent of his class; can you believe that? Our son is such a smarty-pants." Mrs. Daniels beams at Garrison, who lounges back in his chair across from me and sends me a lazy smile he must think looks sexy. He blows me a kiss next, and I throw up a little in my mouth.

"He had offers from law firms all over Georgia but chose to come back to Savannah to be close to family. We are so glad to have him back." Mr. Daniels is just as insistent as his wife about his son being God's gift to everyone.

"You're going to change the world," Mrs. Daniels says directly to Garrison, and he turns the full charm of his smile on her.

"Why, thank you, Mama. That is very kind of you to say."

I take a bite of my lettuce and mock them in my brain.

"What kind of law will you practice, Garrison?" Daddy asks, trying very hard to be a part of the conversation.

"Dupree, Athena, and Fisk mainly practice contract law, but we also have some mergers and acquisitions work for local companies. I'd say that puts me in quite the position to know what's happening and have a say in it."

You have got to be kidding me. Garrison practices contract law? There's not much he's changing other than legal jargon in business documents, let alone the world.

"Paige, what are your plans now that the season is over?" Mrs. Daniels asks.

"I—"

"She'll be preparing for her future," Mama chimes in.

I give her a discreet look of annoyance, wondering why she won't let me answer for myself. She ignores me.

"We're very proud of her for finishing college and making the deb circuit. It's time she took her rightful place working at The Mansion and standing beside the lucky man who'll be her husband."

My fork falls from my hand and clatters against the china plate. "Excuse me?" My voice just hit an octave I didn't know I was capable of, the sound bouncing off the high ceiling of the formal dining room. The entire table turns to look at me, probably seeing the shock on my face.

Husband? Who on earth could she imagine I'm dating to assume I'll be getting married anytime soon?

"Please use your indoor voice, Paige," Mama chastises, and I feel like a child bride she's grooming to be a subservient wife rather than a future business mogul.

"What's this talk about a husband?" I ask at a much more reasonable volume.

"You and me, sugar, we're gonna make some beautiful babies."

My head whips around to stare at Garrison, my jaw going unhinged as I feel positively gobsmacked at his insinuation.

"Don't you worry about the babies' names. Of course, they'll take the hyphenated Fairchild-Daniels name so the Fairchild legacy lives on." He leans back and crosses his arms over his chest with a self-satisfied look on his face.

Oh, no. No, no, no. I can't process his words. It sounds like he's making jokes at my expense, but no one is laughing or countering his lies. I look around the table as blood rushes in my ears. The expressions that look back at me are sanguine. Unconcerned. *Decided*.

My future has been decided for me.

How long have I been the only one in the dark? Is this why he came back to Savannah?

"Daddy?" I implore him as he dabs his mouth with a linen napkin. "Do you have any idea what he's talking about?"

"Your mama and I have given this plenty of thought and discussion. We wanted to introduce the idea to you tonight, though I had hoped to do it a little differently than Garrison chose to." He casts a sidelong glance at the buffoon sending me a smug look from across the table.

Garrison must be loving this turn of events that puts me at a disadvantage once again. He thrives on making others feel small. Helpless. Powerless.

"Sweet Paige, we figured out a way to combine assets from our companies without needing a formal merger," Mr. Daniels says slowly as if I'm learning impaired. "The Xenios Group will invest in the Daniels manufacturing plants, and the raw crops from the Thackery Agriculture farms will move to a processed stage for more income streams. It's a win-win for both our families."

"Yes, I know how integration works. But why does it have to involve marriage?" I bite my lip to stop the flow of words about his son's past actions. This is ridiculous. They're insane if they think I will ever get on board with this. "You can combine assets all you want in business without me marrying Garrison. This isn't how business mergers should happen," I insist.

"For our family, it is. Marriages make stronger alliances than any business deal ever could," Mama says, stopping me from protesting further. "The Daniels's manufacturing endeavors will allow us to process our raw cotton into textiles, a more valuable commodity. You were just talking about vertical integration this afternoon, so you understand. Your father and I had the same choice when we were married. We chose to create a partnership through marriage that benefited our respective ventures." Mama sips her wine like we're having a friendly chat about the weather.

She's so unbothered by the idea of turning her daughter into a business opportunity, I wonder if this has been her plan all along. It really shouldn't surprise me; she's always had one idea or another for what was best for me.

"Of course, we'll allow you and Garrison plenty of time to court before the engagement. You can fall in love the way any young woman would want to. You'll be just the tempering hand he needs in his life. It's so perfect."

I look over at Mrs. Daniels as she finishes speaking. The idyllic smile on her face says she's only seeing the fairytale side of the story she's created in her head. Does she not know her son is a monster, and I would rather drink hot lava than marry him?

"I plan to make you fall head over heels for me. You'll see. I can make your dreams come true," Garrison says, extending his hand, palm up, for me to place mine in it.

I pull back like he's a venomous snake. I want nothing to do with him in reptilian or human form. "That sounds more like a nightmare. I can assure you my dreams don't include you in any way, shape, or form."

I push my chair back from the table and stand on wobbly legs.

"You're all crazy if you thought I would go along with this." I turn my back on the madness that just occurred and walk out of the dining room.

"Paige, get back here!" Mama commands at my retreating back. I hear her own chair pushed back, but I don't turn around.

My steps don't falter as I pass through the house, grabbing my purse and coat from the hall closet before continuing out the front door. My pace quickens as I get closer to the freedom of open air and I run down the last few stone steps and along the path that leads to the carriage house, which serves as the garage. I'm too stunned to have a rational thought other than to get out while I can. Unfortunately, Mama picked me up earlier so my car is at my apartment and I'm left with only one option to get my butt out of here now.

"Everyone in this house has gone cuckoo and I want nothing to do with it," I say to the silent cars in the garage.

I pull the keys to the AC Cobra out of the drawer of the workbench along the wall and walk to the small, dark blue convertible with white racing stripes, my twenty-first birthday present that I received last August. I hop in, buckle up, and hit the garage door opener as I turn the key in the ignition. The roar of the V8 engine coming to life matches the furious thoughts swirling through my head.

"There is no way I'm marrying Garrison Daniels, would-be rapist, and all-around garbage human being," I hiss angrily, my hands strangling the polished wood steering wheel as I floor the gas and shoot out of the garage. A spray of gravel flies from the tires when I hit the long driveway and point toward the road that'll take me away from this house and the strangers inside who took the place of people I thought I knew and trusted. Mama and Daddy have lost their minds.

I drive aimlessly in an angry haze with the mild early December air whipping my hair around my head in a frenzy. It's just cold enough to be invigorating and remove my thoughts from the haze within blocks. Instead of dazed, I'm just furious. Halfway to my apartment, I slow my fuel fest and start to think about what will happen next. It's likely my parents, or at least Mama, will chase me down and hope to convince me that they know best when it comes to my future. She's been that way my whole life. *Because I said so* was repeated so often, I stopped asking her why years ago.

I shudder in disgust. How can either of them insist on this pairing with at least Mama knowing our history? I should have told Daddy all those years ago. Maybe he would be on my side or have stopped this from ever happening and blindsiding me.

Maybe I really am just a way to strengthen the businesses for them. It's an antiquated notion, but the only time the Fairchilds have differentiated their business holdings is indeed through convenient and profitable marriages. Mama and Daddy are the most recent example, but it goes back generations. Could they think this is their only option now that they want to expand the agricultural legacy that comes through Mama?

Mr. Daniels seems to expect a piece of the Fairchild empire in exchange for helping the agriculture legacy with the little bit he added in about an investment. How will this affect the Xenios Group? There are more questions than answers spinning in my brain, but I know there are plenty of ways they could go about this that won't require my participation in a sham marriage. They may have to pay a pretty penny to acquire an existing manufacturing plant or come up with a plan from scratch, but it's feasible. Even my rational thoughts get swept away in the rushing air around me as I focus on the insanity that is my life, and the dinner I just fled.

Where can I go that they won't find me? Not to my apartment. My next thought is to Alex's but he's left for New York, and I can't go to the Whitakers' house because that is the first place Mama would go to hunt me down when she starts her search. It's better to keep them out of it, anyway. I'll have to call to explain why Mama will inevitably harass Mrs. Whitaker for information on me. I have very few friends and even fewer options, it seems.

I drive aimlessly along the dark Savannah River sparkling with the reflection of the streetlights before turning inland when it becomes obvious I can't exactly run from my problems here in Savannah. It's too small, too familiar, and too easy for Mama to know exactly where to find me.

I turn down a dark street, pull over, and finally look up, shocked to find myself across the street from The Abyss, which is dark and the street empty, probably because it's closed on Sundays. I must have driven here without realizing it. At least I'm across town from Mama and Daddy's house, in the opposite direction of my apartment, and far enough from The Mansion that I've removed any possibilities of running into them should they come for me. I park on the street and sit with my hands still gripping the steering wheel. With the engine off, I can hear my phone vibrating from my bag on the seat next to me and I grudgingly fish it out. Of course, it's lit up with notifications and missed calls from Mama. I quickly text Alex.

> Paige: My parents are crazy fools who want to marry me off to, get this, Garrison Daniels *vomit*. I'm in hiding after fleeing Sunday dinner, but you might wanna let your folks know Mama will be on a warpath and she'll start with them in her crusade to get me to bend the knee if I know her at all.

A few moments pass before a message from Alex vibrates the phone I'm tightly clutching.

Alex: *whistles* She's lost it. I knew she was on the edge, but she's the queen of crazy town, now. I'll let my mama and daddy know, but don't you worry. ❌ The Whitakers have your back and my mom knows to protect your privacy after all these years of fielding off your mama's insanity.

Paige: You're my favorite, and I owe your parents something really nice for Hanukkah. I wish I could squeeze you one more time. I hope New York knows what a special person they have in their hands.

Alex: Roger that, Miss Debutante. You'll have to come to visit after the holidays. Maybe New Year's Eve? I think you need a vacation from the South and everything your parents have planned. Sending you hugs and strength. Don't let her win!

My eyes burn as I turn off my phone and bury it deeper into my bag. I wish I could hide out with Alex like I used to in high school when Mama was on a tear. I look around the deserted street in bewilderment. Now what do I do?

I look up at the tall stone building that houses The Abyss to the glass greenhouse of Elysium. *Hayes.* The name whispers through my mind seductively, and I want to bat it away like an annoying mosquito.

He is nothing more to me than a brief acquaintance I may have a raging bourbon crush on. He doesn't owe me sanctuary as I once again run away from something I don't like. He's probably back in Atlanta, anyway.

God, what would I even say if he was in residence at The Abyss? *Hi, can you hide me from my parents and the arranged marriage they think is a good idea?* I laugh bitterly at my thoughts and feel wetness creep into my eyes. I brush away the moisture, refusing to cry over this.

"Paige?"

I jump at the unexpected voice and turn to look over the passenger seat. The Cobra is an open convertible, so I have no shelter to hide from someone who knows me and will inevitably report back to Mama.

"Hayes?" I squeak.

Did I seriously just conjure the man with a thought? If I'm that good at manifesting, how did I end up in this crazy situation with my family wanting to marry me off to freaking *Garrison Daniels* of all people?

"What are you doing here?"

I look at his sweaty T-shirt and the running shorts he's wearing—they are short enough to see his beautiful, massive thighs—and deduce exactly what he was doing and also the absurdity of my question when I'm the one sitting outside of his nightclub.

"I thought you would have gone back to Atlanta," I say in explanation for my dumb question. I press my fingers to my forehead and squeeze my eyes shut. This is so stupid.

"I was planning to go back after my run. Are you okay?" He bends down and plants his hands on the passenger door to lean into the low car, coming so close to me, given the car's small size, that I can smell his divine scent mingling with the sweat from his run.

I blink to make sure the frustrated tears are gone and swipe under my eyes at any running mascara. "Just peachy."

"What's wrong?" he asks, his voice taking on a dark tone that has my eyes snapping up to meet his. "Did someone hurt you?"

I shake my head until my wind-tangled hair whips over my shoulders. "No, nothing as simple as that."

"Then why the tears? A girl like you shouldn't be crying on a beautiful evening like this."

"It's nothing you can help with," I say rather than begging for his help.

I know this is a problem I have to deal with instead of pushing it off on someone else. I'm no damsel in need of saving, but why does it feel like I can pour my heart out to him?

"Do I need to pull you out of this car, throw you over my shoulder, and march you inside to get you to tell me what's going on?" His smooth voice grows gravely, and I feel that weird pull in my belly that zips straight to my lady bits. He makes me feel things I've never felt before with just his voice alone. I shiver involuntarily at the thought.

"Wouldn't that be considered going caveman on me? This is the post-*Me, Too* era; you can't just throw a woman over your shoulder and march her anywhere," I joke, which is easier than admitting how messed up my world just became or facing my confusing feelings where he is involved.

"Honey, if caveman gets you to tell me what's got you crying and lets me fix it, I'll do it. Besides, there's a lot I can and will do, even if you think I *just can't*."

Six

Hayes

I've been thinking about Paige all day.

The innocence of her, the softness, the quick humor she uses to mask who she really is, and most of all, the way she embraced me. It wasn't just a hug. That girl clung to me like I was a lifeline and it made me feel ten feet tall instead of six-two.

Feeling her warm body against mine and her breath against my chest nearly undid my restraint. I wanted to bend her over the Chesterfield and fuck her raw. Instead, I did the honorable thing, for maybe the first time in my life, and sent her back to the party. Then I took an icy shower and jerked off thinking about her red lips on my cock until I was the one feeling raw.

I'm not what she needs in her life. This is an absolute truth that I know, logically.

She should be exploring who she is as an adult post-college, making strides in her career, and dating boys her own age. She doesn't need a cynical and ruthless old bastard like me lusting after her youthful *freshness*.

I was running from my demons and fantasies of what I could do with someone as impressionable and perfect as her when the blue Cobra parked across from the club caught my eye. You don't see them much, especially not in the winter when their lack of a roof means they are always open to the elements. I slowed down to appreciate the automotive beauty designed by Carroll Shelby in the sixties and caught the raven-haired woman rubbing at her eyes. I knew it was her before she even turned her head when I called her name.

Now her car is parked under The Abyss and I've got her in the elevator heading straight to the third-floor apartment. The elevator opens to my flat and I cross to the only door she hasn't been through. I hesitate for a fraction of a second before I unlock it and hold the door open for her. Letting her into my private apartment feels wrong because it would be too easy to get comfortable with her in the intimate space.

Having her in my office was one thing, but my apartment? It was safer having her in an area meant for business deals than one with more surfaces to imagine fucking her on.

I want to stay the honorable person who sends her away, not the lecherous old man who wants her naked.

"So this is where you live, huh?" she asks, looking around warily.

I watch her fingers flex like she wants to touch everything as she walks into the open flat. The kitchen is separated from the living space by a large island, a sofa and flatscreen TV define the small living room, and a massive bed takes up the wall in the far section of the space. It's about five hundred square feet, so by no means is it cramped, but it's not the five thousand square foot Buckhead mansion I'm used to in Atlanta.

"My turn for questions."

I place my hands on her hips and lift her, nearly smiling at the squeak of surprise she lets out. I sit her on the granite island where I can stand in front of her at eye level.

"Who did this to you?"

Her eyes snap and her surprise at being lifted is erased by the fury that springs up. "Like I said, it's nothing you can help with."

"There is very little I'm incapable of doing," I threaten. "Now spill before I resort to creative interrogation techniques to get the answers I want."

I swear her lips pinch into the hint of a grin and if that doesn't make me want to devour her, I don't know what would.

"I'm not a patient man, Paige," I warn, instead of stealing the grin off her face with a searing kiss.

The smile fades and I hate myself for erasing it. She looks away from me, toward the window that overlooks the river.

"My parents cooked up some crazy idea they want me to go along with and I can't do it. It crosses a line I didn't even know I had when it comes to them."

"What could they possibly want you to do?" I ask, searching for plausible options while I wait for her answer.

"This is so stupid I can't believe I'm about to say it." She hides her eyes with a hand. "They want me to marry an awful man to merge our family businesses."

I'm irritated more than I should be. The idea of her being married off grates my nerves. I pull her hand away from her face and see the tears welling in her jade eyes. I keep her hand in mine and squeeze it, hoping to be reassuring when what I really feel is anger that they came up with the idea before I could.

"Marriage isn't the worst thing in the world, or so I'm told. What makes the idea so repugnant to you?" Her parents are shrewd when it comes to their business, pinning a merger on a marriage. I like it.

"It's who they picked."

Her face scrunches up and she looks away as fat tears leak down her cheeks.

"His name is Garrison. We have... history," she pauses and clears her throat. "He... he got me drunk and tried to rape me in high school." She whispers through the pain and obvious shame. Her shoulders bunch up toward her ears with the admission, and she half turns away from me.

I let go of her hand and slam both of mine flat on the granite on either side of her, making her jump.

It doesn't matter that she said *tried*. This asshole wanted to violate her and that's as good as the deed itself. I want to kick one of the barstools out from under the island, throw a chair, flip a damn table because I'm so mad that anyone wanted to hurt her in that way. The innocence she exudes is precious and some entitled asshole wanted to rip that away from her? I'll kill him.

The possessive streak in me is blown wide and she's not even mine to protect, but damn if I won't destroy anything that even threatens to hurt her, now or anytime in the past.

"Do they know?" I demand close to her face, my voice a snarl. "Your parents. Do they know what he did to you?"

Her nod is almost imperceptible, but I'm close enough that I can see each individual eyelash that sits against her wet cheeks through the slight motion.

"Mama knows," she says softly, her words catching on a hitch.

I do kick the stool now. It sails across the room and clatters against the heavy wood footboard of the bed. I stalk toward it like I'll kick it straight out the window next.

"Why would your mother even allow that?" My chest heaves with the anger coursing through me. "No, fuck that. Why would your parents *want* you to marry someone who tried to rape you?"

I have too many questions and enough anger to ruin anyone who wants this fate for her. I want to throttle her father for even entertaining the idea, whether or not he knows the full story. He should know. He should be the one angry and hell-bent on making the sonofabitch pay for what he did to Paige. The drawn-out way I want to hurt the guy who did this is savage and could have me labeled a psychopath if it ever became news.

"Why are you so angry?" she asks, surprising me. I spin and stomp back to the island, pushing my hips between her knees and placing my hands on the granite to lean into her space. She doesn't pull back, but her eyes widen.

"Why aren't you?"

"I am angry!" she shouts in my face. "Why do you think I was parked out there? I was too angry to be driving, but I needed to get away from my family and their insane business dealings." She shakes her head and returns her eyes to me. "Having my future decided for me is one thing. Being told who to marry because it's fortuitous for the family business is a whole new level of screwed up. But maybe it's the only way they think they can get what they want." The sad tone her voice takes lends itself to acceptance and I'm not about to let her roll over and allow them to use her like that.

"What kind of deal would they get from selling you off like chattel?" The energy of her anger crackles between us when I speak, and I encourage it. "You're valuable, so they better be getting something good for this kind of fucked up trade. What does an heiress like you fetch on the marriage market? A couple million? A private jet? Some nice new vacation home?"

The sting of her slap comes as no surprise after my taunts. The burn on my cheek is refreshing, and I wish she could feel that incandescent truth for herself, without the physical pain.

"How dare you!" Her chest heaves against the green silk of her top and I want to send buttons flying when I rip it off her.

Instead, I smile cruelly. "Stay angry, Paige. Maybe you'll clear that pretty little head of yours and realize how fucked your family is to even consider this. You're not a bargaining chip for a business deal, honey, you're the whole damn pot."

The righteous indignation leaves her as she shrinks into herself.

"My family is unusual, and so is the way they do business. They don't see anything wrong with arranging marriages to make a profit or invest in the family business. The way my legacy is passed down is to a *married* heir, so I can see why they're making me get married, and having it be good for their own ends as well."

She blows out a breath and looks anywhere but in my eyes. I want to grab her cute little chin and force her to look at me. I curl my fingers around the edge of the island instead.

"My parents had an arranged marriage to join two powerful empires, just like generations of Fairchilds have done before. To them, it's normal to want to marry me off to another family that would be an advantageous match when it comes to vertical integration."

"Stop it. You're thinking way too rationally about something completely irrational. Listen to yourself, for fuck's sake! Getting married for advantageous vertical integration? This isn't the boardroom, it's your life."

"I'm just trying to make sense of things and see it from their perspective," she snaps. "They have to have their reasons, and I want to be objective about it."

"There's nothing to be objective about with their nasty little plan. They want you to marry a guy who was willing to rape you. What do you think your relationship will be like? Separate bedrooms and lives? No. He'll take full advantage of the situation and your parents will want grandkids, so guess what, you'll be getting raped whenever he wants to have you and it'll be under the guise of your marital duties so you'll have to take it."

Crass and cruel, but it's the truth. Boys who think it's okay to get girls drunk in order to coerce sex from them turn into men who are sick and twisted. I would bet my Maybach the fucker has tried what he did to Paige on others, and I want to hunt him down and trap him like the rat he is.

"I bet he was thrilled about his part of the bargain."

She looks up at me, her big eyes brimming with tears again. "He was."

The crack in her voice nearly brings me to my knees. I don't want this for her, and she shouldn't be forced into anything remotely this shitty.

"You can't marry him." It seems like the most obvious statement I can make, but it needs to be said.

"I never said I would."

"You're still trying to see things from your parent's perspective, so that tells me you're at least considering the pros and cons of going through with it. What happened to that line you can't cross?"

"I was just blindsided, okay? I never imagined they would even suggest something like this, let alone have them spring it on me at Sunday dinner when everyone but me was in on it."

"They're something else." I shake my head, feeling the righteous anger quelling as the need to comfort and protect her wells up. I need to help her through this in whatever way she'll let me. I take a deep, steadying breath to push the anger out of my tone. "What do you want to do now?"

"Run away," she says wistfully.

I straighten up. This I can work with. I have the means to send her anywhere she could possibly want to go. Paris, Bali, Australia. If she names a town I've heard of, I'll send the jet there in a heartbeat. "If you could go anywhere in the world, where would it be?" I will make it happen with the snap of my fingers, but I don't offer that information.

Her cheeks turn pink, and her mouth closes tight. She shakes her head, refusing to answer. What kind of answer would have her reacting like that? I'm more curious than ever about the inner workings of her incredibly sexy mind.

"Tell me, honey. What was the first thing that just popped into your head?"

"Somewhere with you." Her whisper is so faint I have to play it over in my head to realize what she said.

"You can go anywhere in the world and you want to be with me?" I ask softly. I'm floored by the possibility that she feels even a hint of the attraction I do, that she could want me, despite our decade-plus age gap and our obvious differences.

"It's stupid, I know, but you made me answer with what first came to my mind and for some reason, I decided to be honest. I take it back. I want to go to Turks and Caicos."

I grin. "No takebacks. If you want to be with me, you're getting what you want. You want to run away? Good. You're coming with me to Atlanta." I press a kiss to her forehead and saunter across the flat to the bathroom, leaving her stunned on the island.

"Where are you going?" she calls after a few seconds.

"I need a shower. Unless you want to join me, I suggest you get comfortable for the ten minutes it's going to take me."

Her gasp of shock is gorgeous, and I laugh as I close the bathroom door. She's *really* innocent. It's hard to imagine that someone as stunning as she is would balk at being invited to shower with a man. Granted, we only met twenty-four hours ago, and she's just agreed to run away with me, but I had assumed she would be a little more experienced, or at least a little more confident with men. I'm starting to think she's untouched, and that spikes the possessive feelings in me to new levels. If I were an animal, I'd pee a circle around her and fight off any males who dared come close. It also makes me feel like a lecherous bastard. I am way too old for her, and she's far too innocent for me.

I do the next best thing to marking my territory. I pull out my phone and send a message to my assistant. I need more information about this Garrison kid and want to know about the Fairchilds' interesting marriage clause in their inheritance practices. I leave strict instructions to be discreet but thorough, then step into the shower.

Seven

Hayes

"What is that?" Paige asks when I hit the key fob to unlock my car in the garage.

I was a little disappointed she didn't join me in the shower, though I hadn't expected her to. It's these warring feelings and expectations that are going to get me into trouble with her. Being honorable when I'm used to being deplorable is like mixing oil and water. Doesn't stick for long.

"Maybach Exelero."

I love this fucking car. I noticed it in the Jay-Z "Lost One" music video and knew I had to have it. It cost me a fortune, in fact, it was several million more than most people hope to make in their entire lives, but it suits me better than any other vehicle I've driven. There was only one made. The exclusivity made it more tantalizing than anything else available. Except maybe the woman who slides into the black and red interior of the sleek black car. She could be hands down the most enthralling person I've ever met and she's barely an adult. I don't know if it's the innocence she exudes, that she's the key to her daddy's kingdom, or the feeling she stirs in me to care about someone other than myself, but it's intriguing.

"Never heard of it. Guess it's pretty cool, though," she says, taking the seat belt I hand her before I close the door.

I round the back of the long car and climb into the driver's side after I tuck my Louis Vuitton weekender in the space behind the seat.

"Pretty cool?" I mimic.

I start the engine with a roar that threatens to bring the roof crashing down on us with the reverberations from the exhaust.

"That V12, twin turbo engine sound *cool* to you?"

"Okay, it's scary cool." She looks over at me and rolls her eyes. "I've never seen this around town. I'm surprised you managed to stay under the radar driving this death-mobile around."

"Death-mobile?"

"You're like Batman, but with a sleeker, more villainous ride that promises death. Definitely a death-mobile."

I nod in acceptance. "I've heard worse."

She turns in her seat to face me. "Like what?"

I carefully exit the garage and turn toward the airport. "Oh, you know, dream killer, life ruiner, business ender.

Lots of stuff that relates to death, so I guess I need a death-mobile to complete the package."

"Why would anyone say that about you?"

Oh, sweet summer child, I think. She has no clue.

"Let's just say I'm the one who has to deliver the swift death blow to all those failing businesses Olympus gobbles up. I'm not loved as much as my brothers, who get to play with the functional portions we keep and make prosper."

"You're still a part of the most successful holding company in the South. Heck, the East Coast. You have to do what's best for the business overall, even if it means shuttering parts that are no longer producing or congruent with the vision the company takes on."

"Try one of the top five corporations in *the world,* sweet girl."

She grabs my arm that is resting on the center console. "How? I read Forbes. I stay up to date with the business world. How is this news to me?"

"We have many names and faces. You've likely heard of the more public portions of the corporation, but Olympus is privately held and we're quiet about our dealings. There is plenty we can do under any other part of the business that may never link back to Olympus as a whole."

"Privately held and that secretive. Are you in the mafia?"

Surprised laughter bursts out of me, shaking my whole body as I try to compose myself. It takes a moment,

"Hell no. The mafia is chump change. We're about legitimate business, but willing to get as underhanded as we have to be when necessary to get what we want. Legally, of course."

"That sounds like the mob. I won't, like, go to the police or anything if you are. Your secret is safe with me." She squeezes my arm where her hand still rests. I like it there.

"We're not the mob, but I appreciate your vow of secrecy. That's touching, actually. You'd keep my secrets literally the day after meeting me. Have I even earned that loyalty?" I muse aloud. I certainly haven't earned her trust, yet she's placed a lot in me, just by being in this car now.

"You're aiding and abetting a Fairchild fugitive from the parental law, so yeah, you've earned it. Don't say I didn't warn you, though. Mama's wrath is legendary, like, freeze the earth bad when upset, so this could blow up in your face as well as mine."

"That's a risk I'm willing to take." *High risk, high reward.*

I pull onto the tarmac in the private section of the airport, the gate sliding open without me having to stop, and head to my hangar where the jet is waiting. I park the Maybach in the hangar and nod at the armed guard dressed as a mechanic who lives on-site to babysit my toys. You don't just leave a multimillion-dollar car unsupervised.

"Of course, a plane," she says under her breath as she gets out of the car. "I thought we were driving to Atlanta and was planning to spend four hours in the car. I guess it's smarter to fly when you have private jet money," she says, louder.

"Work smarter, not harder. I actually want to get some sleep tonight before work tomorrow, so a four-hour drive isn't ideal."

I follow her up the stairs to the jet and get her settled in a leather chair before I hand over my bag to a flight attendant and take the seat across from her.

"You'll need some things. How long do you want to run away?" I ask. I'm already mentally creating a list of items she may need that I will text to my assistant as soon as I know her sizes.

"As long as necessary to drive home the message that I am *not* marrying Garrison Daniels, no matter how badly they want the business perks that union would bring. So at least a week, I would assume. Maybe longer if Mama puts her foot down and cuts off my trust. Oh, God." She stops abruptly and cringes. "Um, also, I'm probably going to be poor soon, so I may need a temporary loan for some necessities until I can smooth things over with Mama. I'll pay you back, with interest."

"You will have anything you could possibly want, just say the word and it's yours, no payback or interest needed," I promise without hesitation. I know what I'm getting myself into. I'm absconding with a Southern hotel heiress, protective parents be damned, and money is no issue.

She shifts in her seat as the plane begins to taxi on the runway. "Why are you doing this for me?" she asks, a hint of mistrust tinging her words.

I have the opportunity to be brutally honest and lay out exactly what I want from her, or I can temper my response so it doesn't have her jumping out of this plane before it can get off the ground. Given the mistrust, it's probably better to go with the latter.

"I know what it's like to have overbearing parents who plan your life out for you, removing your freedom of choice, and the frustration that leads to when you have differing plans," I begin. It may not be my exact story, but I can relate.

Thatcher and Rula Mae Olsen raised three head-strong, independent, and ruthless men, but they weren't what I'd call the model of doting parents. Calculating and demanding is more their speed. They raised us boys to be the men who would take over the family business and lead it without hesitance. There wasn't much of a choice in the matter for me. I knew what my role would be from the time I understood what the business was.

"I think you need some space from the situation to make up your own mind about how you want to proceed. It doesn't cost me much to make sure you get what you need, and it's my pleasure to give you what you want."

She blushes crimson, so I know she's picked up on the subtle innuendo. It's going to be fun playing with her innocent nature. She clears her throat and tucks hair behind her ear.

"But what do you get out of it?" Her clear green eyes drill into me, demanding a forthright answer, even if she doesn't know what she's asking for.

I lean forward, my elbows pressing into my thighs as I stare into her eyes. "You."

Eight

Paige

$M^{e.}$

Hayes. Wants. Me.

The flight was short and I'm still contemplating his one-word answer now that we are in Atlanta and driving in another of his beautiful cars. The butterflies in my belly have turned into the hummingbirds that visit Mama's sugar water feeder daily and a flood of warmth washes over me from head to toe as I replay what he said for the ninetieth time. This accomplished, driven, secretive *man* wants what I have to offer. Which is what, exactly? A recent entry into society, domineering parents, a long wait to inherit my family legacy, and no sexual experience to speak of. What could he do with a virgin? Oh, wait...

I pull my bottom lip into my mouth with my teeth and twist a button on my blouse with worrying fingers.

Hayes drives us through the dark streets of Atlanta in the Mercedes SLR McLaren that was waiting for us at the airport. I had to ask him what it was, just like with the Maybach. I know without Googling that it must be expensive and rare, as that seems to be his taste with automobiles.

Now we're headed to *his house* in *Atlanta*, a place Mama calls a hell hole. Will he expect me to have sex with him when we get there? I mean, I'm not against the idea, but it seems a little soon and I'm not prepared for this in the least. I would have gotten a bikini wax and worn pretty lingerie over freshly showered and lotioned skin. I want my first time to be perfect, after all. Dropping my panties and crawling into bed with Hayes after learning my parents want to marry me off for a business deal isn't exactly what I had in mind.

"What's warping that brain of yours, honey?" he asks, his hand reaching over to find mine and freeing the button from my torture before it comes off in my fingers.

I don't mind the way he calls me honey. It's far sexier coming from his mouth than I've ever heard it said, and it makes me feel closer to him somehow. For all I know, he could call every woman honey in order to avoid the faux pas of a forgotten name, but he uses my name just as frequently, so I doubt that's the case.

A shock of cold breaks through the cozy feelings that have turned my brain to mush. Thinking of him calling another woman honey, whisking her away, or interlacing his fingers with hers as he does with mine drives a wedge of rage right through my center. I tighten my grip in my moment of jealousy over a freaking possibility.

"Are you going to tell me what you're thinking about, or just crush my hand a little more until I can get you home and force you to tell me?" he growls.

I release my death grip, but he doesn't retract his fingers from mine.

"Are you seeing anyone?" I want to know if he's sleeping with anyone, but that's not a polite question for a proper lady to ask, so I work around it. If he is, I need to turn right around and get back to Savannah, because I am not about to ruin a relationship.

"That's what has your head in knots?"

His thumb smooths over my knuckles and I huff out a breath as I look out my window.

"Paige, look at me."

I stare at the ceiling of the sports car and take a deep breath before I turn my face in his direction. "Yes, I want to know if you're in a relationship. Or, you know, frequently indulge in a casual kind of thing." My words grow more mumbled as I speak, and I fight to not turn away from him immediately in my embarrassment.

"I could lie and say I've been a celibate bachelor for years, but I think you actually need the truth. Brace yourself, baby girl."

He gives my hand a tug, so I glance at him and catch the set of his lips and the intense look on his face. I nod to tell him I'm ready to hear what he has to say.

"I fuck any willing woman I want whenever I feel like it."

I suck in a breath and want to jump out of the car to get away from the mortification that is burning my skin.

"Thank you for being honest," I whisper.

"I'm not finished. The women I sleep with see only my Amex black card and what they can get from me, so I treat them in kind."

"Gotcha." I try to pull my hand away from his, but he stops me with a slight tightening around my fingers.

"I would love to see every inch of your body trembling under mine as I turn you inside out with pleasure. I want to trace kisses across your body to map your soft skin and find every spot that makes you moan and call out my name."

By the time he stops talking in his deep, sandpaper rasp, I'm breathing heavily with sweat beading on my forehead, a drop tracing its way down my spine. My thighs rub together, looking to find some relief from the heavy pull in my center that floods my panties with warmth.

"Wow," I breathe out. When I risk a look in his direction, I catch his tongue darting out to wet his bottom lip the same way I'm dying to.

"Does that sound remotely casual to you?" His voice takes on a gravelly quality that continues the barrage of feelings that drag me into his undertow.

I stay silent.

"Answer me."

"I-I don't think so." My voice is a husky whisper of its proper volume, but I'm unable to give him anything more.

"Trust me, it's not."

I simply nod my acceptance because I don't have the capability of forming a coherent sentence.

"Have you been with a man before?" His question is soft, looking for confirmation.

My cheeks heat and I look down at my lap, my brain going from incredibly intrigued to embarrassed with the flip of a switch. What if he doesn't want to be my first? I could be too inexperienced, too fragile and new.

He likely wants a woman who knows her way around a man's body.

I don't know how to please someone like him. I don't even know the mechanics of what the first step would be to achieve that. I could never meet his expectations for a lover, and he's going to hate it if we do sleep together. I'll be a disappointment.

"Paige, are you a virgin?" he asks again, more directly.

I nod my head, too flustered to speak the acknowledgment.

I hear a groan and think he's offended, regretting his decision to help me at all, regretting telling me what he would do to me, and wishing he had stayed silent. I risk a glance in his direction, my cheeks hot with shame now. He returns my stare, but his mouth is a sensual smile and his eyes are intense.

"I would love to be your first. I will absolutely, and with happiness, ruin you for any other man if it meant you were mine. None of that will happen unless it's exactly what you want, and when you want it. I won't touch you until you tell me when you're good and ready for me."

He clears his throat and returns his attention to the dark road. The implication that I will be ready for him at some point hangs between us like forbidden fruit. I'm already *this close* to reaching for it to see how good it would taste, damn the consequences.

He just promised to not only take my virginity but turn me into a sensual creature he'll worship *when I'm ready*. Praise Jesus, I just found a man willing to wait until I'm comfortable and begging for him. Sorry, Jesus, I don't mean to invoke you when it comes to sex, but hallelujah!

"We're here," he says a few minutes later, turning into a driveway and pushing a button that causes a heavy wrought iron gate to swing inward and allow our passage.

I lean forward to catch whatever view I can in the flashes of the headlights as we wind back into the heavily wooded property.

"Are we still in Atlanta?"

"Northwest Atlanta, yes. I have a few acres of property, so it feels more rural."

"I wouldn't say rural, more like an enchanted forest, but okay, Hayes."

He slows and I turn back to catch sight of the huge, modern home constructed of glass, wood, and steel.

"What the heck?" I say out loud.

"What's wrong?" He pulls the Mercedes up along the front of the house and shuts off the engine.

"Nothing's wrong, exactly. It's not what I was expecting, I guess." I look up as I step out of the car. The house is three stories in one section and two in the rest and is very wide with sharp angles everywhere.

"Which was?"

He holds his hand out to me and I take it with a bit of hesitation. We're about to walk into his house, in Atlanta, hours away from Savannah where my parents expect me to be. I feel far removed by both time and space.

"An estate, I think. I'm not really sure what to expect from you. I'm used to the Antebellum and Victorian architecture in Savannah, and your apartment there was in a historic building, so I guess I assumed your house would be some classic stone mansion. Maybe a few gargoyles and definitely split into wings so you would have to tell me to avoid the west wing. Wow, I just up and ran away, didn't I?"

He chuckles at my non-sequitur. "You're something else."

He opens the front door for me, but before I can get a look at the interior, a huge black dog rounds a corner and comes to a skittering halt that blocks our way in. I do what any stranger in a dog's face does and freeze. The dog is muscular and thickly built with ears that are cut to stand up straight from its blocky head and smart whiskey-colored eyes that are focused on me with an intensity that would have anyone peeing their pants. I tighten my bladder to avoid that fate and the humiliation that would come with it. I swallow with an audible gulp.

"Are you a good boy?" I ask the dog in a soft voice.

He whines and paws at the ground.

"You are a good boy!" I say in my most pathetically indulgent baby voice, because when you have a giant dog in front of you, you better make friends with it, fast. The dog pants and shimmies a few steps back and forth as his butt wiggles in excitement.

"Good boy, Cerb. Sit," Hayes commands.

The dog obeys instantly, sitting back on his thick haunches, and looking at Hayes for his next instruction.

"He likes you."

"What dog wouldn't like me? He probably knows I'm a sucker and I'll share all my food with him and give the good belly scratches."

Hayes laughs and shakes his head. "You're going to spoil my dog, aren't you?"

"Absolutely. Don't even tell me where the treats are, I'll find them on my own and you'll have a fat dog before the week is over."

The big dog barks and paws at the ground.

"I hear you, big guy, you want all the treats. Come on, lead the way."

He happily springs up from his perfect sit and sprints the length of the big open hallway and turns a corner with a four-paw slide in his excitement.

"He's a big softy, isn't he?" I look up with a smile at Hayes and catch his appraising look.

"No. He's a guard dog, but I think you broke him."

I laugh out loud and leave Hayes at the door to follow the dog, who is poking his giant head around the corner, waiting for me to follow.

"What kind of dog is he?" I call over my shoulder.

"Cane Corso Italiano. His name is Cerberus," Hayes answers, following behind while I take my time and look all around at his house.

"I love that. It's perfect for him. Hey, Cerberus, did you find the treats, sweet baby?"

He gives me a *barroo* of a response and I smile. I follow the dog into a big modern kitchen with slick marble surfaces and glossy cabinets set against stainless steel appliances, white tiles on the walls, and slate gray flooring.

"I think I'm going to like it here."

"I like you here, too."

I stop and look over my shoulder at Hayes. He's leaning against the doorway to the kitchen, his arms crossed over his chest. I smile softly and turn away as my cheeks heat with a blush.

I go to the door Cerberus is standing by, wagging his nub of a tail and looking back at me expectantly. Inside I find a big walk-in pantry that is full of items, but Cerberus leads me right to the container of dog treats. I reward his helpfulness with a few treats as he performs all the tricks I can think to ask him.

"You taught your dog to play dead?" I ask after I've pointed a finger gun at him and said bang. He is still on the ground, his tongue hanging out as he waits for me to tell him to get up.

"He's had extensive training. He knows everything," Hayes answers with a grin. "Cerberus, place," he says, pointing at a rug near the sink. The dog jumps up, gallops to the rug, and sits, pushing the rug across the floor in his haste to do what his master has asked.

I toss a treat at Cerberus for being such a good doggo. He catches it with a snap of his jaws and crunches happily.

"I think that's plenty of treats for you, big guy." I shake the box of crumbs and set it on the counter.

"I'll have more sent tomorrow. It's getting late. Are you tired? Hungry? Want to kill me yet?"

I look up at the weird question and shake my head.

"You went out of your way to help me. The last thing I want to do is kill you."

"Good. Let's go to bed."

My eyes widen. "Bed, as in together?" *Is this it?*

"Relax, there's more than one bed in this house." He motions with his chin at the door and whistles sharply for the dog, who pops up and trots out of the kitchen.

I follow Cerberus up the stairs, knowing Hayes is right behind me. I hesitate at the doorway to the bedroom Cerberus walks through and look back.

"Is this where you want me?"

Hayes walks right into my space, and I back up until I'm against the doorjamb with the heat of him along my front. He brushes my hair over my shoulder and traces his fingertips against the skin of my collarbones and up my neck until his fingers are threaded in my hair and he's cradling my head. His thumb strokes over my bottom lip, and my mouth parts.

"Why does that innocent question from your lips sound like the most sinful suggestion?"

My body grows warm and quivers in nervous anticipation. I raise my chin and look up at his lips, slightly parted and so freaking kissable.

His eyes burn hot with a need that terrifies me. I grip the doorway behind me to keep my hands from pulling him closer and starting something I won't know how to finish. This man is sex appeal incarnate, a walking wet dream, and I'm too afraid to act on anything because what if I don't live up to his expectations? He's had *any woman he's wanted*, and I'm sure they've all been sex goddesses who knew exactly what to do with that hot desire in his eyes. Whereas I have never even been kissed.

He drops his hand and abruptly moves away.

Disappointment is not what I was expecting to feel, but it washes over me in a wave of regret for not having pushed up on my toes and brought my lips to his the way I had imagined. I follow a moment later, walking into the sleek room punctuated with dark furniture and a huge dog bed in the corner. He moves through the space without the hesitance that I do, turning the light on when he enters what I assume is the closet. The bed is just as big as the one in Savannah and topped with a pristine white duvet that balances out the dark wood frame and the gray textured wallpaper wrapping the room that lends a cozy feel.

What does he look like stretched out on that bed? I imagine his tan skin standing out against the stark white, his hair rumpled from sleep, and his green eyes doing that burning emerald thing again as he takes me in.

"Here."

I jump and look up from the bed cover I was just smoothing my hand along, imagining his skin under my fingers. He's holding a stack of clothing.

"Thought you might want something to sleep in."

I take the T-shirt and flannel pajama pants from him and hug them to my chest protectively as my heart hammers against my ribs.

"I probably should have picked up some of my stuff, huh?"

He smiles. "We can take care of that tomorrow." He rubs the back of his neck. "You can go shopping while I'm at work, or I can have some things brought in for you."

I bristle at the thought of someone else picking out clothes for me, like Mama would. He would probably have some gorgeous assistant do it.

"I'm perfectly capable of buying my own clothes."

He nods. "That settles it, then. Good night, Paige."

"Wait." I grab his arm as he turns to leave. "You want me to sleep in your room?"

He must have a guest room somewhere that would be easier than giving up his space for me. It's an inconvenience I don't want him to have to endure for my sake.

"It's the most comfortable, so yes. What's mine is yours for as long as you're here. If you need anything, I'll be across the hall."

I'm at a loss for how I feel thanks to the kind gesture, his words, and how accommodating he's been for an interloper who invited herself into his life without any warning. From the little I know about him from the business world, he's known as uncompromising, ruthless, and devastating. Instead of experiencing that, he's shown a much kinder side to me. I don't hold back when I put the clothes on the bed and cross the small space to him. He opens his arms for me in anticipation just before I wrap mine around him and tuck my head into his chest. Hugging must be my love language for how I resort to it to convey my appreciation to him.

"Thank you. For everything."

He wraps me against him in strong arms for a moment before he sets me away and leaves the room quickly.

I'm left standing in the room alone, feeling empty and confused, knowing that could have gone better. I look over at Cerberus, lying in his bed and watching the doorway through which his master left.

"Not exactly what I wanted, but oh well," I say to him.

He pulls himself up with a grumble and walks over to me, nudging his head into my hand until I pet him.

"Guess you'll have to do in a pinch."

Nine

Hayes

Cerberus looks up at me from where he's sprawled out on my bed. Paige has a bare leg kicked out from under the covers and it's resting on one of Cerberus's massive paws. He looks quite content to be cuddling with the heiress I stole from Savannah and not at all guilty about the fact he's not supposed to be on the bed. A cloud of Paige's dark hair is spread over the pillows, her face peacefully asleep in the early morning light.

I cross the room silently to the bathroom where I shower off my morning workout and quietly dress for work. Paige is still asleep when I stand at the end of the bed and fit my silver cufflinks on my shirt. I had hoped she would stir, roll over, and tell me good morning before I left her here for the day, but it's probably better if she doesn't. I woke with my dick hard as a rock and taking care of myself hasn't alleviated the need I feel for her body that calls to me like a siren. I am liable to act on my inclination to run my hands up her soft leg and see where it leads if she so much as smiles at me right now.

"Take care of her," I whisper to Cerberus, the traitor who normally doesn't leave my side but now has a new favorite human.

I leave a note on the nightstand for Paige and drive away from the house with an unusual feeling gnawing at me. I wake up, get shit done, and eat business acquisitions for breakfast with a smile on my face, but I'm not at all excited about leaving for work today. The gorgeous debutante in my bed is to blame for my lack of desire to do a job I normally love.

"Welcome back from the sticks," Zander says when I exit the elevator and enter the executive offices of our downtown building. "Bring us any souvenirs from your antebellum wonderland?"

"A little birdy told me he brought himself back a pretty present this time," Payton pipes in, walking over with a cup of coffee in his hand.

I take the cup from him, and he protests.

"What fucking birds are you listening to now?"

I'm going to have to check which loose-lipped staff member needs a reminder of who pays their salary and replace them immediately. I operate under the utmost discretion when it comes to my private life, and if someone on my staff is willing to share details with my nosy brother, they will more than likely spill other secrets to someone outside of the family. That's unacceptable.

"I have my sources but relax. It's on the Atlanta Haute List, not someone from Olympus."

He pulls his phone from his pocket and shows me the local gossip site with a dark photo of me helping a woman into my gull-wing Mercedes outside of the jet at the airport. The headline reads, "Billionaire playboy Hayes Olsen is living the after-hours life, jetting into town with a new plaything on his arm". At least they don't know my 'plaything' is a hotel heiress who is fourteen years younger than me. Once they get wind of that, the real press vultures will descend.

"Check the airport staff. This wasn't taken with a telephoto lens, so someone was too close to the hangar. Find the person responsible and get rid of them," I say, handing the phone back to Payton.

"That's your role, big bro. You do all the firing and nasty work. I stay on top of the gossip and set you loose when the real shit hits the fan." Payton grins smugly and I'm glad I stole his fucking coffee.

"Is she a liability?"

I turn to look at Zander, standing stern-faced in the doorway of the office I want very badly to enter and shut them both out of. Look at the pot calling the kettle black.

"When have I ever entertained a liability?" I spit.

He's the one I'm normally cleaning up after, paying off bitter exes and issuing NDAs to every fresh-faced model who doesn't want to leave his penthouse apartment when he's finished with them. If any of the Olsen brothers should be called a playboy, it's the youngest, Zander.

"You know we're under a deadline to roll out phase two. If we start making waves in the news that tanks public perception, it's going to cost us. Even I'm on my best behavior which means it should be a piece of cake for you to keep your nose clean. If you fuck this up, we're back to square one and we lose out on a cash cow."

"I'm well aware of our business dealings and needs, so shut your fucking mouth before I shut it for you." I loom over him with the threat, using the extra inch of height to my advantage.

Zander's gray eyes flash dark with his temper and likely the frustration of staying out of trouble. His trouble usually involves long legs and willing pussies, so I can only imagine the pent-up aggression he's holding at bay.

I'm a little pent-up myself and the gorgeous girl probably just waking up in my bed has everything to do with it.

"Get your asses in the boardroom and quit giving me shit. We have meetings to run and deals to make." I point at the heavy black doors that lead into the room where they can stay out of my business. And now I have to hunt down a leak at the airport and deal with that mess.

Payton whistles. "Look at this elusive fucker not answering our questions about the woman. He really doesn't want us to know about this one."

I glare at Payton, ready to deck him if he doesn't quit his middle-child meddling.

"Let's see. You flew in from Savannah, so she's someone you met there. That's a mixed bag of social elite and backwater busted. She top tier or bottom barrel, Hater?"

I grit my teeth at the stupid nickname. They will keep at this until they figure it out, and it's better heard from me where I can control what they learn than from one of their minions who will be sent out scouting on their behalf.

"Fucking crème de la crème, leagues above your own standards, Payton." I pause and double down on my resolve that this is necessary. "It's Paige Fairchild," I finally bite out, hating to give this piece of information up when I wanted to keep it all to myself.

Payton pumps his fist in the air. "Holy shit! Hayes has gone after the woman set to inherit the very legacy he wants to steal. You've got mad cojones, man. This is conniving, even for you."

"You think you can fuck the hotel deal out of her? She the kind of girl who would prefer a fat check to running a hotel empire?" Zander asks, a hint of awe lacing his crude words. Even he hasn't attempted to sleep with someone to cement a potential business deal, which is probably for the best.

"I think you need to drop it and move on. Don't you assholes have work to do?"

"I like your tactic. Just don't let it blow up in your face and ruin our chances of adding a hospitality sector to the business. This could definitely fuck up phase two like Zander said."

"Thank you for your astute observations, Payton. Now get the fuck out of my office and let me work." I push them both out the door and slam it in their faces. This is what I get for working with my fucking family. I'm stuck with them forever when all I really want to do is fire their asses.

Ten

Paige

"Where in heaven's name are you?" Mama's screech is an unwelcome start to my day, but it's time I called her back. Turning my phone on after waking up in Hayes's bed with his big beast curled up next to me was an unfortunate responsibility that had to be tended to. So when I pulled on the flannel pajama pants Hayes lent me and padded down the stairs to let Cerberus outside, I finally found the courage to do it.

"I'm safe in Atlanta."

Mama lets out a groan of despair. She hates Atlanta with a passion, avoiding the capital city with fervor, so it's an extra slap to the face to know her only daughter has bolted straight for Satan's very gates.

"Your father and I have been worried sick looking for you. Now we find out you don't even have the decency to tell us you would be leaving town after you ruined our family dinner. We reported you missing, Paige!"

Alarm floods my system and I have to take a seat on a lounge chair by the gorgeous deep blue lap pool. Unfazed by the yelling coming through the phone, Cerberus trots around the acres of green grass, looking for the perfect spot to do his morning business.

"You reported me missing? Mama, I've been gone for less than twelve hours. It's not like I would have been tossed in the river as soon as I left your house."

"You took the Cobra. You could have been killed in an accident with that coffin on wheels," she insists. "And you weren't at your apartment, and no one has seen you or the car. What was I supposed to think? I cried my eyes out all night worrying about you. The sheriff is out searching for you this morning. I'm going to have to call him and tell him you left of your own accord trying to give me a heart attack."

The guilt trip is heavy, but it's not a burden I should have to shoulder alone. Her actions pushed me to leave and refuse to tell her anything more, so she brought the worry on herself.

"Well, call off the dang search. I'm fine."

I try to keep the snap out of my voice, but I'm finding it hard to feel the sympathy she wants.

"You went too far, Mama."

"So this is all my fault once again? You always do this, Paige. There are certain customs you have to adhere to when you come from a family like ours. Like it or not, you have responsibilities other girls don't have to assume."

"I won't marry a would-be rapist, Mama. Even you have to realize that can't be one of the responsibilities and customs on my shoulders."

She makes a strangled noise and I wonder if it's possible to cause a stroke with a phone conversation.

"Garrison Daniels is a wonderful man from a good family. Your alleged assault story from years ago is the only time he has ever been bad-mouthed by anyone in our town. It's about time you get over the fact you made a mistake and led a boy on at a party and were confused by the events that took place because of it."

Alleged assault? I led him on? Confused? I think I'm now the one at risk of an aneurysm. Hot tears prick my eyes as my own mother blames me for something I had very little control over.

"I can't believe you. Your ambition to make something of the minor part of our legacy knows no bounds. You would rather marry off your only daughter to a predator to save what's left of a dying industry. All for what? More money?"

"This isn't about money, it's about your future! You need to be with a man who knows how to take care of you the way we have all your life, and Garrison can do that. It's just an extra blessing that his family can augment the legacy you will pass on to your own children.

You'll understand, someday, how hard it is to give your children the best they deserve."

I pop up from the lounge chair like it electrocuted my behind and pace the stone pool deck in a rage.

"I deserve a lot more than Garrison Daniels, Mama. I'm staying in Atlanta until you realize that for yourself."

"That's it. You've pushed me too far. I'm cutting off your trust. You won't get anything from the family you're shaming with your atrocious behavior."

I take a deep breath, knowing this was the likely course of action she would take to force my hand.

"Mama, I love you, but I don't like anything about you at the moment. Cut off the trust if that's what makes you feel more in control. I don't care and it won't make me come home any sooner. I hope we can have a better conversation in a few days when you can see the cutting your hair with kitchen scissors crazy you're being right now."

She makes a squawk of outrage as I end the call with shaking fingers. I've never stood up to her like this before, and the unease I feel at going against my mother's wishes is agonizing. I stop my pacing and wipe my wet cheeks. Cerberus sits at my feet, his back against my legs, his head scanning the yard around us.

"I'm glad you're here, buddy," I tell him, bending down to place a kiss on his head.

He rewards me with a few licks on my hand before getting up to walk to the house. He pauses and looks back to see if I'm following him.

"Yes, you bossy thing, I'm coming, too."

I feed him breakfast and rummage through the refrigerator for something to eat. It's fully stocked and fresh. Who does the grocery shopping for Hayes while he's away in Savannah? Does he have a service, or maybe an assistant who keeps him stocked in organic oat milk and fresh produce?

I settle for avocado toast and eggs, using items from his stocked fridge and gorgeous kitchen that's a dream to work in. I lose no time in making myself right at home among the glossy surfaces and high-end equipment. I'm not the greatest cook, and I always make a huge mess, but Mama and the chef at The Mansion made sure I knew my way around the kitchen like any proper Southern lady should. I could probably make Hayes a five-course dinner with the food in the kitchen and a bit of Googling to figure out a menu.

I clean up after myself and decide it's time to get started on that shopping I told Hayes I could accomplish on my own. He left a note with instructions to use the Amex he provided for me and to take the Mercedes SUV in the garage for my driving needs. He's quite the accommodating host and full of Southern hospitality for an uncompromising billionaire. There's a part of me that feels a little too much like the women he's been with before, who used him for his money. Unlike them, I fully intend to pay him back for any purchases I make with the black card in my hand. Just as soon as Mama gets over this coup I've staged and gives me access to my trust again.

But what if she doesn't get over it, and decides I don't deserve unfettered trust access, or she puts me on an allowance, like I'm still twelve? I could really use a contingency plan should Mama not budge on her plans to marry me off. Would dating Hayes be enough to keep her off my back about Garrison? Hayes's pedigree is pristine, he's got the deep pockets she seems to think I need, and he's a shrewd and accomplished businessman who could help me figure out another way to fortify her family's agriculture interests.

Okay, new plan in addition to paying him back. Get Hayes to fall in love with me.

It's a task unlike anything I've taken on before and will likely be the most difficult thing I have done in my twenty-one years. I'm nothing if not ambitious and willing to do anything I have to do in order to achieve the goals I set. But with this, it seems a little daunting. I've never been in love, so I'm unsure what it takes to start. All I have going into this is a raging crush, a flimsy goal, and the threat of marrying Garrison to keep me motivated.

That should do it, really.

A few keystrokes on a web search for high-end shopping led me to the Shops at Buckhead where I'm currently trying to decide what exactly I'll need for a week in Atlanta with Hayes. I decided against a quick Target wardrobe because, like his garage full of shiny supercars, Hayes probably has expensive tastes in dining and activities. I want to be prepared for whatever he may suggest this week. Also, the whole make him fall in love with me thing may require pretty underwear. Thus, my first stop is at a lingerie store.

I have an armful of silk and lace panties, a slip, a silk robe, and bras hanging off my arm when a salesgirl approaches to help me.

"Girl, you better be going on your honeymoon or intent on seducing a man with that haul."

I laugh nervously. "Something like that," I offer. "I'm in town for a week without my clothes, so I have to make do."

She takes the garments from me and leads me back to the dressing room with a knowing smile.

"Sure. How about I pick out a few racier pieces to compliment your ladylike choices, just for fun?"

I smile and nod shyly. "I guess I could use something a little outside of my comfort zone."

She leaves me for a few minutes and returns with a new armful of items.

"Your coloring would look so good with red. Why you only had pale pink and white is beyond me. I added some super sexy black pieces, too. Tell me if you need additional sizes or anything. I'm here to help."

I take in the selections she's arranged in the dressing room and my cheeks heat. I stare at myself in the mirror wearing a pink silk slip, then at the straps and lace bits that make up what she brought in, and feel like I need to sit down. Is this what Hayes would want? Corsets and tiny thongs? Bras that barely cover my nipples or are completely see-through?

I try on a few of her selections to see if any of them feel like *me* and get a good laugh. Definitely not. But surprisingly, I do love a red lace babydoll nightgown and a black lace and mesh bodysuit. I bring them out with the pale pink and white I had originally picked and pay for my new luxuries with Hayes's card without incident.

I spend the next few hours collecting a small wardrobe for a bevy of scenarios; if needed I can come back for anything I haven't thought of. I keep all my receipts so I can pay Hayes back for my decadent splurge once I have access to my trust again. I like designer goods, but the shopping here is truly upscale and there's not much I'd consider inexpensive.

I wait at the valet for the car and smile when the Mercedes AMG G 63 rolls around the corner. It felt positively pedestrian and safe compared to his Maybach and Mercedes supercars, but it works for me as I have my own smaller, less expensive SUV, which really isn't in the same category when compared to this high-end G-wagon. I cruise through Atlanta back to the house, singing along to the radio and feeling far better than I should for the events of the last twenty-four hours. Cerberus greets me at the garage door when I come inside with my bags.

"What does your daddy like to eat?" I ask him after taking my bags upstairs and changing into leggings and a soft, cream-colored sweater.

He tilts his head at me, and I laugh.

"Thanks for the help. Guess I'll have to figure it out on my own."

Eleven

Hayes

I've had a shit day. As promised, I traced the loose thread at the airport and had to fire a longtime employee because they got greedy and allowed someone where they had no right to be. I'm technically the CFO of Olympus International, but I've always been the one to carry out the hard decisions and punishments we put in place. It never gets easier having to let an employee go or shut down a business. I know what a job means to some and taking that away makes me feel heartless and cruel, even when it's the best possible choice. We can't have businesses hemorrhaging funds or employees who aren't loyal.

Beyond that, I had to sit through hours of negotiations with a company we want to acquire in order to expand our precious metals mining capacities in overseas markets. We have mining operations throughout the world, but we saw a need to invest in the leading metals that are used in everything from computer chips to jewelry—platinum and palladium. Payton has led the negotiations up to this point on a few mines in South Africa, and he's been working on this deal for months now but pulled me in to secure the deal.

The fuckers are playing hardball, though, and aren't giving up as easily as Payton had assured me they would. We've had to schedule more meetings this week to revise our contracts and meet certain demands while finding a way to get exactly what we want in the bargain. I was hoping this could have been finished today so I can focus on my next goal of a smooth rollout for phase two. That phase expands our business holdings to include the hospitality sector, which includes Paige's daddy's Xenios Group, among other small, privately held businesses. We want to corner the market on exclusive boutique properties, and the Fairchilds have the Eastern Seaboard locked down on that front. They're the biggest hotel group we're looking at acquiring, and everything hinges on their acquiescence.

All I want is to go home to my dog and have a glass of bourbon without interruption before I move on to getting Paige to fall for me. If I can work out the details of this marriage clause in her inheritance, maybe the hotels would come easier. So far, it doesn't look like things would transfer the moment she is married, just that she has to be married in order to inherit the legacy. Small difference in wording, big difference in execution. Either way, I don't think it would hurt to have her madly in love with me when I make the offer to her father for the Xenios Group.

Cerberus doesn't meet me at the door when I walk into my house and I'm instantly on guard wondering what's wrong. Has something happened to Paige? Could she have gone out with the dog and something, or more likely someone, have happened?

The smell of cooking wafting from the kitchen quickly allays those fears, as Cerb is likely right next to Paige where I want him because that's where the food is.

"Honey, I'm home," I call out with a genuine smile on my face. I like the idea of coming home to someone who cares enough to cook for me. I'd never demand or even expect it, but this is an interesting change of pace from what I have available every week by the nutritionist who does my grocery shopping and stocks my fridge with professionally prepared food so I don't have to.

I hear a clatter from the kitchen.

"Oh, damn!" Paige swears.

I think that's the worst word I've heard out of her sweet Southern mouth, but I'm betting I'll get a few more, eventually. I set my jacket on the metal banister of my floating staircase and head back toward the kitchen, following the noises coming from that direction. The sight that greets me has genuine belly laughter shaking my whole body in an instant. Cerberus's normally sleek black fur is covered in flour as he licks up what I assume is a beaten egg from the slate floor. Paige is on her hands and knees, trying to beat him to the mess, but he keeps rotating his body to block her from his find.

"Cerberus, out," I command. He leaves the mess on the floor and trots out of the kitchen to sit in the hall looking like a demonic ghost. I shake my head at him for being naughty, but watching him lick his chops trying to get the flour and egg mixture off his face is pretty hilarious and I laugh again.

"What happened in here?"

Paige peeks up at me from her knees, her hair falling down in dark ribbons around her face from the messy bun on top of her head. She blows a piece of hair out of her mouth and gives me a defeated look.

"You scared me, and I dropped the bowl of flour I was trying to throw away. Then I put my hand in the bowl of eggs and flipped it off the counter. Now I've got a dog ready to be baked into chicken cordon bleu and a mess on the floor."

I cross the kitchen and grab a towel off the counter. I crouch down in front of her and pull her hand from the floor, taking her soiled paper towels and using mine to clean off her egg-covered fingers. Once her hand is clean, I pull her up with me.

"Forget the mess. It can wait. This can't."

I lean down and place my lips over hers as I hold her sweetly surprised face in my hands. What I meant to be simply a chaste kiss quickly takes a hot turn when she sighs against my mouth and opens her lips to flick her tongue out against mine. That's all it takes to unleash every dark desire I have for her into the kiss, slanting my lips over hers and plunging into her mouth.

I pull back slightly as she stiffens, but she moves toward me for more and I comply. I worship her luscious lips, her tongue playing with mine curiously when I sweep through to taste her deeper. I let the kiss take on every strangled need I've felt for her in the past few days, taking a piece of what I've denied myself, making sure she feels the intense appetite she stirs in me.

When I finally force myself to pull away from the hottest damn kiss of my life, her eyes stay closed and her lips are a reddened pout. Her eyes open lazily, a haze of lust settling over her face as she looks at me.

"Wow," she manages in a husky whisper.

The sound of that one word has me dying to set her up on the counter so I can pull her against the erection that strains my slacks and dry hump her until she begs me to stop. The tone her voice takes when she's turned on is my new favorite thing, and I want to hear her calling my name in that hot rasp.

"W-what was that for? You haven't even had dinner yet, so it can't be that I cooked for you."

I lick the taste of her from my lips and swallow hard.

"Just how I wanted to say hello to you."

"Mmm. Well, hello to you, too, handsome. That just blew all of my expectations for my first kiss out of the water."

My heart nearly stops. *I'm her first kiss?* My God, I get *all* of her firsts. A possessive thrill runs through me, and I look at her with new eyes. She will be all mine and more and I want to make sure she is ruined for anyone who would dare to follow me.

"That's just the beginning. It will get even better. You deserve the best and I can certainly offer that and more."

She tucks the strands of hair that have escaped her bun behind her ears and takes a steadying breath as her eyes clear.

"Well, if that's going to happen every time you come home to me, I don't think I'll mind having you leave quite as much."

Home to me. I savor that thought, rolling it around on my tongue. I've never liked the idea of going home to someone before, as I like my house in order, without the messy unpredictability of another person in my space. But the thought of coming home to Paige produces a feeling so far in the other direction from my usual that I can imagine it vividly and with an unfettered desire that surprises me.

I want to share everything with her. My house. My life. My dog. Maybe even my heart. The sobering thought has me evaluating how it could have even crossed my mind just now. I'm tight with my emotions, preferring to catch flights, not feelings, but this is something else. She's something else.

I redirect my misplaced thoughts and look around the kitchen. She has a steaming roasting pan of chicken cordon bleu cooling on the island next to a bowl of broccolini with red pepper and parmesan flakes. Farther down, there's a platter of roasted potatoes glistening and sprinkled with parsley.

"You did all this?"

She looks around and cringes. "I had hoped to have everything cleaned up and the rest of my messy cooking habits hidden before you got home, but I wasn't sure when that was, so I guessed wrong. I have a sink full of dishes to do, and now this." She gestures at the paper towel, flour, and egg mess on the floor.

"It can wait," I remind her. "Thank you for going to all this trouble. I wasn't expecting it, but you just made a bad day better."

Her smile is angelic, bright sunshine and flowers, and I want to devour her again, or eat her pussy out for dinner instead to really show my gratitude.

"It's the least I could do. Oh, and you might want to add flour to your grocery list if there is someone who does your shopping." She pauses and bites the tip of her thumb in thought. "Or I could shop for you if you want," she says around her thumbnail.

I nod, pulling her thumb away from her mouth and kissing it. I would've liked to suck it into my mouth and give her a preview of the things I can do with my tongue, but salmonella is a bitch.

"Wash up. Let's eat."

After her delicious dinner, I help clean up the kitchen, doing the dishes as she dries from a seat on the counter next to me. She's so fucking cute perched up there I can't help taking my time. She's at the perfect height for me to be able to pull her ass to the edge, wrap her legs around my hips, and plunge into what I am sure is a perfect little pussy. I have to forcefully pull my thoughts away from eating her out and fucking her on the kitchen counters so I don't accidentally move faster than she's ready for. Instead, I think of the dry-as-hell legal contracts and terms for the acquisitions we're working on for Olympus and I slowly regain control of my absurdly hard dick.

"You feel up to helping me give Cerberus a bath?"

"Given that I'm the responsible party for why your demon spawn looks like a ghost, of course I'll help."

"Demon spawn?" I chuckle imagining what that even is or why she would use it for Cerberus.

"His little cropped ears look like horns and his eyes kind of have a reddish-brown glow. With his glossy black fur, he's totally a hellhound of some sort, but he's just the sweetest and he's yours, so demon spawn works."

I shake my head at her comfort with a dog that is trained to take down a 200-lb man and subdue him until other means arrive. He's jumped over cars in pursuit of a mark, and his surveillance skills are better than any tech system I could buy, not that I don't have a top-of-the-line system in place.

The way Paige handles him, and how he responds to her, is unique. He acts more like an oversized golden retriever with her than the born and bred bodyguard he is. I'm still taking the Vegas odds that he would decimate anything that tried to hurt her.

I call Cerberus to me, and we all go up to my bedroom and into the expansive bathroom.

"In," I tell him, opening the frameless glass door to the shower.

He drops his head and looks up at me with what can only be called puppy dog eyes that look entirely misplaced on a hundred-pound guardian.

"I'm not buying it, big guy. You're a mess and need to get cleaned up for bed."

I unbutton my shirt, remove my cufflinks, and shed the shirt on the vanity next to the sink. I step out of my shoes and pull off my socks. I'd strip down to my boxer briefs, but I assume that would be a little too much for Paige's sensibilities, so I just empty my pockets on top of my shirt and turn to her.

She's pulling her sweater over her head, exposing a white camisole with lace trim that stretches with the sway of her breasts that look to be held in place with a soft lace bralette that doesn't provide much support or hide her chill. She's in leggings and already barefoot, so when the sweater is gone, she appears like she's about to say something, only her jaw drops open.

I look down at my bare torso and flex my abs a little for her. Not every thirty-five-year-old can rock an eight-pack, but I put in the grueling hard work to maintain this one. Her look of awe is all I need to make sure I'm up again at dawn tomorrow, getting in a workout in my home gym.

"Good Lord almighty, this is what you look like under your clothes?"

"Come here and I'll let you touch me to see if you're dreaming," I tease.

"I'm not passing up that offer," Paige mumbles, her steps already bringing her closer.

A tremor of anticipation runs through me, and I don't remember the last time I felt something like that. Fuck, I want her hands on me.

Her fingers reach out tentatively, softly brushing over my chest before she flattens her hand against my skin, and I burn at her touch. Both of her hands now run across my chest, her thumbs caressing over my nipples unexpectedly, sending a shiver down my spine and alerting my cock to her proximity. She slowly drags her hands along my obliques with her thumbs pressing against my abs, stretching out the anticipation that jacks up my heart rate.

I breathe shallowly, forcing myself to stay still. The last thing I want is to scare her with the desire that races through me and drives me to pounce on her, pull her clothes off, and mount her in seconds to take my fill of her gorgeous body.

Her fingers dip with my abs and work even lower, toward the hard bulge in my pants begging to be released. When her fingers and her eyes reach my waistband, she pauses and looks up at me.

"You want me?" She says it in a breathless, unbelieving way.

It has just become my mission to remove the doubt from this innocent woman's mind and ensure her that she is, in fact, the most delectable, gorgeous, perfect example of everything I could possibly want wrapped up in a cotton candy package.

"Wanting you doesn't even begin to touch the depth of what I feel. I want to do very bad things with you, things that would shock and scare you even," I growl, remaining still by some act of God that has nothing to do with my own self-control. "But not tonight." I take a short step back, which is physically painful, and watch as her hands stretch with me, and then fall from my skin.

"Why?" she asks, her naturally pink lips pouting.

My attention is focused there, but all I can think of are her nipples and if they match this delightful color and what they would look like after I spent some time licking and sucking on them.

I rake both of my hands through my hair and allow myself a moment to breathe. Contracts and terms. Not her hard little nipples or the pussy below that I want to strip bare and rut into without thought. Unsexy contracts and stupid terms.

"You're not ready. Remember what I said?"

She nods, but I catch the look of longing. *Just you wait, baby.*

Cerberus barks, the sound echoing through the bathroom and bringing me out of the Paige spiral I was lost in. He's standing at the shower door, his eyes fixed on us. He paws at the door and snorts.

"Yeah, yeah, we'll stop messing around already." Only, this is just the tip of what messing around with Paige could lead to. "Grab a couple of towels from that cabinet," I direct, motioning to the linen closet. Paige turns on her heel and quickly moves to do as I ask.

I open the glass door and Cerberus moves back into the large enclosure, looking up at the multiple shower heads. I only turn the tap for the handheld and wait for it to warm up. The shower door closes with a soft thump, and I turn to see Paige has stepped into the shower with us, her leggings pulled up to expose her calves. I didn't think I could find ankles or calves hot, but she's proving me wrong at unexpected turns, so now I have an ankle fetish I need to exercise.

"There's dog shampoo on that shelf," I tell her, instead of falling to my knees and taking her foot in my hand to kiss that damn calf.

I turn back to the big dog.

"Time's up, buddy. Let's get you clean."

Paige helps soap up Cerberus as I rinse off the flour that made him a spotted gray specter of himself. *Demon spawn*, she called him. That would make me a demon. I wonder if angels fall for demons. I move to shut off the water and I'm about to tell Paige to grab a towel when Cerberus shakes his big body, showering us with the water from his fur before she's ready. Water drips off her nose and her white tank is doused, the print of her lace bra showing through, along with her pointed nipples. They are pink, perfect little buds, just like her lips. My dick is stupidly hard as I stand observing her, making no move to help her dry off when I like her wet so much more.

"I should have expected that," she says. She shakes her hands off and pushes back the wet hair that sticks to her face, unaware that she's my living, breathing, completely wet dream.

Twelve

Paige

I kick the duvet off my legs and feel Cerberus shift on the bed, instantly alert after snoring a moment before. It's very early, judging by the weak gray light barely edging out the dark night. I'm uncomfortable, and it's not the plush bed. No, there's a pulling, rolling *need* in my center and it's all Hayes's fault.

I have resolutely managed to not touch or be touched by a man intimately since that awful high school party, and I very infrequently explore my own body since there's not been much that enticed me to, or maybe it's not wanting to open a door I can't close.

But Hayes has ignited a furnace in my lady bits that throbs and burns to be touched, and I think it's time I put in some work before I end up mounting Hayes in his sleep and not knowing what to do next. He'd probably laugh at my eager inexperience, and that thought keeps me from trying it.

"Cerberus, place," I whisper, sending the dog off this bed to his on the floor. I don't need him judging me for what I intend to do.

My heart hammers in my chest and my hands shake. I place my hands against my chest, my eyes closing as I remember the feel of the muscles and warm skin on Hayes's body. I can already imagine the unforgiving hardness and the way my soft curves would mold against his muscled planes.

I glide my hands down my silk slip, crossing my belly as it trembles in nerves and anticipation under my fingertips. I inch the material up over my hips and slowly trail my fingers lower, feeling the swollen folds and slickness of my desire. I press my fingers against my center and heat blooms.

I think of the bulge in Hayes's pants, how hard it feels against me when I cling to him, and how he readily admitted his desire for me without moving further. My fingers circle slowly, pressing harder on the little bundle of nerves, already primed like a trigger, waiting for me to pull it and set off my need for Hayes.

I remember our kiss in the kitchen—my very first, and what a first kiss it was. The force of it was breathtaking. His skilled tongue moved against my hesitant one, guiding me, taking me, demanding I take as much as he was.

I gasp quietly, my fingers switching direction as I allow my mind to wander through possibilities I don't have firsthand experience with, but can imagine nonetheless. I move one of my hands back to my breast and squeeze through the sheer lace, the scratch of the material just the right texture I need to have my legs clamping together as my release surges over me. I roll to my belly and grind out the waves of pleasure against my fist, my hair sticking to my sweaty face as I let the pillow absorb my low moans and the one name that forces its way out of my mouth.

"Hayes!"

It's a plea and a low moan and a hiss all at once. I stop moving and breathe into the pillow, my breath coming hot and labored after what could be the most explosive orgasm of my life. Or of the few I have coaxed from my body, at least.

Smiling, I roll to my back, brushing hair off my sweaty face, content and finally free of that all-consuming need. Movement in the dim room catches my eye, and I look to the doorway. I sit up like I've been hit with a hot poker and gather the duvet against my chest. Hayes is framed in the doorway and I'm not sure how long he's been standing there. *Did he just see... all of that?*

"You're so fucking beautiful," he says, the words given a physical weight as they wash over me in the dark room.

I expect him to stalk to the bed and kiss me savagely, maybe more, but instead, he walks quickly through the bedroom to the bathroom. I catch his bare torso and red athletic shorts when he flips on the light, but he closes the door behind him and his body is lost to me.

"Oh, my God," I whisper in mortification, my hands covering my face.

Hayes just caught me touching myself in his bed. What must he think of me? If I'm lucky, he wants me just as badly as I want him. It's just as likely I did something wrong, and he is far more aware of my inexperience and inability to do anything that will be what he wants in bed. Either way, how he can have the patience of a saint with looks that burn like the devil, and not touch me, is beyond comprehension.

I need to explain myself, somehow. Tell him I'm dying to feel his touch where no man has touched me before, but I'm so caught up in my own head about the expectations, the mechanics, even, that I'm holding back. It's so frustrating. I don't know when I'll be ready, but I hope he is still waiting when I get there.

The shower turns on in the bathroom. A part of me, okay, a really big part, wants to walk through that door and give myself to him right now, inexperienced or not. The hesitant side is growing smaller, and the arguments not to, weaker. I don't know what compulsion takes hold of me, but I slide out of bed and tiptoe to the door, resting my forehead against it as my heart pounds. Am I brave enough, bold enough, to open it? What happens if I do? Without logical answers, my hand turns the knob and slowly opens the door. I keep my eyes shut tightly until the first breath of steam meets my face. When I open my eyes, my mouth drops and I can't look away.

Hayes has his naked back to me, thick legs spread, one arm braced against the wall as the other works himself roughly at his front. Water from several shower heads pelts him as steam gathers and swirls through the big glass enclosure. His muffled groan is primal, his exquisite behind clenching as his hand slows the motion at his hidden front. His head drops forward, his shoulders rising with his breaths through the last pump of his fist, his release washed away by the shower.

As he straightens, I back out and softly close the door, running to the bed and jumping in like monsters are after me in the dark. I nearly scream when Cerberus jumps on the bed and settles in next to me, his great head resting delicately on the pillow beside mine while my heart hammers against my ribs.

"Your daddy is sinfully hot and he's going to make sweet love to me, someday," I tell him, knowing it's one hundred percent true.

I lie in bed, too amped up to fall back asleep even though it's early, and listen to Hayes in the bathroom. When he comes back into the bedroom fully dressed, I feel the need to apologize. I sit up, Cerberus's head rising at my movements.

"I'm so sorry. I don't normally do that. I'll wash your sheets today."

Hayes slowly walks toward the big bed, clasping a watch to his wrist. He sits on the edge of the bed, angled toward me.

"Don't you ever apologize for doing something that feels good. Not anything."

He doesn't ask for my acknowledgment, but I still nod.

"I should be apologizing for invading your privacy by watching you. I'm sorry for not being able to look away."

My cheeks heat, but I have to come clean to him now, even if I have to admit it in a whisper and feel the shame wash over me in cold torrents.

"I watched you, a few minutes ago in the shower. I guess we're even."

His head tilts and the ghost of a smile crosses his mouth. "You watched me in the shower? What did you see?"

I look away and swallow. It's time to speak now or forever hold my peace. "You were... pleasuring your-self," I whisper. I can't get out the words that would accurately describe the brutal power of his body and the sounds he made that caused my stomach to drop and my body to tighten with need again.

"Honey, that was punishment, not pleasure. You don't want to know the things that were going through my head at that moment, that I was working out of my system."

"I do want to know," I admit in a rush. And it's true. I want to know the thoughts he had that pushed him to release so quickly, and if it was thoughts of me that did it.

"If I start talking about it now, I'll need another shower. Just know I had very dirty thoughts of what I wanted to do to see you feel that good again."

I smile in triumph and look down at my hands clutching the duvet. The feeling of success overrides any embarrassment I felt. I was the one who nearly brought him to his knees, even if only in his thoughts.

"You like that I was touching myself, thinking about you."

It's not a question, but I nod, my smile fading as heat flares in my belly.

"What were you thinking about when you touched yourself?" His low voice is a caress across my skin in the dark.

I swallow audibly. I screw up the guts to tell him, because the triumph I feel knowing I've got him twisted up feels good enough to share.

"You. The way you kissed me. And, well," I pause, forcing myself to just say the words, even if it feels foreign to admit it. "How hard you get around me. The promise of what's to come."

"Baby girl, it's you who's going to come. I'll make sure of it." He smooths back his hair and looks away.

I see the bulge in his pants and know he's affected even now. Maybe it's having watched him, or the wisps of sun that filter weakly into the window giving the moment a surreal quality, but I blurt out, "Can I touch you?"

His head turns to me quickly. "How do you want to touch me?"

My eyes dart to his crotch and I nod at the bulge. "I want to feel you right now."

He groans. "Baby, you can touch me anytime you want." The heat from his stare is searing in the quiet bedroom.

I slowly rise, pushing the duvet off me, and move toward him on my knees. I sit back on my heels when I'm beside him and tentatively reach out my hand. It shakes and I nearly snatch it back, but the thought of missing out on this moment is greater than my trepidation. I lightly place my hand on the bulge, and it flexes hot under my palm. I curl my fingers down his front until I'm cupping him, but he doesn't even fit in my hand.

"Oh, God, you're big," I say out loud before I can stop the words. My eyes snap up from my hand in his lap to his face and I catch the measured breath he takes.

"It'll fit. You'll see," he grits out. The strain in his voice is a testament to whatever restraint he's employing at the moment.

I move my hand around like a blind woman mapping a new room. I'm looking for a beginning or an end, but I only feel solid flesh and heat through his slacks that don't give me an idea of what he could look like, or how he could possibly fit inside of me the way he promised. I press harder and he groans. The urge to crawl into his lap is so strong I actually do, moving my hand so I can straddle his legs on the edge of the bed as my slip rides up my thighs.

His hands rest lightly on my hips. "What are you doing to me, baby?"

I shake my head and slowly lower my center to rest on the bulge in his pants. His hands grip me tightly as his head tips back and a hiss escapes his mouth. My lady bits are pulsing, my whole body hot and ready to take over where my mind loses the ability to function. My hips rock once, gently, and I sigh.

"Why does that feel so good?"

Hayes moves one hand from my hip to my back and flips me onto the bed, his weight settling over me, the bulge I was just touching now snugly nestled between my legs. My heart thumps heavily in my chest and my fingers tingle, but I'm not afraid of him in this moment. He smooths hair out of my face and kisses my cheek before he moves his face next to mine with a deep inhale I can feel through my entire body.

I rub my cheek against his face like a cat and my hips rock up to rub against him. He meets my body with his, grinding against my center, and I gasp. I press harder, wrapping a leg around his hips to bring him closer. I want more of that contact and he obliges, rolling his hips into mine in a rhythm that makes my gasps come quicker.

"Kiss me, please," I beg softly. His mouth moves from my hair to my lips as he rises above me. It changes the angle of our bodies just enough that when his tongue enters my mouth, I cry out as pleasure rocks me. He swallows my whimpers of satisfaction as his hips continue to rub against me until I finally fall away from his kisses. I lie languidly beneath him, basking in the afterglow until he stills.

"You're going to be my undoing, baby." He rolls off me, sitting at the edge of the bed, and breathes deeply.

I roll to my side to face him. "I really liked that."

The pulsing has receded and I'm feeling more in control of my body now. What I just did feels like a huge step forward. I wanted Hayes and I took what I wanted. I didn't let my fears of inadequacy or not knowing what to do stop me, I just went with my instincts and it was so good. Maybe I'll be a quick learner and will figure out what he needs from me to be satisfied.

He leans over and touches his lips to mine.

I thread my fingers into his hair and keep him close before he can pull away, and the kiss deepens. I kiss him fiercely and hope it sears him the way it does me.

His hand traces up my throat until his fingers cup my jaw and he slows the intensity, reining it in so it's soft and mellow. When he pulls away, my lips feel the loss and want more. He traces my bottom lip with his thumb, his eyes dark and fixed on my mouth.

"If I could get away with staying in this bed kissing you all day, I would."

"You have to go, don't you?" I brush the hair off his forehead and run my fingers through the soft hair at the nape of his neck.

He nods once. "But first I have to change my pants."

I glance down and notice the wet spot on his pants. "I did that?" Mortification races hot through me and I cringe.

"We did. Bodies self-lubricate when turned on, and you're very good at turning me on. I'm gonna have a hard time walking when I get up as I tell my dick to calm down and get to work."

"Remember when I said I wouldn't mind you leaving so much if you kissed me when you get home?"

He nods.

"It's not true. I'm really bummed you're leaving right now and want to beg you to stay, kiss be damned."

He laughs. "Same page, same book."

I make him honey garlic glazed salmon with jasmine rice and green beans and the kitchen is sparkling when I expect him to be home. I sent Cerberus to his place as I cooked and cleaned so I wouldn't end up battering him again and needing another shower this evening. Not that I'm complaining because that allowed me to see Hayes shirtless and he let me feel his chest and abs without any barrier under my hands, but I don't want him thinking I'm always making a mess. Because it's only most of the time, not always.

I'm lighting taper candles I found in a box in the back of a drawer, the table set so well my mama couldn't even find fault, when I hear the door open and Cerberus whines from the mat in the kitchen.

"Honey, I'm home." I hear from down the hall. It's not even close to sounding like the fifties television phrase he stole it from. Instead, it sounds like more of a rumbled promise he intends to keep.

Hearing that phrase from him does silly things to my insides and gives me a major case of nervous butterflies. I smooth my hands over the white shirt I managed to keep stain-free during dinner prep and turn away from the table and start toward the hall to meet him.

"Go ahead, big guy," I tell Cerberus with a smile. He sprints out of the kitchen. I follow, nearly as eager as the dog is to see Hayes. He gives the dog an affectionate scratch under his chin when Cerberus gets to him. He straightens up and continues down the hall, the giant black dog on his heels.

"Did you cook dinner again?" He looks into the kitchen, which is spotless, then looks toward the dining room where I lean against the doorframe.

"I have a handful of recipes under my belt and I plan to make as many as I can while you let me stay with you to show my immense gratitude."

"Here I thought you were a hotel mogul in training, but you keep surprising me with your vast talents."

I give him a patient look. "I'm a proper Southern lady. I am incredibly talented and can do anything you can do, but backward and in heels," I drawl. "I could run a multi-million-dollar business by day, then cook you a gourmet dinner, entertain your work friends, and plan a charity function at night." I laugh and shake my head, not even able to take myself seriously with that pitch that would have made Mama proud.

"Mmm," he growls, stalking closer. "You really are the perfect woman."

My laughter stops abruptly when he buries his hands in my hair and tips my head up, his mouth on mine in a hot second. His kiss ravages my lips, his tongue sweeping against mine and leaving me breathless. He uses his thumb to turn my face to the side and kisses along my jaw, making his way to the sensitive spot below my ear that I am only just now aware of.

Holy wow, the vibration of his exhale on my neck sends a shudder through me that makes my knees weak, which I always thought was just an expression used in

Nanny Fairchild's romance novels until this very moment.

One of his arms drops to my waist and pulls me tight against him, the entire length of our bodies touching as he nips at my earlobe.

"I could eat you for dinner, Miss Fairchild." His voice is a rumble of pure sexiness.

My brain short circuits in that moment. I can't think of a word to say and I make this humming noise in my throat that I hope conveys the appreciation for his masterful use of the art of seduction. It works. I am so seduced and know what his bedroom voice sounds like. I like it, maybe too much, as my panties grow damp and I squirm in his arms.

"I like when you make those noises. It makes me want to find out what others you will make when I have my mouth on you." He grazes his teeth down the side of my neck. "Do it again." He bites the spot where my neck meets my shoulder and I moan. *Me.* I just moaned. He licks over the light bite. "That's my good girl."

He gives me another bite-kiss on my neck and steps back, leaving me up on tiptoes, his shirt fisted in my hands keeping us connected. When did I grab his shirt? I must have blacked out from the overstimulation of having Hayes hold me, kiss me, and talk to me like that. I'm a live wire, an exposed nerve, all feeling and energy and nowhere for it to go except to course through my body in shivers and racing adrenaline.

I loosen my fingers and let my hands slide down his chest to his stomach and then, with a little regret, leave his body and return to my sides. I'm still a little hazy and at a loss for words as he watches me with eyes smoldering and so deep green that they remind me of a jungle, wild and dangerous. I take a deep breath to clear my nose of his manly scent, all expensive cologne and whatever he exudes that my body is hardwired to respond to, making me crazy for him. This might be biology at work, but it doesn't fully capture his allure and the attraction I feel for him. That is something else entirely.

"Y-you're really good at that," I croak, my voice as unsteady as my legs.

"That's how I want to greet you every night you are here. You don't even have to make dinner. In fact, I'll take care of dinner the rest of the week, because I don't want you thinking you have to lift a damn finger or earn your stay. You're my guest, and I want you to feel comfortable here."

"You sure know how to make a girl feel welcome." I don't mean it as a joke, but I feel my smile pulling at the corners of my mouth anyway.

"There are a lot of ways I could make you feel even more welcome, but that might take all night, and you already went through the trouble of making what smells like an amazing dinner. So instead of throwing you over my shoulder, marching you upstairs, and doing all sorts of unspeakable things to you, I'll calm down and be good company."

"When you put it like that, I may be tempted to abandon dinner plans." I look down at my hands, fingers twisting together nervously. I'm more than intrigued. I imagine this is a state of heightened arousal, and my body wants all of the unspeakable acts he mentioned to take place right this moment.

He catches my chin and lifts my face again. "I'll rein it in. I'm sorry for being so forward. I didn't mean to overwhelm you."

I feel my cheeks flush in embarrassment, and don't want him to think that because I'm inexperienced I don't want this now. "It's a little overwhelming, and fast, but... I like it."

"I'll slow down. There's no rush." His hand leaves my chin, the backs of his fingers caressing down my neck to my chest, where he flattens his palm over my heart. "You need to be ready here, not just here." His hand slides down between my breasts and over my stomach, his fingers turning down as he softly cups between my legs.

I make a surprised sound, but my legs spread of their own accord allowing him more access to the heat that is pooled right where his hand is and he can probably feel it through my leggings.

He drags his hand up through my heat and finally rests it on my waist, in a safe spot between the parts of me that are hot and throbbing for his touch.

"Slow sounds good." My voice wavers, not quite on board with the plan despite knowing it's for the best. He's right. My body is responding much faster than I imagined it would, and if I act on every instinct and desire, I may regret it when my brain and heart catch up. I shake my head and take a deep breath, blowing it out slowly when he speaks.

"Let's eat."

He takes my hand and leads me into his dining room, the table set for two, the candles glowing in block holders I found for them, giving the low-lit space a cozy feel. He pulls a chair out for me, scooting it in as I sit, rounding the table to take his place across from me.

"This looks amazing. I'm impressed. It's like you know the way to a man's heart is through his stomach," he says, smiling at me before he takes a bite.

I look down at my plate feeling foolish for thinking exactly that. I must be entirely transparent. There is nothing I could attempt that would take him by surprise or even be a sly way of getting closer to him or making him fall for me. Want me, yes, but actually fall truly, deeply in love with me? Unlikely. I sigh in vexation at my own thoughts.

"Why that look when I compliment you, angel? You're supposed to smile and preen when I tell you how good you are, not look defeated. What did I say?"

"It's nothing, I promise. I'm glad you like it." I take a bite of my own dinner, not wanting to have to explain myself while my face is bright red. I swallow and look for a way to change the subject. "What do you do when you're not working?"

Hayes takes a sip of the dry Riesling I paired with the salmon after going through his wine fridge and doing a web search for what would work best. "Good pick." He sets the wine glass down. "I work a lot, so there's not too much outside of that I do with any regularity."

"Workaholic," I chide with a fond smile.

"Guilty." He smiles, his cheek dimpling in a delicious way. "I work out every day, but that's for vanity and health reasons, not really because it's an interest."

"I can attest to the effectiveness of your workouts, so if vanity is the reason, I support it." I take a bite of a green bean to hide my smile.

"You like what you see?"

My eyes dart up to his, watching as they take me in, invested in my answer.

"Obviously," I scoff playfully. "You're chocolate fudge cake."

"Chocolate fudge cake?" His brows furrow and he tilts his head as he tries to discern my meaning.

I feel a blush creep up my neck and into my face but take the topic very seriously. "Chocolate fudge cake is my most favorite food in the world and I could eat far too much of it because I can't stop when it's available. I have to moderate myself around chocolate fudge cake. I have to carefully pre-portion the cake and hide it away so I can make it last. It's the food I would request as a celebration, as commiseration when life doesn't feel fair, or as my last meal. I am a glutton for chocolate fudge cake."

"You really like what you see," he replies in understanding. "But you're afraid of what will happen if you let yourself indulge."

I nod vigorously, blinking a few times to help me keep my brain on track. "What do you do besides workout and work, though? What do your weekends look like? You have to have a hobby or something that lets you relax. It can't all be work and no play."

His eyes darken and he gets a mischievous look. "I am not a dull boy, if that is what you're insinuating."

I shake my head, confused. "No, that's not what I mean at all," I stammer.

He laughs. "I was finishing your quote: 'All work and no play makes Jack a dull boy.' It's from *The Shining*."

"I've never seen it." I'm so relieved he doesn't think I think he's dull for being a workaholic.

He pulls back and gives me a look of shock. "It's a classic Kubrick film based on the Stephen King novel.

Jack Nicholson and Shelley Duval? It's a great horror movie. We can watch it after dinner if you want."

I clap my hands and point at him. "That's something you can claim as a hobby; you're a movie buff! There is no way you aren't by how you just went on about that movie," I tease. "I'm intrigued. We can watch it, but I will warn you now, I am the biggest scaredy cat and don't usually watch horror movies because I'll probably freak out and scream."

"I'll hold you if you get scared."

"Deal."

We finish dinner in record time and do the dishes together. He picks me up and sits me on the counter to dry again tonight. It's a quick process as I already cleaned up after my cooking mess so it's just our plates and the serving dishes. As I'm about to hop down from the counter, he stops me with a hand on my thigh.

"Come here, princess, I'll give you a ride to the couch." He turns his back to me and hitches my legs around his hips, intent on giving me a piggyback ride.

I laugh and wrap my arms around his shoulders to pull myself close to his broad back. "Such service. Who knew I'd get a prince and a steed in the same pretty package."

He scoffs. "I'm the guy who would beat up the prince for being a little pussy. I'd rather get my hands dirty on the battlefield. I'm not afraid to do the hard things, whatever they may be." His hands are bands of steel on my thighs, and I believe him.

"A morally gray knight, then. That works for me, since I'm no princess."

"You'll always be my princess." He squeezes my thighs and I smile against his back as we bump down the hallway.

He deposits me on the soft leather sofa in the den, grabbing one of the soft throw blankets from the back and dragging it over my legs.

"You sit tight. I'm going to change out of this suit so we can cuddle."

"Promise?" I call, smiling in pleasure at the thought, and watch his retreating figure. He's dreamy.

I'm searching through the movie channels looking for *The Shining* when he returns and the remote falls from my hand when I get a look at him. He's wearing gray sweats that show off his powerful legs and a black t-shirt that stretches across his chest. I can't help noticing the bulge in his crotch on display as he walks despite likely not being aroused in the slightest. He's big even when he's not hard. The blood rushes into my face and my whole body grows hot. Hayes in athleisure wear is a whole different level of sexy. And far more comfortable for him than a suit, I'm sure.

He settles next to me, his back pressed into the corner of the couch. He shakes his head like he doesn't like the spot, throws the blanket off my legs, and scoops me up just to deposit me in his lap as he stretches his legs into my vacated spot. Then he drapes the blanket over the both of us. He shifts my hips around until I'm snuggled between his legs, my behind backed up tight to the crotch I was just ogling, letting out an exaggerated sigh.

I can't fight the smile that's plastered to my face during this whole precious ordeal.

"That's better." He pulls my back flush against his chest and wraps his arms around my middle. I feel him press his face into my hair and inhale. "Now we're ready to watch a movie." His words are exhaled right above my ear, and I shiver.

I do, in fact, scream during the movie. It freaks me out enough to turn my back to the screen and bury my face in Hayes's chest, my arms wrapped around his middle and my legs straddling one of his thighs.

His big hands keep up a steady caress along my back until the music on the screen lets me know the scary part has passed and I'm able to pull my face away again. When I look up at him, ready to apologize, I catch his intense stare and watch as he lets his bottom lip roll out between his teeth. His lip is slightly wet, and I want to taste it with a fierceness that has me feeling hot all over. I raise myself up to straddle his hips and catch his lip in my teeth this time, feeling him groan at the contact. My hands snake behind his neck, sliding into his hair and pulling his head forward so I can kiss him. His hands settle on my hips, clenching as I tentatively delve my tongue into his mouth and find his waiting, expectant and eager, to meet mine.

I forget all about the movie as I take my time learning every detail of his lips, how our tongues can clash or move together, and the drugging taste of him that has my hips moving over his, feeling him grow harder in response. I don't know how the movie ends, or if Jack ends up being a dull boy after all, but I do know what it feels like to come apart in his lap, my moans swallowed whole by his mouth.

Thirteen

Hayes

My mind keeps wandering back to Paige when I should be focused on meetings. Instead of strategy analysis and market research for phase two, I'm still thinking about her whimpers and the way her body moves with mine each time she straddles my lap, or lies below me, always fully clothed, and finds her release through the friction we create.

She's a natural, every sincere and unpracticed movement like she's been pulled from my deepest fantasies and washed to be the cleanest version of what I long for. Even the way her body fits against mine, it's just... perfect. It's going to be so much sweeter when the clothes are removed and she's ready for me, but I'll take what I can as she grows more comfortable and confident exploring what our bodies can do together.

It's been decades since I dry-humped a girl like this. My sexual experiences usually move from foreplay to fucking as the mood strikes within the session, never thinking that I wouldn't end up inside my partner at some point in the span of the evening.

There's something different about moving slowly with Paige that keeps me from rushing in. I'm savoring every first with her and building the tension that will break in sweet release when it's time. And I'm jerking off more than I have since my teens. Thank God I haven't come in my pants, but it's been a close thing on several occasions now.

"Hayes, we need you focused on what's going on here, not whatever the fuck you're thinking of instead."

I cut my eyes to Zander and glare. I hate that he's being the fucking voice of reason.

"Are we buying a fleet of rental yachts or not?"

Payton shakes his head. "Profit margin isn't high enough for the investment and operating costs. We're back to just the boutique hotel chain. Your girl's business is still on the docket, along with six others, to make it the largest chain in the U.S."

I nod. Without the Xenios Group properties, we'd have to cobble together several more acquisitions and risk spreading our investment too thin. We can make the most impact with our plan A, and it requires Xenios.

"I'll work on it," I promise. "As for the others, how are the acquisition plans going?"

"Southampton, Royal, and Atherton are all barely treading water, so they should take the first lifeline we throw without a fight. We'll be doing them a favor," Zander says.

"My sources say the other three are amenable to the prospect, but will put up more of a fight, so we'll have to go in low and work to the deal we planned on. They'll take it eventually." Payton grins, turning his attention to me. "So, has the Xenios princess taken you out at the knees, or is she still fighting? You're crankier than usual, so I think she's playing hard to get. Or she's not that good."

"Shut your fucking mouth," I growl, crumpling a P&L sheet for one of the hotel groups in my fist.

"You're so touchy when it comes to her. Why so secretive, Hater?" Zander presses. "Afraid if you brought her up more, I'd slide into her DMs with a dick pic and steal your girl?"

I glare at Zander, murderous thoughts racing through my head at the very notion of him, or any other man, sending a photo of his dick to Paige or coming anywhere near her. At least she doesn't have social media for him to act on his threat out of pure spite. I crack my knuckles in anticipation of knocking the smug look off his face.

Payton leans back in his chair, fingers steepled as he gives me a knowing look. "He's got it bad, Zand. Hayes hasn't been one to do relationships, but I think this one could be different. Don't threaten to send your junk to your future sister-in-law. It would make things weird at family gatherings."

I fire the crumpled ball of paper at Payton's head. He ducks and laughs.

I'm not thinking that far ahead.

Am I?

True, I've considered marrying her to make getting my hands on her legacy that much easier, but I've known Paige for less than a week and she's only been at my house for five days. We haven't even had sex, so there's no way I should be thinking long-term. Still, the thought curls seductively around me, much like Paige does when we sit on the couch and watch movies together. She can squeeze her five-foot-six frame into my lap with ease. The make-out sessions that inevitably take precedence over the movie are getting hotter and hotter.

She's becoming more comfortable with me by the day. Her newfound boldness is stealing the space where shyness existed when I met her, and she's asking for more. A future with her isn't hard to imagine, and it's brighter than the bleak monotony of business takeovers and the continued corporate expansion I've made my mistress.

"I'm done with you jokers. You get after me for my thoughts wandering but you can't stay serious for an entire meeting and just end up wasting my time." I push my chair back and stack my files. "I'll keep working on the Xenios Group. Their team has been tough to crack, but my people are on it."

"More like she's cracking your nut," Payton quips.

"His little person is on it, that's for sure," Zander adds. They both laugh as I leave the boardroom fuming.

"Just fucking do your jobs," I toss over my shoulder before the door closes.

I check my watch. It's a few hours earlier than I normally call it a night, but I'm done with these fools and I... miss Paige. I shake my head at the thought. I'm no good here when my head is at home, so I tell my assistant to handle things and run a few things by my SVP before I leave. My team is more than capable of handling anything that could come up without me.

I stop by Underworld Spirits on the way home to check on my new pet project. The distillery is cranking out liquors in anticipation of our official launch on Saturday, and they want me to try out a new bottle of the reserve bourbon. I take it home with me, thinking Paige will like the flavor, and grab some red roses while I'm at it. If my mind is walking into the future with her, I should be taking the steps to make sure she's on board with the idea.

The red Audi parked in front of my house is the first sign of trouble. The sound of women's voices from the kitchen is the next. I'm already in damage control mode by the time I make it into the space and catch Paige sitting stiffly on a stool at the island, Cerberus attentive at her side, while Maisie, my nutritionist, places the lid on a glass storage container with more force than necessary.

"Oh, you're home early," Paige says when she sees me in the doorway. She smiles when she sees the roses, but it's tinged with anger. "I was just keeping Maisie company while she made your meals."

Her words feel like condemnation and I immediately want to refute it, to tell her she's got it all wrong, but I feel oddly guilty.

Maisie's blonde ponytail whips as her head turns to find me. She saunters over in her bright workout clothes that cling to every augmented inch of her, and wraps me in a possessive hug, plastering that body against mine in a very familiar way.

"I was getting to know your friend. What a surprise it was to see her here. You should have told me. I would have bought enough groceries to make two servings."

Goddamn loose ends, Hayes. You know better. I step out of Maisie's arms without returning the embrace. Paige's face is stricken, the betrayal in her eyes accusatory.

"You're right, I should have told you I no longer need your nutrition services. It slipped my mind because I've been fully preoccupied lately and hadn't even thought about it," I say, hoping to convey the truth to both women.

Maisie stiffens next to me. "Is that so? Have you fallen off the health wagon and gone to fast food?" she asks sharply.

Paige turns her face away from us, the pain echoing from her expression before she can hide it by petting Cerberus.

"Not fast food, something far more pleasurable, and homemade. I'll pay you for the rest of the month for the inconvenience of my late notice and be sure to recommend your nutrition services should anyone ask."

Her heavily made-up blue eyes crackle in fury at the dismissal. This could go wrong in so many ways. I'm trying to treat her like any of my business deals, but she's more attached than most.

"It's Christmas in a few weeks." Maisie might as well be standing with her hand out.

I look at her calculating face and sigh. Just like every woman before her, Maisie sees dollar signs where I'm concerned. It was a mistake to sleep with her in a moment of weakness, and then allow her to continue to cook for me. It was convenient, but a bad fucking idea.

"I'll make sure you get a bonus as well. Thanks for your time. Drive safe."

I step aside and motion toward the door. I'm as obvious as I can be without telling her to get the fuck out.

Maisie rolls her eyes and picks up her canvas tote bag.

"Good luck, Paige. Hope it works out better for you. I had the longest run with this one, so you better offer more than just *friendship*," Maisie calls over her shoulder as she leaves the kitchen. She pops her head back in a moment later. "Oh, feel free to give my number to your brothers. They may be needing my services, and since I have more free time now, I can take on more *clients*."

"Leave." The growl in my voice betrays my irritation. I'm done with her and need to face the next, more important, gauntlet—Paige's devastation.

I wait for the door to slam shut before I turn back to Paige. I put the roses and the bottle of bourbon on the island between us. Now it's a peace offering when it should have been a *just because I was thinking about you* gift.

"Paige."

"Don't. Please," she says, her proud face set. "You don't have to say anything. I'm nothing but a runaway you're harboring because I'm too immature to accept my fate. I appreciate it and I won't ask you for a Christmas bonus when I go home."

I don't like the idea of her having a home that's not with me. The fear of her leaving mixes with the anger at myself for allowing Maisie to show up today, desperation flooding my thoughts.

"Paige, stop," I command sharply, coming around the island because I can't stand the separation. I want to pull her into my arms and kiss her until she sees that Maisie means nothing to me and all I want is her. I stop short when Cerberus growls and stands between us, blocking me from getting any closer.

She really did break my dog. He's more loyal to her than me and I raised him from a pup.

She places a comforting hand on his neck. He licks his lips and looks back at her.

"Thank you, buddy, but I got this."

He relaxes and lies down at her feet but keeps his eyes on me. Damn traitor.

"You're nothing like Maisie," I begin.

She raises an eyebrow at me in confusion.

"I hired her for a service. Yes, I let it go too far once because I'm used to taking what's offered, and she was offering."

Paige scoffs and rolls her eyes. "Oh, that's rich."

I push on. "I let her continue to work for me after that, and maybe she expected more, but that's on her because I was honest about my intentions."

Just saying this makes me feel like a slimeball and I know I'm not worthy of Paige with this kind of attitude toward women. I've never hated myself, but I'm discovering it's possible as she judges my morality in her steely silence.

"Got it. You can have any woman you want, whenever you want them. My memory is just fine, so I don't need the crude reminder, Hayes."

"I don't want anyone but you." How can she not see my willingness to change my whole way with women because I want to be different for *her*?

Her bright green eyes flash at me angrily.

"Well, that's the thing. I'm not like the women you're used to. I'm not interested in dropping my panties whenever you feel like it so you can have your way with me and continue about your life. I'm a true-blue, love 'til it hurts, in it for life woman, and I'm not for sale."

I push my fingers into my hair and pray for patience because it's not my forte. I'm taken at my word without argument. I bark an order and it's followed. I see, I want, I get. End of story.

With Paige, nothing is that simple. She may be the only thing in the world that's worth the effort it takes to keep a level head and sensitively navigate this landmine subject.

"I don't want to buy you," I grit out.

"I think my crush on you was blinding me to how different we are and just how much I don't fit into your life."

I'm done with this. "You're overreacting."

She jumps off the stool to stand, shaking in anger.

"Sorry if I'm overreacting to having one of your booty calls walk right in like she owns the place and treat me like dirt. Guess my little feelings got hurt because I thought we were..." She trails off and looks away, her face blushing scarlet as her eyes show her disappointment. She paces a few steps away and I follow.

There is way too much to unpack in what she said, but I have to start somewhere.

"What do you think we are?"

She shakes her head and refuses to look at me.

"Paige," I warn.

"I thought this could be something special, okay? Call me a fool, but I thought you were taking your time with me because you actually care about me, not just about getting into my panties. That's on me for not taking you at your word when you told me what kind of man you are."

"There is literally no one else I even want to take my time with. Don't you get it? You're different, and it's making me reevaluate everything. *I* want to be different."

"Glad I could be a catalyst for change for you. I hope the next girl appreciates my part in your reformation."

"Woman, you're infuriating!" I snap.

"Good! Now you know how it feels!" she snaps right back, her tiny frame squared up to mine.

I take a step back as it dawns on me. "This isn't just about Maisie."

She opens her mouth to refute it, but something stops her prepared tirade. Her shoulders slump and she turns away from me with a look of defeat.

It fucking breaks my heart to see the fight go out of her like that.

"Baby, come here."

She waves me away but I pull her into my arms and she tucks herself in without protest.

"What is it?" I ask gently.

"I was bought and paid for a long time ago."

Her broken voice slices through my heart and my arms tighten around her.

"I don't understand."

She pulls her face away from my chest and wipes under her eyes. "Mama's been keeping more from me than I realized."

"What would that be?" I work to keep my tone even because I don't have much patience for Paige's parents after the shit they've pulled with her.

She takes a deep breath and leans back against the island. Cerberus crawls on his belly to her feet and I have to hide the smile that wants to unfold at the big dog's desire to be closer to her. *I feel you, buddy.*

"Mama's family's agriculture investments haven't been doing well for a while, but I never thought it mattered because we have the hotels. The ag money Mama gets goes right into the hotels, so when it started to dry up years ago, we were looking at losing a lot more than some cotton crops."

This isn't news to me, as I've had my team looking into this for a while. It's part of the reason we targeted the Xenios Group for acquisition. The revenue stream from the agriculture side may have bolstered the company at the start of what I now know was the marriage between her parents, but it's been less and less of a boon recently and made them ripe for taking a big deal like what Olympus is willing to offer.

"Go on."

"I think the prospect of losing everything made Mama desperate. Mama confronted the Daniels when… *the situation*… happened, and they offered a lot of money to keep things quiet. Mama took it."

Her voice cracks as tears well in her eyes.

"Mama seems to think we owe them for their unintentional bailout, and the price is my marriage to Garrison." A fat tear slips over her lashes and traces a path down her cheek.

Shit.

"She told you all this?"

Paige nods. "I called her again today. I was hoping we could resolve everything between us, but she was stark raving mad and said I had a duty to keep if I wanted to save the family legacy." Her eyes screw up tightly as more tears come. "I never thought my parents would sell me out to keep the business profitable."

I've had my team working on cracking not just the Xenios Group, but also getting the scoop on the history with the Daniels family. There was indeed a sizable donation made to Thackery Agriculture from the Daniels corporation six years ago, which confirms what Paige said. It doesn't fit with the typical Xenios dealings but is seen several times since in the Daniels's finances. I think Mommy and Daddy Daniels wanted to cover up their son's indiscretions to keep his image clean, and Paige wasn't his only victim.

"I'm going to fix this," I promise. There is way more resting on me fixing this for her than she could ever know.

"I appreciate it, but I don't know how you can undo something that happened years ago and has been in motion ever since."

"I have my ways."

I can't keep my eyes off her mouth. I move my body against hers, my hands on the island and my lips an inch from hers.

"Right now, I need to fix those tears." I hesitate, the unfamiliarity of having to ask permission instead of taking what I want slowing my natural instincts. "May I kiss you?"

"That's all I want, and that makes it really hard to stay mad at you."

I stop her words with my lips, tipping her chin up with my hand. She sighs into my mouth when I sweep my tongue against hers. The little noises she makes dissolve my restraint. I haul her up so her ass is on the island and pull her against me.

She wraps her legs around my hips, crushing me to her center, and my hands push into her hair, tipping her head. The kiss heats, our hands roving each other's bodies. Her fingers work on the buttons of my shirt as my lips wander the skin of her throat, tasting her neck. She tugs at my shirt, and I break away long enough to shrug it off and return to her.

I lift the hem of her shirt, needing her skin on mine, and pull it over her head. My thumbs brush over the lace of her bra, her nipples already straining the thin material. I roll them in my fingers, her back arching as a moan escapes and I dive in, replacing my fingers with my mouth. Her hands grab my hair and hold me close as I lick and suck at her.

"Take the dang thing off. I want your mouth on my skin," she whimpers.

I work at the clasp of her bra, untangling it from her arms to pull it away. I take a moment to appreciate the sight of having her bare from the waist up for the first time.

"You're a goddess. You look so fucking good, I want to eat you up."

A blush blooms on her skin as she looks up at me from under her dark lashes. "Will you, please?" she whispers.

"Fuck," I groan, gathering her into my arms and starting for the stairs.

If she wants me to eat her out, I'm putting her in a more comfortable spot than the marble island. I take the stairs two at a time and kick open my bedroom door so I can lay her out on my bed, her dark hair fanning out over the white duvet. Nothing has ever looked so at home in this space than she does, half naked and blushing.

"You ready for this?" I ask instead of dragging the pants from her legs and diving in the way I want.

She nods once, but her arms cross to cover her breasts as her modesty cools some of the passion we just flamed.

"Honey, I'm not going any further than you want me to. I'll gladly hold you if you just want to lie here and cuddle."

"No, I want you. Please," she begs, rising up on her elbows as she unbuttons her jeans and starts to wiggle them over her hips.

My dick kicks in my pants and I groan. I gently replace her hands and slowly pull the hem of one leg and then the other until her jeans slide off. She's wearing pearly white satin panties with lace sides that are sexier than any thong or G-string I've ripped off a woman. I don't skim my hands up her legs and spread them wide the way I would have in the past. Instead, I lie beside her and pull her into my arms, brushing my fingers through her hair and down her back. I settle a big palm over the dimples on her lower back and kiss her pink lips until she's writhing in my arms again.

I raise up on my forearms and slowly trace kisses down her body, stopping every few seconds to allow her to get used to my lips and tongue on each new patch of soft skin. Her nipples pebble and goose bumps cover her chest when I lick the undersides of her round breasts. Her hips are rolling under me and her body quivers when my mouth finds the fabric boundary of her panties. Her arousal is potent, the warm, wet promise of her so close I could blow my load just laying on my dick wrong. I look up her body from between her legs and catch her green eyes following my every movement.

"Tell me what you want, honey," I say with a devilish smile as my chin brushes her center with my words.

Her head tips back, eyes closed and mouth open in a moan. She returns her gaze to me, a little hazier this time.

"I want your mouth on me. I want to know what it feels like to have your fingers inside me and your lips kissing me... there." Her cheeks burn bright red, but she holds my heated gaze.

"Good girl."

I hold her stare as I dip my mouth and slowly drag my tongue over her panties from her wet center to her clit. She squeezes her eyes shut when I suck at her clit, her hips bucking. I drag my hand up her thigh, holding pressure against her skin when I get to the junction of her legs. She's quivering, her breaths raising her chest. I rub my thumb over her satin-covered opening.

"You're soaked, baby," I say against her.

"Touch me again." Her shaky words are low and full of heat.

I slip my thumb into the leg of her panties and brush over delicate skin that parts and allows my thumb to slip into her wetness.

"Goddamn," I groan as the slick heat covers my finger.

Her thighs tremble as I stroke through her lips and press her clit gently. I shift my position to ease up on my rock-hard cock that is aching and pulsing with each pass my thumb makes through the very spot I want to bury myself.

Her hands tug impatiently at her waistband, pushing her hips up to free her plush ass and settle back once her panties are around her thighs. I drag them down her legs with one hand to free her from the barrier and when I look back, she's on her elbows again, watching me. Slowly, she opens her knees and bares herself to me.

"Fucking hell, Paige," I growl.

I move back up and lower my face to her perfectly groomed pussy glistening with need. I've been holding back, trying not to scare her, but there's something about the way she parted her legs that breaks my resolve. The primal need to coat my face in her slickness drags my mouth straight to her center. Her squeak of surprise at the ferocious way I eat her pussy is quickly replaced by loud moans when my fingers play her clit in harmony with my tongue lapping at her sweet and tangy taste and fucking her opening.

"Oh my God," she cries, her hips lifting until I press them back down with a heavy forearm.

I slowly slide one thick finger into her tight opening, my tongue circling her clit as she gasps. I gently drag the pad of my finger along the front of her pussy, settling into a rhythm that turns the gasps into pleasurable sounds. Her arousal drips down my hand and I use it to gently add a second fingertip to her opening. Her body protests, my fingers held snugly in place.

"Relax, baby. Stop pushing me out," I coax, my fingertips gently motioning inside her.

"I'm trying. It's just a lot."

"If you want my cock in you, you'll need to be able to take at least a few fingers now." Her pussy grips, then slowly releases my fingers as more juice escapes her. I dip my head and lap it up, moving my tongue between my fingers and back up to her clit as she relaxes and allows my fingers to slide in with ease.

"I'm so full," she gasps. "It's so tight."

I close my eyes at the best goddamn words I've ever heard and smile.

"Just wait."

I work my fingers in and out of her in a slow rhythm as I continue to kiss, lick, and suck at her clit. I can feel her body growing close, her tight pussy trying to strangle my fingers as her hips roll under me. I push my fingers in to the last knuckle and suck her clit hard when it finally hits.

"Holy Jesus, sweet tea and vodka!" she screams, jacking up off the bed as an orgasm grips her. Her hands latch onto my head as she falls back against the duvet in the thrall of her pleasure, her body rolling out the final waves until she's panting and everything goes limp.

I wait until her pussy stops pulsing to pull my fingers out of her. She jumps with the motion and I smile, loving every reaction she has to me. I scoop her naked, completely relaxed body into my arms and move to the pillows where I hold her tightly to my chest.

"How are you so fucking amazing?" I ask quietly, my lips pressing each word into her hair as a kiss.

She wiggles in my arms until her head is on my shoulder and she can kiss my neck.

"You stole my line, minus the F-bomb."

I laugh, the sound deep and loud in the quiet bedroom. I stop when her leg hooks over my hip, pulling my still-hard dick right into her tight center and stretching the ability of my slacks to restrain the monster that wants to pound inside of her.

"Careful, angel. I'm real close to that threshold of not being able to stop when I want."

Her hands reach between us and she unhooks my belt.

"Maybe I don't want you to stop."

I shut my eyes and groan, because all I want is to push the restrictive fabric off my dick and plunge inside of her. I breathe heavily trying to remember why I shouldn't as she works on the button and zipper, her hands sending electric currents up my spine each time her fingers touch my cock. She moves her leg off my hip to sit up and tries to push my pants down, but she only manages a few inches because of how I'm lying.

I take her hand in mine, and though it goes against every instinct to get naked and fuck her stupid, I make her stop.

"Baby, you're going to be my undoing." I sit up and pull her into my lap. "How about we slow down? It's Friday night. I want to take you out. Let's get some dinner and have a little fun."

She wraps her arms around my neck and leans back to look into my face.

"Aren't you"—she pauses and looks down at the still evident bulge of my dick that's not on board with my plan—"unsatisfied?"

I smile. "Did you like me touching you?"

She nods quickly.

"Then I'm plenty satisfied."

"Won't you, like, explode or something?"

I laugh and kiss her nose. "Let me handle that in the shower. If you're a good girl, I'll let you watch since I know you like to. My little voyeur," I tease.

Her face blushes crimson and she immediately covers it with her hands. "Hey, that was one time, and I didn't even know that was what I'd see," she mumbles through her hands.

I tilt my head. "I still think you liked watching."

She spreads her fingers over one eye and glares at me. "I don't even know what I like."

I pull her hands away from her face and kiss each of her fingers in turn.

"We're going to find out exactly what you like. Just give it time."

"Let me watch you. I'll stay outside of the shower, but I want to actually see what you do this time."

"I knew you enjoyed watching. My perfect, pretty little voyeur." I pet her hair affectionately as my cock strains my pants, thinking of getting off to her watching while I imagine the feel of her perfect pussy. "Too bad I want to take you out tonight and need to be quick. Sit tight."

Fourteen

Paige

I don't watch Hayes handle himself in the shower, but I do sit wrapped in the duvet in the middle of the bed and imagine every stroke of his hand. When he comes out, a white towel wrapped around his hips and water droplets dotting his muscular chest, I nearly faint.

"Why do you have to be God's gift to women?" I say appreciatively under my breath.

Hayes pauses on his way to the closet, having heard me.

"You don't think the same is true about yourself, Miss Fairchild? You're a total smoke show wrapped up in Chantilly cream. Just knowing your exquisite body is naked under that duvet is threatening to undo all the hard work I just performed in the shower to get rid of this hard-on." He grabs himself over the towel and my heart pounds like the hooves of a racehorse.

"You look like one of those models on the cover of the grocery store romance novels my nanny likes to read.

They're always shirtless and, like, a pirate or duke or something." I guess muscles and a shirtless billionaire work just as well.

He moves his hand away from the towel and laughs. Shaking his head, he goes into the closet. I'm half tempted to follow him inside and force him to take me when he drops his towel, but I don't. It meant everything to me that he was able to slow things down when I was letting my hormones, not my heart, guide my body again. I had hoped I could make Hayes fall for me, but I think I'm the one falling, and hard.

"I like your clothes next to mine. It's more colorful having your bright clothes looking so cute and little next to my suits." I hear from the closet.

I pull the duvet up to my face and laugh. "Sorry, I just took over. I didn't know where else to put my things, so I made a spot."

The duvet is pulled down and Hayes's face appears. He slowly pushes me back on the bed and crawls over me, trapping me in the duvet.

"Good. Don't just make a spot next time, take the whole closet. Stop trying to make yourself small to fit into my life when you're the biggest part of it."

I melt. If I was wearing panties, they would have fallen right off. I slowly shake my head and grin a big, cheesy smile.

"Next time? You expect me to run away from home again?"

His face takes on a serious look as his eyes dart away in thought.

"I guess I was just thinking of the next time you go shopping. I like you here with me."

A sobering thought invades the protective cocoon of the duvet and the fairytale idea of running from my problems. This was supposed to be temporary until I could get Mama and Daddy to see that I wouldn't marry Garrison. I've been gone for over five days and they're only doubling down on their insistence and maintaining the stalemate. What do I do if they don't see it my way, even after this impulsive flight from the future they want for me? I'll have to tuck my tail between my legs and go home to them. And Garrison Daniels. I shudder.

"Come on, let's get you dressed so we can get the city's best pizza."

He rolls off me and pulls away the duvet.

"Good Lord almighty. On second thought, maybe you should just stay naked."

He tips his head appreciatively and I roll over onto my stomach to hide.

"Hell, that's an even better view."

I feel teeth nip at my bare bottom and yelp.

"Hayes!" I roll again and take the duvet with me as I climb out of bed. "Give me fifteen minutes."

"Just enough time for me to rub another out," he says.

I turn to see if he's serious and stop with a sigh. He's wearing dark jeans and an olive-green T-shirt that sets off his tan skin and does things to his dark green eyes that must be magic. He's so pretty it hurts something deep inside of me. He's the most attractive man I've ever met, and here I am playing house with him. It's going to break a part of me when I leave, but I guess Mama and Daddy don't need me whole, they just need to save their business.

"Hayes, you're something else," I say wistfully.

"Now you're stealing my lines, angel."

Hayes holds my hand as we walk into the restaurant, just like he did on the way here. He's using every opportunity he can to touch me, and I'm not complaining. It feels good. I had expected something greasy and casual when he said we were getting pizza, but this place is gorgeous and looks like it could have been taken off the pages of a design magazine with its decor. The big wood-fired pizza oven is open to the restaurant, giving the place a romantic glow. It's busy, but the hostess leads us to a table as soon as Hayes walks up and gives his name. I sit across from Hayes and look up when a waiter appears immediately with a bottle of wine.

"The usual, Mr. Olsen?"

Hayes nods and I give him a look as apprehension settles in my belly. I take the glass of red wine the waiter pours for me and sip. Of course it's good. Hayes has exquisite taste and there's nothing he hasn't perfected as far as I can tell. I pick up my menu and slouch in my chair, finding a way to hide from Hayes while I collect my thoughts.

"What's wrong, honey?"

I pull the menu down just low enough to see him.

"You have a usual."

I raise the menu up again. It's snatched from my hands, and I'm forced to meet Hayes's perturbed scrutiny.

"Tell me what you really mean. Don't play the *guess what I'm thinking game* with me."

"Do you take all your dates here?" I hate the slimy jealousy that slithers through my thoughts and tinges my words. It's hard not to think this way after spending hours with Maisie and hearing all sorts of stories. I have no idea if half of them were true, but from her perspective, she and Hayes *really had something special,* and she was just waiting for the right time to settle down with him. Hayes's explanation was a little more realistic, but I can't help thinking of those women he's had *whenever he wanted.* Who knows how many have sat right here in my chair across from him.

"I usually bring Cerberus here when the weather's nice and sit on the patio. This is my favorite restaurant.

I invested in the place early on, so the staff goes out of their way to accommodate me."

I nod. "So, a lot of dates, then."

His eyebrows draw together sternly. "I've never brought a woman here before you."

Guilt washes over me for assuming the worst about him. Why do I keep doing that? Maybe because I don't know much about him other than he's been hospitable to a Southern belle fleeing an arranged marriage and he has more money than God. Oh, and he knows his way around my body better than I do. I blush at the thought.

"I'm sorry, that was uncalled for."

He rubs his face and then props his chin on his hand.

"I guess I deserved that. I've made it quite clear I have a bit of a past and you haven't had much to go on otherwise." He shakes his head. "Let's start over. I want us to really know each other."

I sit up straighter, hope buoyed in my heart at his interest.

"You go first. I feel like I've told you so much about my family and our troubles, but I don't know anything about you or the brothers you've mentioned."

"They're dicks," he deadpans. "But they're my family and I wouldn't trade them for the world."

"That's quite the ringing endorsement."

"I wouldn't trust either of them alone with you. Let's just put it that way." He raises an eyebrow at me, and I nod knowingly. "Payton, my middle brother, is a year younger than me at thirty-four and thinks his job is stirring the pot. Zander is the youngest at thirty-three but likes to act like the top dog. He's the biggest womanizer and damn proud of it."

"Okay, okay. Stop making them sound so appealing." I prop my chin on my hand and roll my eyes at Hayes.

"Fine, I'll try to find something nice to say about those pains in my ass."

He pauses and looks away, his fingers tapping on the table in a staccato rhythm.

"Payton is the most fun-loving person I know. He knows everyone and everything, so he can ensure we always do something epic no matter where we are. He's a genius with tech and has a chokehold on the image of the company through amazingly clever marketing plans. I don't know how he manages those two things simultaneously, but I'm not about to ask him to pick one over the other when he's obviously doing fine managing both sides of the company. He loves the water the way I love cars. You should see his boats. If we ever get to the ocean, it'll likely be on his yacht."

"That was better. Keep going," I encourage. I sip wine and watch as he runs a hand through his hair, smoothing it away from his face in thought.

"Zander is, well, Zander. We don't get along well because we're both so uncompromising and like to be in control."

He spends a moment in thought, obviously digging hard for something nice to say about his youngest brother.

"He's beyond protective of the things and people he cares about. He somehow always manages to get his way, so he's the best negotiator I can bring in on a deal. He'll know it inside and out and find a way to get what we want while keeping the other party satisfied. Outside of the office, he's the adrenaline junkie, off climbing mountains, base jumping, or finding a new intense hobby that could easily kill him. You wouldn't catch me doing any of that, but you can always trust that Zander has done the craziest shit and doesn't back down when something new is offered. I admire his determination."

"That took you a bit to find the good in him."

"Like I said, we don't get along well, so I've focused on the qualities that bother me more than what I can tolerate. Our mother says we're too much alike, but she's dead wrong."

"What are your parents like?" Knowing my own relationship with Mama and Daddy, I wonder if his are even remotely as stifling.

"Dad is happy to be retired. He was a workaholic until he had a heart attack ten years ago and Mom forced him to give control of the company to me. It was just precious metals and mining operations at the time, so it was easier to handle."

"Mining?"

"Yeah, my grandfather bought out a mining outfit in the sixties that managed to make good during the Georgia Gold Rush back in the early 1800s. Of course, that was mostly exhausted by the time my dad got to it, but they discovered other metals like iron, manganese, and later aluminum, before Dad took the company global, so our operations are still in existence. When it was handed off to me, I figured it wouldn't last forever and we needed to diversify, so I created Olympus International with my brothers and branched out into other endeavors."

"That's amazing," I say, thinking of my own family's sordid history of plantation life before the Civil War. It's not a pretty legacy when you go far enough back, but you can't undo the past actions of relations, only hope to make better ones and do your part to ensure no one is taken advantage of again. *Unless it's a daughter you want to give in exchange for hush money.*

"Your mama must be a tough woman to have three sons like what you've described."

Hayes widens his eyes and nods. "My mama came from nothing. A real ball-buster of a lady my daddy met in the Appalachians of Lumpkin County where some of our mining operations are. She'll tell anyone she didn't need no rich man to sweep her off her feet, but he certainly needed to be managed and she was the lady for the job."

I laugh imagining someone as demanding and successful as the man who sired Hayes needing to be managed.

"She sounds like a hoot."

"More like scary." He shakes his head appreciatively.

Our waiter brings a pizza that we didn't order to our table, and I look up at him in confusion.

"Your usual, sir. Ma'am, would you like anything else to drink?"

"I'm fine, thank you," I tell him. I look at Hayes. "I can't even be mad at you for ordering for me, because they didn't even let you do that. But what if I have an allergy or aversion to something?"

"Do you?" he asks, serving me a piece of steaming pizza with melty strings of cheese that stretch before he pulls them off with his fingers.

"No, I guess not, but you didn't know that."

"You would have told me. If you don't tell me, I'll never know because I'm not a mind reader. But everyone likes pizza."

I look at the puffed pockets of crisp crust with longing. Yes, I love pizza. I make a mental note to not assume he's a mind reader and dig in.

Hayes wipes his hands on a cloth napkin and steeples his fingers in front of him.

"So what are you gonna do?"

I choke on a bite of pizza and take a moment to wash it down with a sip of water.

"As in immediately with my pizza, or some vague time in the future?" I clarify.

"What's your plan? I know what your parents want for you, but what do you really want?"

I take a bite of pizza and chew thoughtfully.

"I'm supposed to start working at The Mansion in the new year as the general manager to get my feet wet in the operations and management side of things. Then I'll run the Xenios Group, eventually, when Daddy retires. It's my legacy, what I've been raised to do, and what I want most is to take over and expand it into something bigger, something that helps more people somehow. I want to leave my own mark, you know? Hospitality is in my blood. I don't see anything else even remotely as fulfilling."

Hayes taps his steepled fingers against his bottom lip and nods once.

"What about the plans your parents have for you?"

My shoulders slump. "I don't see a way around them, honestly. If I want that legacy, I have to do what they say, even if it kills a part of me to do it. I'll have to go home eventually and face the music."

"Stay here with me."

"And what, become estranged from my family in the hopes they'll see clearly eventually? I don't think you understand the lengths they will go to in order to en-sure the survival of their company. This marriage would ensure the financial stability they crave and branch the business out into other endeavors, which aligns with my own future aspirations. Not that I'd ever willingly marry for it," I assure him.

"What if the Daniels weren't able to provide that financial stability your parents are thinking they're getting by arranging your marriage?" He says the last part like an accusation, and I can't help but agree.

"If you know something I don't, that would help my case, I'm all ears." I lean my elbow on the table and sip my wine.

"I'm working on it. Don't give up on me."

"I don't think I have much time. I'm maxing out the bounds of your helpfulness in keeping me while I negotiate with a tyrant, and it's not exactly fun hiding out. I miss Savannah. The sea air, the small-town charm, the historic buildings, being able to walk everywhere, and the Spanish moss draped on every tree. I miss home," I say wistfully.

Hayes reaches out and covers my hand on the table.

"There is no limit to what I would do for you, angel. You're not maxing out anything by staying with me."

I smile. "Thank you for that. I'm forever grateful that you would help me out in a time of need. It's really my own unease with putting that on someone else that's getting to me. Fairchilds don't overstay their welcome, even if it's open-ended."

"How about I put you to work so you're not counting tiles all by yourself in the house next week?" he offers.

"What do you have in mind?" I'm curious what he thinks my ability is.

"I have a few projects at work that could use your background and honestly, your feminine touch. Think you'd like to learn more about Underworld Spirits?"

"I don't know the first thing about liquor distribution, but I can tell a good whiskey from tequila."

He chuckles with me when I smile.

"This is the place that makes the bourbon we had at my ball, right? The exclusive one only available at The Abyss?"

"The very same, but it's a full-scale distillery making that delightful bourbon as well as a smaller-scale production of craft vodka and gin. We'll move into tequila when I can get the perfect agave supplier and start production in Mexico because it has to be just right, or you get bottom barrel shit that leaves you on the floor with a hangover."

He rubs his temples like he's had the experience, even though his wealth should have assured he never touched anything less than Patrón Silver.

"Such a large operation for one retailer?"

"We're beginning the mass production and distribution portion next week. We have a launch party tomorrow, with a gradual rollout planned to keep demand high. I was actually hoping you'd be my date to the party." He squeezes my fingers and smiles his blinding white, panty-melting grin.

"A real date instead of staying tucked in your cozy home? What is this, a trick question?" I laugh because it's easier than admitting to the bubbly high that hit me with his request. It's one thing to know he trusts me to work on a project for him, and another entirely to know he wants me on his arm at a big party he'll be in the spotlight for.

"It's a black-tie affair. We can go shopping tomorrow to make sure you have something comfortable to wear."

I laugh out loud. "Comfortable black-tie? Have you seen an evening gown? Comfort is the last thing that comes to mind when sequins, glitter, corsets, and trains are involved."

His eyes burn with liquid emeralds and a predatory grin cracks his face, showing off white teeth.

"Mmm, corsets. You want to take dessert to go and let me unlace you?"

I tap my nose and smile. "I don't have a corset with me, but I may have other surprises that still allow me to breathe that you'd find equally appealing. I hope your usual includes something chocolate."

Hayes looks around for our server and raises his hand. When the server arrives, he says, "We'll take the soufflé to go and a box for the leftovers, please." He hands off his credit card and returns his heated gaze to me. "I like the idea of surprises when it comes to you."

It doesn't take long for our dessert to be brought out. Hayes packs everything up and holds his hand out for me. We leave the restaurant and he drapes his arm over my shoulder, pulling me close to his side on our walk back to the car.

"This is really nice. Thanks for getting me out of the house." I snuggle closer and look up at him from his side.

"I enjoyed sharing my favorite pizza with you." He places a kiss on my head. "I'm actually looking forward to the Underworld Spirits party tomorrow. I was dreading the publicity, but I think I'll manage if I have you there with me." He stops at the car and lifts the gullwing door of the Mercedes to put our boxes in the back.

I lean my back against the car and cross my arms.

"So you don't mind being seen out with a much younger woman who has questionable parents?" I tease.

"Are you kidding? I'm honored you'd even entertain an old man like me," he jokes right back. "I mean, it's only fourteen years, right? It's not like I'm twice your age, which isn't uncommon for some of the people I've done business with."

I consider his words. Had I been asked a week ago what I thought of a woman my age dating an older man, I probably would have wrinkled my nose in distaste. My small worldview is expanding the longer I spend with Hayes, and I'm not mad about it.

"Okay, old man, come here and kiss me." I grab his T-shirt in my fist and tug him to me.

He traps me against the car with his arms and leans his face close to mine. "Are you starting dessert early, Miss Fairchild?"

I pull his hips flush against me and wiggle. "Maybe."

His lips crash into mine with a passion that leaves me breathless. He takes what I've started and proves that he truly is the one in control and I'm along for the blissfully beautiful ride. When he pulls away, it takes me several slow blinks to register that we are not alone.

"Hayes," I say quickly, patting his back in my growing alarm.

He turns quickly and sees the man creeping closer, light from the streetlight glinting off the knife he holds at his side. Hayes shoves me into the car and stands in front of the door. I'm too freaked at the moment to care about the unceremonious movement, but it registers that he's doing it for my safety.

"Nice ride, man. Gimme the keys."

"You're fucking with the wrong guy tonight. Walk away and this is over. Step closer and I'll end you," Hayes growls.

"Not how this works when I got the knife," the man replies, thrusting the weapon between them.

Hayes kicks out, his long leg making contact with the man's fist and sending the knife clanging to the ground. The man lunges for Hayes, his fist swinging out and catching him in the ribs. Hayes gives a grunt of pain but shoves the man away and kicks again, catching him in the stomach and doubling him over. In a flash, he's back up and swinging wildly. Hayes dodges one fist but catches the other to his ribs and I scream as the thud echoes in my head. Hayes pushes the man and follows so they're out of sight.

I dig through my purse blindly while searching for the men around the car. My fingers close around my cell and I pull it out, fumbling to get my fingerprint to register. I shake so badly it's hard to pull up my keypad to dial 911. I have never struggled so much to dial three numbers correctly, but after several attempts, I press the call button and hope to God they answer and can get here quickly. I hear another thud and I'm not sure who took the hit this time.

"Nine-one-one, what's your emergency," the dispatcher says.

"Please help! There's a man trying to steal our car."

I look up as the scrape of metal against concrete rings ominously in the air.

"Oh my God, he's got a knife. He's going to hurt Hayes."

"What's your location?" she asks calmly.

"Um, it's the Buckhead area." I look around for any indication of street names but see the sign for the restaurant instead. "We're outside of Napoletana Pizza, near Peachtree and Piedmont," I say, finally remembering the cross streets.

"Officers are responding. They will be there short-ly. Stay on the line."

I listen for sounds of the fight but it's grown quiet and I hope to God Hayes isn't lying hurt and the attacker's taken off.

"I can't see them anymore," I say, scanning through what I can see of the lot.

"Ma'am, do not go looking for them. Stay where you are safe," the dispatcher cautions, but I'm already out of the car and looking around wildly.

"Oh my God, they're gone. Hayes!" I shout, my head whipping around in search of where they could have gone.

"Ma'am, officers are less than a minute away, do not get involved."

I scan the parking area and see an alley behind the building. I hear sirens wailing in the distance as I run toward the alley and pray I won't find Hayes in a heap.

"Please, please, please," I beg quietly.

"Ma'am, officers are almost at your location, do not leave," the dispatcher says, just as I enter the dark alley.

"Hayes!" I scream again, listening to my voice bounce off the walls.

"Right here," he answers from midway down the alley, kneeling on the ground in the shadows.

"Oh, thank God!" I turn toward him in relief.

"Paige, stay there!" he calls sharply, halting my steps.

"Ma'am, officers are looking for you, please make contact," the dispatcher instructs me.

I freeze in indecision, wanting to run to Hayes but needing to find the officers.

"The police are here," I call down the alley.

"Go to them, honey. I'm okay," he says quietly.

I turn and run out of the alley, red and blue lights lighting up the parking lot as four officers turn toward me, weapons drawn. "I'm here, I called!" I yell, my hands going up in the air as my phone drops to the concrete. The screen cracks, but the call is still live.

"They're down the alley," I say, my voice shaking as one officer moves toward me, pistol outstretched while the other three move toward the alley behind me.

A voice comes through his radio spouting codes and words I can't follow, and he lowers his weapon.

"Ma'am, come with me, please." He beckons me toward him and I follow, even though my heart is stuck in the alley with Hayes.

It feels like hours as I sit in the police car, recounting the events as best I can for the officer while I shake and search for any sign of Hayes. When an ambulance arrives, I bolt upright and scream for Hayes, but the officer keeps me with him. The stretcher that comes back ten minutes later is carrying a man, but the paramedics are working over him and I can't see if it's Hayes. I break down, cold tears streaming down my face as I sob hysterically.

I wail Hayes's name and wish this were a horrible dream I could wake up from.

Fifteen

Hayes

When I walk out of the alley escorted by two police officers, I don't see Paige. I quickly scan the area and nearly lose my shit and start screaming for her.

"Where's my girl? Where is she?" The frantic tone is loud in my own ears.

"Cool it, buddy, she's in the shop," one of the officers says, pointing at the police car flanking my Mercedes. One door is still open, making it look like a bird with a broken wing.

"Hayes!"

I turn when my name is called and see Paige clambering out of the car and running toward me. Relief as I've never known rushes through me to see she's safe and nothing happened to her. I meet her with open arms, catching her flying figure as she launches herself into my chest.

"Baby, you're all right?" I ask, pulling her tight to me while she sobs.

"I didn't—you were—so scared," she cries, her words disjointed and hysterical.

"I'm okay. I just have to give a written statement and we can go home, got it?"

"What happened?" she asks. "You're covered in blood!"

"It's not mine, I'm fine," I assure her gently. I glance down and notice my shirt and hands are bloody and it's now on Paige where she was pressed to my chest, smeared on her cheek and streaked on her sweater. The sight turns my stomach more than the adrenaline of the fight did. I don't like seeing her marred by blood, especially the blood of a man who threatened her safety, no matter the outcome.

"Mr. Olsen?"

I look up when I'm called and see Antonio De-Sano, the owner of Napoletana, coming over.

"Everything okay out here? I came out when the cops showed up and saw your car. I wanted to make sure you're all right."

I look at the police officers with me, wondering if I'm allowed to talk about it. The closest one shrugs and leaves me with the remaining cop.

"It's good now, Antonio. I'm sorry this happened here. It's a good area. I never expected to get carjacked in Buckhead."

I shrug and my shoulder blares in pain. I reach over and feel the warm wetness of an injury I wasn't aware of. I look at the last cop.

"You have a first aid kit? I could use a little patching up if we're not going to have an ambulance here."

Paige pulls away and looks at my shoulder.

"You're bleeding! He cut you?"

"Apparently," I answer, keeping calm for her. Truth is, I came out of that far better than the other guy. He left with a pretty bad stab wound thanks to falling on his own knife after I kicked him. I seem to have managed only a few bruises and a slashed shoulder. It could have been worse. I could have lost Paige.

My brain replays the instant my world became black and white, then went red. When the carjacker showed up with a knife, threatening Paige's safety, something just clicked. My first priority became to keep her safe over anything else. I went on instinct, but I saw the wrathful haze of red when the fucker continued to fight when he didn't get the hands up acquiescence he had hoped for. My own safety was a far lower priority and I leaned on some Muay Thai I did in my twenties to make sure that fucker stayed away from her.

But I'm too old for this shit. My ribs burn with every inhale, so I'm thinking I may have bruised a few, and my shoulder is throbbing. Both are injuries that wouldn't have kept me out of the gym the day after a brutal sparring session, but a decade later feel debilitating as the adrenaline leaves my system. I'm just glad I had something to rely on when I needed it and didn't end up stabbed and missing a car, and possibly without my girl.

I get my shoulder cleaned up and it thankfully doesn't need stitches but will probably leave an ugly scar right across the top. I write out my statement for the officers and give them all of my contact information in case they need to get in touch with me. They likely will, as the criminal investigation will lead to a trial and all sorts of opportunities for my name to be dragged along in the press. I'm not looking forward to the news tomorrow.

It's not every day that a billionaire fights off a carjacker who leaves the scene in an ambulance.

When the police release us, I tuck Paige into the car, shut the door and make a call to Payton.

"Aww, Hater calling after hours. Miss me?" he asks when he answers the call.

"Hardly, but I need you on a situation."

"What happened?" He's alert and all trace of humor is gone from his voice.

"Some fucker decided he was feeling extra brave and wanted my car tonight after dinner at Napoletana. It wasn't pretty and he left in an ambulance. Get our PR team on this immediately to make sure it doesn't get out of hand."

"Are you hurt? Oh, shit. Did something happen to Paige? That would be so fucking bad," he finishes almost to himself.

"Just a little cut and bruised, nothing too bad. Paige is fine, but this will get ugly when her parents find out." I scan the area and notice a few bystanders with phones out, recording video and snapping photos that will likely be all over the news, or worse, the gossip sites, tomorrow. "We can't stop our names from getting out, so we need to tighten up at Olympus for the takeover."

"I'm on it. Take your girl home and make it up to her. Damn, your first public appearance together had to be a big one, huh?"

"Not really my intention," I grumble.

"Yeah, yeah, I know. Night, Hayes."

I hang up the call and pocket my phone. I look over at Antonio standing near the restaurant, his arms crossed as he surveys the continued commotion the police presence brought to his doorstep. I walk over and extend my hand. He takes it in both of his for a moment and gives me a worried look.

"I'm sorry Antonio, this is a shitty situation to drop on you. Let me know if it affects business. I'll make it up to you."

"Oh, no, I'm more worried about you, man," he says, his hands held out in front of him. "Can't have my best customer and investor attacked right here. I'm going to look into security for the lot. This is unacceptable."

"Everything will be fine. You couldn't have stopped this."

"Looks like the police are leaving now," he says, looking over my shoulder. I turn and catch the cruisers pulling away from the lot.

"I guess I should get going, too. Thank you for checking on us."

He nods and motions for me to go. I wave as I turn and walk back to the car.

I slide into my seat and start the car. I reach for Paige's hand and hold it in mine, scanning her head to toe to make sure she is okay. She seems fine, physically, but I can tell she is exhausted. The late hour combined with the emotional adrenaline dump leaves her wasted and quiet in the seat next to me. I keep her hand in mine, fingers laced tight as I drive home. Every time I lose her touch, panic surges.

Cerberus greets us at the door when we get in, his stubby tail wagging as he smells us. His tail stills and he growls low as he looks out the door behind us until I shush him. "They didn't follow us home, you badass, but thanks for having my back. I could have used you earlier."

He follows at my heels all the way up to the bedroom where I help Paige undress in the bathroom. I crank the shower on and return to where I left her leaning against the sink. It takes two seconds to pull my shirt over my head and get out of my pants so I can help her into the shower.

Her bleary eyes open wide when the water hits her, but she doesn't move except to bring her hand to my shoulder where bandages cover the three-inch cut. It's really not that bad. I feel like I need to get a tetanus shot, but I'll figure it out in the morning. Right now, Paige is my priority and I'm focused on removing the blood from her creamy skin and washing the bad night off of her. Once she's clean, I duck under another showerhead and scrub my body raw, trying to get the smell of the alley and the carjacker's blood off me.

I kept pressure on his wound after he fell. Partly because I don't want to be even a little bit responsible for anyone's death, even a criminal. Also because it will be much easier to deal with a trial where he's on the stand for attacking us, not me being grilled for killing in self-defense.

"Oh!"

Paige's voice has me rubbing water out of my eyes and looking over at her.

"You're naked." She brings her hand up to cover her mouth but doesn't look away.

I chuckle, glad to have her innocence bringing me back to the present. I wash the soap suds from my body and turn my back to her so I don't wake the beast between my legs that would like to scoop her up and impale her against the shower wall. I shut off the water and grab a towel to wrap around my hips and a second to dry her off.

She stands still, water droplets falling off her chin and down her back from her hair as I smooth the towel over her skin. Once she's dry, I pass the towel over me quickly and wrap her up so I can carry her to the bed. She doesn't object and rests her head on my chest until I set her on the side I now think of as hers and go to the closet. I pull on pajama pants and grab a T-shirt before returning to her and slipping it over her head.

"You okay, angel?" I ask, a little worried.

"I was so scared," she murmurs, her hand brushing wet hair off my forehead. "I thought I had lost you." Tears well in her eyes, making the clear green brighter.

My heart clenches in my chest and a fiercely protective emotion rises up in me as I wrap her in my arms.

"I'm not going anywhere. You got me, honey." The only flaw to my statement is if someone else takes away my ability to be here for her. It was too close tonight. That's not happening again.

The sun streaming through the curtainless windows wakes me before I'm ready. I squint and pull a pillow over my eyes at the slight.

"Fucking sun, how dare you," I growl hoarsely.

Normally, I'm up before sunrise, so not having curtains has always been an aesthetic thing. Now I'm rethinking my design choices. I must have overslept, likely due to having Paige's warmth curled against me in my bed where I tucked her in last night. I couldn't go to the guest room after what we went through. That would have been too far away. I reach for Paige now, wanting to pull her right back into my arms, but all I get is a handful of cool sheets.

I sit up, my eyes opening wide. "Paige?" I call.

I look around the room and notice Cerberus is gone, too, so at least he's being a good demon spawn shadow, wherever she is. Still, my heart jackhammers away in my chest when she doesn't reply. I'm out of bed and pounding down the stairs in a sprint as my mind delivers every fucked-up scenario it can to explain her absence.

"Hi," she says, her hands wrapped around a mug of coffee when I skid into the kitchen.

She leans against the counter wearing my old Vanderbilt T-shirt, her hair messy and rumpled, with Cerberus at her bare feet. It's the most beautiful image my brain can comprehend after the panic that flashed every worst-case possibility through my mind.

My eyes close and my lungs exhale a great breath I must have been holding.

"Fucking scared me, baby. I didn't know where you were."

"I'm sorry I scared you. I thought coffee would help with this awful headache I have. Here, I poured you a cup, too, but I don't know how you take it, so it's still black." She holds out a second mug to me.

I gladly take it. Caffeine sounds excellent. I palm the back of her head to bring her to me to kiss her forehead good and long.

"Thank you."

She tips her chin up and catches my lips with hers.

"That was a rough night."

"Let's not repeat that. Ever." *Or anything remotely close*, I tack on silently.

I catch sight of dozens of wilted red roses and the bottle of bourbon abandoned on the island from last night. I push her chin with a finger in the direction of the floral carnage.

"That was for you."

She laughs. "I know. They're still pretty. I can probably nurse them back to health if you have a vase big enough for me to get them in water." She pauses and looks at me. "You think you got enough roses?"

I shrug. "It was a *just because I was thinking about you* gift, and I wanted you to know I was thinking about you lots."

"Hayes Olsen, you're sweet on me," she teases, pressing her fingertips against my bare chest and batting her eyelashes at me.

"Try crazy about you," I reply, serious as a heart attack.

Her teasing look softens, and she smiles.

"Is this fast? I'm not too sure how feelings with relationships work, but this feels pretty fast and dirty."

"Do you want it to be fast and dirty?"

I'm invested in her answer, hoping we're on the same page. That thought surprises me. I started the week with ulterior motives that benefited me at her expense when it came to having Paige in my life, but she's hard to resist. Her sweet innocence is addictive, and taking my time getting physical with her has made it, dare I even say it, *better*? I know the moment she lets me sink inside of her will absolutely be worth the wait. She's taught me a lesson on delayed gratification and the strength of my own willpower that's worth its weight in gold alone. Not to mention, the valuable knowledge that there are some things in life more important than personal or professional gain.

"Right now, I just want you. I don't care if it's fast or slow. I'm not exactly a relationship expert, but... I do think this is special, even if it wasn't supposed to happen, and fate had other plans."

"You think the fates would have it so wrong that we weren't supposed to happen? I call bullshit. We make our own fate. I'm good with the way this is working out."

She smiles at me fondly. "Me, too."

If I start thinking too hard about a future with her, I'm liable to go down a rabbit hole and then she will really know the meaning of fast. "You ready for some fancy dress shopping?" I ask to change the subject.

She shuts her eyes and shudders. "I guess so."

I blink dumbly at her half-hearted reaction. "You're not chomping at the bit to buy some crazy expensive dress and get all fancy?"

She shrugs a shoulder and it raises the hem of my favorite shirt, exposing more of her soft thighs that I want wrapped around my head. Or hips. "I've had to wear far too many crazy expensive dresses Mama picked out. I guess it's just not as exciting because of that."

"You're saying you've never picked out your own dress?"

"Oh, I have, it's just been under Mama's direction, or straight up picked out for me when she didn't approve of my choices."

"That's it." I pat my pajama pants, then look around the kitchen for my phone to no avail. "You have your phone on you?"

She looks down quickly. "It broke last night. I dropped it when the police got to the restaurant. The screen is cracked, but it still works."

She walks to the counter where her purse is and pulls out the phone, the screen shattered and ready to shred her pretty little fingers to ribbons the minute she tries to use it. That won't fucking do.

"We're stopping at the store for a new phone before we get you a dress of your choosing."

She tries to protest, but I cut her off.

"I don't care if that phone is usable. Every time you pick it up, you're going to be thinking about last night, and that is psychological torture." Not to mention physical, given the condition.

Her shoulders slump. "I think you're right." She brightens, her eyes flashing with humor. "What's another receipt to add to my tab?" she says, pulling out a handful of paper from her purse. "It'll feel so good to write you a fat check once my trust is active again."

"Unacceptable," I state. Her mouth drops open, but I continue. "I'll rip up any check you try to write me. I don't want you to pay me back for anything, ever, got it?"

"But—"

"But nothing, sweetheart. I told you I would take care of you, and that includes anything you could possibly want or need."

Sixteen

Paige

Hayes is a man of his word. He buys me the newest version of my phone with a screen protector and a protective case on top of it, and we search for places to find formal dresses last minute that won't look like I'm going to prom or a wedding as a bridesmaid. Thankfully, Atlanta has far more dress shops than Savannah, so we have a few options. I look through their websites and decide on the one that looks like a good start.

"Are you coming into the shop with me to weigh in or do you want to be surprised?" I ask as we pull up to the cute shopping area and park near the store.

He looks around at the shops and then appraises me for a moment.

"I want to be surprised. I'll go to that coffee shop and get some work done on my phone while you shop."

"Wish me luck." I blow him a kiss that he catches as I hop out of the Mercedes SUV.

This should be interesting. Mama always insisted on shopping with me and would veto me from even trying on dresses she felt were inappropriate *for a lady of impeccable breeding and social standing.*

"Hey, sugar, welcome in," a perky blonde in a pink shift dress says as I walk into the airy store.

I smile at her and look around. The store is so pretty and familiar in a way that makes my heart yearn for Savannah. It has white-washed brick walls, industrial chic hardware, and exposed lighting setting off the racks of dresses. I'm instantly comfortable and starting to look forward to this shopping trip after all. Hayes says we make our own fate, so why can't I?

"How can I help ya?"

"I'm going to a black-tie affair this evening and I want a showstopper of a dress," I say bluntly. "Like, make my man fall on his face, amazing. Do you have anything that fits that description?"

Her eyes light up and she practically vibrates in excitement.

"I've been waiting five years for someone to come in and say just that! Oh, this will be fun. I'm Angela. Haute Belle is my place, and we're going to make your man trip over himself by the time we're done here."

"I'm probably a size six or eight depending on the cut," I offer as I follow her around the store.

"Four, max," she replies, pulling see-through garment bags off racks with lightning speed.

"Do you have magic dresses that are super forgiving or something?" I know my own dress size, and a four would make me look like a popped can of biscuits as the best-case scenario.

"Nah, sugar. I have corsets and magic seaming in these dresses. You'll fit a four, promise."

"Do you design the dresses?" I ask in astonishment as I look around at the veritable rainbow of gorgeous gowns.

"I sure do! I do most of the alterations, too, but I send my designs out to be manufactured because ain't nobody got time for that."

She leads me back to a big dressing room with really good lighting and starts hanging up dresses on the bar along one wall.

I look at the sequins and beading covering a navy gown next to me and shudder. My fingers hurt just thinking of the labor that went into it. I give in and hope something will work.

"Okay, Angela, do your thing."

Two hours later I am nipped in, hemmed, and had bra cups sewn into the bodice of a stunning size four gown that is unlike anything I've ever worn before. Mama would most definitely *not* approve, but I think Hayes is going to be rolling up his tongue. Best of all, I feel incredible in it.

"Angela, you really are a miracle worker. I can't believe how fast you work."

"Girl, you've got a party to go to. Time is money. If you need anything, you know to come right back to me and I'll get you all fixed up. I do bridal, too, if that man of yours knows what's good for him when he sees you in this dress."

A blush warms my cheeks as I grin. "I'll keep that in mind."

"Now, get! You have a man waiting on you and probably need to go to hair and makeup soon, anyway."

My eyes widen. I hadn't even thought that far ahead.

"You wouldn't happen to know an artist that's available today, would you?" I can do a decent job on my own hair and makeup, but this calls for something only a pro can deliver.

"Today must be your lucky day. My girlfriend is the best and I know for a fact she's loafing around at home right now crying about a last-minute cancellation. Here, let me text her and get it set up for you. She makes house calls. That okay?"

I smile. "That's even better."

She gives me a tablet and pulls up the social media handle for her friend so I can look at her work. Oh, she'll definitely do. I think she specializes in glow-ups because her before and afters are incredible. I let Angela call and arrange everything for me, supplying Hayes's address when asked. I hope he doesn't mind a stranger coming over.

I leave Haute Belle with my garment bag and shoe box carried delicately in my arms and head across the street toward the coffee shop Hayes went to. He's sitting at a table that looks out the window directly at Haute Belle, so he waves as I approach and takes a last sip of his drink before he meets me outside.

"I take it that went well?"

"The best. I even have a hair and makeup artist coming to the house later. If that's okay?" I tack on.

He shrugs. "Whatever you want to do is fine by me, honey."

"If that's the case, I want to eat leftover pizza for a late lunch and then start my beautifying routine. This dress requires some high-maintenance grooming."

"I'm intrigued," Hayes says, taking the dress and tucking it into the backseat of the G-wagon for me.

He hands me my seat belt and waits for me to buckle before closing my door and walking around to his side.

My new cell rings that awful telephone ringer from my bag and I jump to get it just so I can stop the noise. I much prefer something softer that still gets my attention without scaring the heck out of me. Or just plain old vibrate to not have to hear it at all. I cringe when I see the screen.

It's Mama.

"Oh, Lord," I mutter, staring at the screen in resignation after I've muted the call.

Hayes looks over. "Uh oh, Mommy dearest. Go ahead and take it. I don't mind."

I grimace now that he's removed my option of ignoring her.

"Hi, Mama," I answer.

"Paige Kore Fairchild, what in heaven's name are you doing with *that man*?" she screeches over the line. I pull the phone away from my ear and turn the volume down.

"What are you talking about, Mama?" How can she know I'm with Hayes? I've only told her I was safe and with a friend, without supplying any additional information.

"That god-awful Atlanta Haute List gossip site is reporting you were with that scoundrel during a carjacking last night. How dare he put you in danger like that! And how dare you not call to tell me you were okay immediately. I had to find out because Levitica Johnson's daughter Melanie was telling everyone in Savannah."

"What's the Atlanta Haute List?" I ask Hayes with my hand covering my phone.

He groans and fishes his own phone out of his pocket, tapping away while I listen to Mama decry the evils of Atlanta and the dangers lurking around every corner. He shows me a slick-looking mobile site on his phone with the titular name splashed across the top of the page and the very first story having a big old picture of me at my deb ball last week next to a photo of Hayes from what could be a business journal article.

"Debutante Hotel Heiress Nabs Atlanta's Most Eligible And Elusive Bachelor Billionaire," reads the headline.

"Holy smokes," I drawl, my eyes widening. "This is bad, right?" I whisper to him.

He gives me a maybe yes, maybe no head wag.

"It's a gossip site, so not everything they print is true, but this is pretty spot-on, so I'm going to do some digging to see what they're reporting."

I watch over his shoulder as he scrolls into the article, Mama still not exhausted on the line. I throw in a "Mmhmm, okay," just to show her I'm still on the line.

"Paige Fairchild, heiress to the multimillion-dollar Southern darling hotel chain, The Xenios Group, was spotted getting cozy at trendy Atlanta pizza spot Napoletana Friday evening with none other than Olympus International CFO Hayes Olsen. Sources say the two are a new item, and Fairchild could be the unknown brunette Olsen flew into town on his private jet just last weekend from her hometown of Savannah. The young heiress has yet to be linked with any of Georgia's elite, so to make her debut and instantly find herself canoodling a billionaire seems too good to be true. The lucky lady found herself in trouble as the billionaire's favorite Mercedes SLR McLaren was the intended target of a carjacking gone wrong. Sources say the attacker left the scene in an ambulance while our new love birds drove away from the restaurant together, seemingly unharmed.

Is our own Olsen Atlanta's newest Batman? He does only seem to be spotted under the cover of night, and he's got the Bruce Wayne bucks to pull it off, so anything is possible. The story is still developing, so hit Like and Subscribe for all the Haute gossip."

"Oh my God," I whisper shriek. "How do they know so much about me—about us?"

"Welcome to Atlanta, where your status as an heiress is as good as a headline." He grimaces. "I'm not helping you out, any. They love following my brothers and me around to see what we're up to. Eligible bachelors and all that," he finishes, visibly disturbed.

"Paige! Are you even listening to me?" Mama yells.

"Sorry, Mama. I dropped my phone," I offer as an excuse for not answering whatever question she expected me to. "Will you please repeat that?"

"I said you need to come home right now. I'll send you a plane ticket for this afternoon. That lecherous child predator is only after one thing. You have a humble, good man here just desperate to have you home."

My spine straightens and I rear back as if slapped.

"Hayes is an incredible *gentleman*," I emphasize. "Garrison is not a good man and he's most certainly not desperate to have me anywhere. I'm not coming home, Mama. Not until you get it through your pretty head that I won't marry that awful man or be traded for financial gain."

"You leave me no choice, Pai—"

I end the call before she can utter her threat and silence my phone in case she calls again.

"Well, Mama knows about you."

"I heard. Guess I'm not exactly her pick of the litter?"

"I don't see why you wouldn't be, given that any business alliance forged through our relationship would benefit the Xenios Group far more than any from Daniels Industries. I think that's too pragmatic for Mama, though. She prefers hush money to a legitimate business deal not carried on my back as a bought and paid-for bride."

Hayes coughs, turning from me with his fist covering his mouth, and I pat his back, probably unhelpfully. I hope he's not coming down with anything. I want to really wow him tonight, but I'd rather nurse him back to health at home if he's not feeling well.

Seventeen

The Atlanta Haute List

S potted: The Bachelor and the Belle

Our favorite billionaire businessman was seen out and about in Atlanta, in the light of day! Yes, mysterious and secretive Hayes Olsen left his Buckhead compound during daylight hours on a shopping trip with new flame Paige Fairchild. The two visited a Peachtree shopping area, with Olsen parking himself in a café, much to the delight of baristas in the know, while Fairchild spent hours at Atlanta darling Haute Belle designer dress shop. What could she have picked up and will she be stepping out in it anytime soon? We're just as curious as you are, so send all your tips to HauteGossip@TheATLHauteList.com and we'll be sure to share. Remember to hit Like and Subscribe for all the Haute Gossip.

Eighteen

Paige

Hayes is working out in his home gym on the first floor while I shower and wait for the makeup artist to get to the house. I'm just pulling on leggings and a loose tank when I hear the doorbell ring.

"She must be early," I say to Cerberus as he perks up at the sound and goes on the alert.

"Let's go meet the woman who will take this," I say, motioning to my bare face and wet hair, "and turn it into something your daddy calls a smoke show."

He trots at my side as we go downstairs. I pull open the heavy door with a smile ready to meet the artist Angela spoke so highly of. My smile falters and my heart stutters to a stop before resuming a breakneck pace when I get a look at the person standing on the stoop.

"Garrison?" I shriek. Cerberus growls low and nudges past me to stand between us. "What on God's green earth are you doing here?"

Garrison eyes the huge, menacing dog warily and takes a step back. Smart.

"I've come to take you home, sugar," he says, the hint of fear trembling through his prepared bravado.

"You're a few bricks shy of a load if you think I'm going anywhere with you. What are you even doing here? *How* are you here?" How could he have tracked me down to Hayes's house?

"Your mama sent me to look for you. She's worried sick and you need to be home in Savannah where we can start that beautiful relationship of ours that's going to be the perfect blending of Southern breeding and smart business."

"Crazy, the lot of 'em," I say to Cerberus, the muscular dog posturing and still growling low in front of me. "Garrison, I will not be going anywhere with you, and I most definitely will not be marrying your sorry excuse for a behind."

"You'll love it in time, trust me." His self-satisfied grin turns my stomach and I gag.

"I just threw up a little in my mouth when you said that."

He's undeterred by my rude remark.

"Paige, I've wanted you for years. It's meant to be and our families are all on board. We just need you to see the writing on the wall and come on home where you belong. It's what's best for everyone."

I roll my eyes. I'm dang tired of other people deciding what's best for me without so much as consulting me about it.

"I don't care how much money your mama and daddy paid to keep your bad behavior quiet. I'm not a business deal and I won't be a pawn in this farce."

My voice trembles in rage and Cerberus takes a taut step closer to the unwanted visitor in front of us, his posture stiff and his shoulders bunched, ready to attack if I so much as breathe the word. Garrison doesn't respond to my comment on his family paying off Mama.

"Not that simple, sugar. The deal is as good as done whether you accept it or not, so you might as well relax and enjoy the ride. I might even make it pleasurable for you if you're good."

I don't know what kind of stupid he's made of, but he tries to reach for me right over Cerberus's head. The dog snarls, his ferocious bark loud and evil. His jaws snap at the hand before it can graze my skin and Garrison yanks it back.

"Cerberus, you're a very good boy," I say quietly.

The dog stops snarling but doesn't look away from the potential threat in front of us. I look up.

"What kinds of commands do you think he knows? I haven't tried them all out yet, but he's a smart boy and he doesn't like you any more than I do. You better start walking back to that car out there if you want to keep both of your hands."

"I'm not leaving without you," he says, anger and fear creating an irrational and scary gleam in his brown eyes.

"Everything okay, Paige?"

I turn at the sound of my name and give Hayes a grimace before it turns to appreciation. He's shirtless and toweling sweat off his chest as he walks down the hallway. His perfection isn't even marred by the bandage on his shoulder. He just looks more beautiful, and incredibly dangerous.

"I've got a visitor from Savannah set on seeing me home, thanks to my crazy mama's scheming."

He stops beside me and opens the door wider, taking in Garrison's frozen form in front of a growling, slavering Cerberus, who takes a step closer to Garrison, edging him off the porch and onto the top step of the stairs.

"You're on private property, boy." His words snap with authority. "That dog doesn't seem to want you here anymore than we do. I suggest you see yourself off it if you know what's good for you."

"I'm taking my girl with me if I'm going anywhere," Garrison challenges, his chest puffing to extend like the paunch that hangs over his belt.

I scoff and take a step back, aligning with Hayes in the doorway. Garrison is cuckoo crazy if he thinks that's going to fly.

Hayes shakes his head slowly. "She's not now, nor has she ever been, your girl." His voice is deadly quiet and lower than normal, reverberating with dangerous intent.

"I should gut you just for showing up here after what you did to her all those years ago. It might actually teach you a lesson you've taken too long to learn."

"You can't touch me," Garrison throws back, but his tone is much less convincing.

My eyes widen for Garrison, because this is not a side of Hayes he should be making angrier than he already is. I have seen Hayes in action now. I know what he's capable of when threatened, and I highly doubt Garrison is ready for the punishment that would be doled out if he tried to touch me right now. Hayes might spring on him if he so much as looks at me wrong, for all I know.

"There's a lot I can do and you'd still deserve worse. Leave, now."

Garrison's lip hitches up in his own snarl. "You're just a bump in the road to our future together. She's got a duty to her family and a role to play, just like I do. She'll see it soon enough, if not today."

Hayes steps forward, his anger palpable. "You've got some fucking nerve. I have enough dirt to put you away for years. The other inmates will treat you just like you've treated the girls who were paid off to stay quiet about your proclivities for date rape."

Garrison's face pales and he shifts nervously from one foot to the other. "I don't know what you're talking about," he denies.

So much for being a lawyer. He isn't convincing me of anything other than his own guilt. Still, my head swings to Hayes, wondering if it's true. *I wasn't the only one?* I look back at Garrison, really appraising him now.

"Go home while you still can, Garrison. Tell my mama I won't be a part of this sham and she can write me out of her will for all I care."

Hayes and Garrison break their staring contest to turn to me as I prop my hand on my hip.

"I'd rather be penniless and working a normal nine-to-five than accept any part of this godawful archaic clause to secure my own legacy."

"You're going to regret that, Paige," Garrison says, dropping his attempt at wooing me with more smarmy Southern charm. "Say goodbye to everything you've ever known or wanted, because there's no way in hell your mama and daddy will let this slide. You'll never so much as step foot in The Mansion again for how you're breaking your mama's heart."

"Don't say another fucking word to her or I'll rip your tongue out of your head and shove it up your ass."

Hayes takes a step closer to Garrison on the porch, Cerberus right at his side, and I'm not sure which is more intimidating at the moment. I follow a step behind, a little scared that Hayes may really take the opportunity Garrison presents to fight. True, Garrison would deserve every punch Hayes lands, but I don't think it's the right move unless Garrison does something incredibly stupid. Given he showed up here today, it's not unlikely.

"Oh, good, right on time," Hayes says, looking over Garrison's head as a police cruiser comes into view around a bend and rolls down the long driveway to the house. Cerberus snaps his jaws again and forces Garrison down, step by step, until he's standing on the driveway.

"You called the police?" I ask Hayes mildly. I don't mind the thought of Garrison being carted off in a police car in the least. In fact, I relish the idea and would very much like to see that happen. It would be about freaking time.

"My security system alerts me to anyone who drives through the gates when they're open like we have it for the makeup artist," he explains rationally, like we're not witnessing the Atlanta Police Department roll up with Garrison in their sights.

Garrison turns nervously to watch the police car park next to the Lexus he must have driven here.

"I didn't like the looks of a strange man walking up to the door when we were expecting a woman. I called preemptively, and I'm glad I did, because I was this close to having to bury the fucker out in the back forty."

I smile. "I like the way you think," I tell him, rising on my tiptoes to place a grateful kiss on his cheek. He catches me around the waist and keeps me close.

The police officers get out of the car and approach with their hands resting ominously on their gun belts. I highly doubt Garrison would do anything to warrant them drawing a weapon on him, but their seriousness in dealing with trespassers wins my approval.

"Garrison," I say to drag his attention back to the door instead of on the police. "You're done. If what Hayes says is true, and I believe it, everyone in Georgia is gonna know what a pig you are. Even my mama and daddy will have to admit they pinned their hopes on the wrong man."

His eyes grow big with what I hope is a newfound respect for me after assuming I was just going to be a wilting pushover forever. Or maybe it's just plain old fear. It feels good to threaten him with what I only hope makes him feel as helpless as I have been at his hands.

I look over at Hayes and sigh. Not only is he pretty, but he's defended me two days in a row.

Watching Garrison get escorted by the police to his vehicle and run out of Atlanta is a sight I will treasure for the rest of my life.

Nineteen

Hayes

I'm straightening my cuffs and preparing to put on my tux jacket when Lindee, the makeup artist who's spent the last two hours with Paige, comes down the stairs. I rush to help her with her big bag that I can only assume holds the entirety of a makeup store inside with how heavy it is. *Fucking hell, how does she cart that thing around on a regular basis?*

I set her bag down in the wide-open foyer once I have it down the stairs. I smile as I open the front door to an empty doorstep, thinking of Garrison Daniels being escorted off my property by the Atlanta PD. It was amazing to watch Paige dress down that dirtbag in her sweet, genteel way. Even when she's hoppin' mad and fed up with people, she's still polite. She seemed lighter and more confident when he was gone, a change having settled over her after standing up for herself and accepting whatever fate came of it because it was what *she wanted,* for once.

"Thank you for coming at such short notice."

"Paige really saved my butt after I had a cancellation, so it's me who's thankful," she responds, brushing short black hair behind her ears. "Would you mind if I waited for your reaction? She looks so good I want to see your face when she comes down."

I laugh, but the uncomfortable, unfamiliar feeling of nervousness sets in, and I look at the stairs like they're the gateway to heaven. They are, in a way. Paige is every bit a celestial being of beauty and goodness, so it fits.

"Yeah, of course. Can I get you something to drink while you wait?"

She shakes her head. "No, thanks, she's not going to take long."

As if on cue, I hear the unmistakable sound of a stiletto hitting the stairs and I turn expectantly, my palms sweaty. With the way the stairs make two turns, it takes a moment to catch the first sight of Paige's slender ankles—that I have some new fetish for—come into view with slim black heels emphasizing her high arches and perfect little toes.

I swallow hard from just her damn feet alone and know Lindee wasn't messing around when she wanted to watch my reaction. The hem of a glittery red dress brushes the step behind her feet as she descends carefully, and I already know I'm going to have a hell of a time not slinging her over my shoulder and finding an appropriate surface to lay her out on with the striking color and slinky elegance of the fabric. The matchsticks of her heels alone make me want to rush up the stairs and scoop her into my arms to avoid a potential fall, but she's the epitome of Southern grace as she expertly navigates the stairs.

Of course she is. My girl is a Southern goddess.

Paige rounds the second landing and I see her in all her glory. The lights reflect off the sparkles of the red gown that follows every luscious curve of her body, the front hem slit to mid-thigh on one side so every other step exposes her long, toned leg beautifully. I continue my appraisal higher, loving the way the fabric stretches over her hips and exaggerates her small waist, giving her an incredible hourglass shape. The top is draped low so just a hint of her cleavage is evident while being sexier than a full-on tit show. The thin straps disappear over her shoulders and, I'm sure, continue to the back of the dress somewhere I'll need to explore with my mouth before the night is up.

Her full lips are painted the same red she wore to her Debutante Ball and her face is expertly shaded so her cheekbones are radiantly enhanced and her eyes smolder in sparkly eyeshadows that make them look twice as big even with the thick, dark lashes that have been added. Her clear green eyes catch the light even more than her dress, dancing in mirth as she catches my stare. I bite my lip as I take it all in. Her softly waved hair is brushed tightly behind one ear while loose and voluminous everywhere else, looking so silky I want to run my fingers through it now.

I open my mouth to compliment her, but I'm at a loss for the words that would adequately describe just how stunning she truly is.

"Wow," I breathe instead, because that's all I can manage. A lifetime of speaking and advanced degrees couldn't have prepared me for this moment.

Lindee claps excitedly beside me, but I don't look her way. Instead, I pull out my money clip, peel off several hundreds, and hold them in her direction.

"What? No! Paige already paid me," she refuses.

"Take it. This is worth every penny and far more because that gorgeous woman still looks like the girl I adore under that incredible smoke show."

Lindee laughs and takes the cash. "If you say so. She's stunning, right?"

I just nod, still enraptured with Paige as she smiles timidly at me.

"What do you think?" Paige asks, doing a slow twirl in front of me that shows off her backside, the dress open to mid-back and her ass looks like a perfect peach. My hands strain, like my dick, and I want to cup that luscious ass and do some nasty shit to her.

"I think I need to throw you over my damn shoulder and march you right back upstairs so no other man can get a look at this perfection." I'm so close to doing just that. No one else deserves to see Paige looking this smoking hot. I'm likely to end up punching anyone who dares.

"Then you'd miss the launch of your new business. Not happening, boss."

Fuck the launch. I just want her. My hands move to her hips without my acknowledgment, and I hold her for a second.

"That red lipstick was a good choice. I don't want to mess up Lindee's work, so I'm going to have to refrain from kissing the ever-living hell out of you."

"That's my cue," Lindee says, opening the door wider and letting herself out. "Awesome dog, by the way. He was such a good assistant. He even let me dust his face with a makeup brush. Seemed to like it, too," she says with a laugh as she closes the door.

"Where is Cerberus?" I ask, looking for Paige's trusty shadow.

"I told him to wait and he's being a good boy," she says, looking back up the stairs. "Cerberus, come," she calls.

The big dog sprints down the stairs and slides across the slick floor to us. Paige bends down and places a kiss just above his eyes and rubs his ears while he pants happily. I didn't realize I could be so jealous of a dog. I shake my head in amusement. Any woman who can win over my ferocious dog so thoroughly is one I never want to give up.

"You ready?" I ask.

I'd say fuck it and peel the tight dress off her body and have my way with her, but duty calls and I guess she does deserve to be shown off with how amazing she looks. I'll just have to keep my hands to myself.

"I'm ready if you are," she says with a smoldering look, and my heart and balls tighten simultaneously.

Fucking hell. This woman is perfect.

I hand my Mercedes over to the valet and extend my arm for Paige as we walk up to the event space. I'm dismayed to see the line of reporters and camera crews lining the black carpet that stretches to the door with the Underworld Spirits logo splashed on the brightly lit white backdrop behind it. No one told me there would be a photo op and press like this. I make a mental note to figure out who slipped up and reprimand them appropriately. I need to know exactly what I'm walking into, always.

"Hayes," Paige says my name nervously and I look down to catch her eyeing the press gauntlet we have to walk through.

"You don't have to answer any of their questions unless you want to. They're going to take photos of us whether or not we like it, so we should do our best to smile and look like we're happy to be here at the very least."

She nods and swallows. "I can do that. But what if they ask about us?"

"I'm okay with telling them we're dating if you are." Anticipation rises unexpectedly in my chest, the make-or-break moment taking me by surprise.

She looks up at me and my nerves subside some with the smile she gives me.

"We're dating. I like that. A lot."

"Good. It's the truth, and I like it, too."

I press a kiss to her smooth cheek and stand up tall. I have a ravishingly beautiful woman on my arm who just agreed that we're more than friends. I haven't been in a relationship since my twenties, having turned to brief flings as business picked up, but this feels so *right*. A relationship with Paige is exactly where I want to be at this stage.

We approach the press vultures and I set my face into what I hope conveys jovial boredom.

"Hayes, is it true you stabbed a man last night?"

My mask of indifference slips a little at the unexpected first question, but I don't have time to give it much thought, let alone an answer before the questions converge on us.

"Paige! When did you meet Hayes?"

"Mr. Olsen, don't you think she's a little young for you?"

"Miss Fairchild, are you moving to Atlanta?"

"Hayes, when did you buy Underworld Spirits?"

"Paige! What about your fiancé back in Savannah? What does he think of your new relationship with Hayes?"

Paige turns at that question, finding the reporter who asked it and smiles while I clench my jaw hard enough to crack teeth.

"You must be mistaken," she says with a laugh. "I've never been engaged, and I assure you, there is no fiancé, nor anyone whose opinion matters, to object to my dating such a proper gentleman." She turns away from the reporter and faces the others expectantly.

They eat it up, quickly calling more questions at her now that they know she'll respond.

"Were you scared during the carjacking?"

"Of course. Anyone would be in that situation," she answers, looking at me. "I'm safe today because of this man's heroic actions. The world needs more people like Hayes Olsen, but this one's mine. I'm keeping him."

I don't even hear the rest of the questions or bother to answer, fully in awe of this woman beside me. Paige is perfectly poised and at home selectively answering what she wants and redirecting those she doesn't with ease. We pose for various photos and slowly make our way through the press and into the venue thirty minutes after our arrival.

"I'm making you head of the PR team for Underworld Spirits. What you just did was brilliant. You're a natural."

I could keep flattering her for hours because the list of her qualities is endless, but she stops me with a kiss.

"I just told the truth and made sure to mind my manners. Anyone can do it."

"More people should, you mean."

I absently run my thumb across my lips to check for lipstick and smile when it comes away clean.

"I was kind of hoping you'd cover me in red lip prints later, but whatever you used isn't budging."

"That was the point. I'll paint on a sloppier option and mark you up anytime you want, though."

She looks around at the party, full of people dressed to the nines holding glasses of our liquor.

"Y'all really know how to throw a party."

I snag a couple of tumblers from a tray as a waiter passes and hand one to her.

"This should be the double barrel bourbon. It's incredible."

She takes a sip and closes her eyes. "It really is. There's a candy flavor to this one."

I smile proudly at her discerning palate.

"Come on, I want to introduce you to the leadership team."

I lead Paige around the party, introducing her to the Underworld Spirits vice presidents and the executives who oversee the operations. I kept everyone on when I bought the company because I trust their vision and direction. They've proven a good investment and a loyal group who just want to see their brand of liquor become successful.

"Is this the belle everyone but you is talking about, big brother?"

I turn at the question to find Payton standing with his own glass in hand and a mischievous smile on his face. I sigh, knowing there is no avoiding my brothers now.

"Paige, I'd like you to meet Payton Olsen, every inch the middle child he is, and Chief Operating Officer of Olympus International. Brother, this is my beautiful Paige." I place emphasis on *my* and hope to God he doesn't try to pull some bullshit that will need to be put down.

"Pleased to meet you," Paige responds.

Payton holds his hand out and she takes it firmly. Instead of the handshake she was expecting, he raises her fingers to his lips and kisses them suavely.

"Oh," she says in surprise, taking her hand back once he releases her fingers.

"I've heard so much about your adventures with my brother online that I had to meet you in person. God knows he won't tell me anything himself."

Payton gives me a look that I know means he's been working overtime controlling the media with the carjacking last night. God, it feels like an eternity ago when barely twenty-four hours have passed.

"Don't believe everything you see online," she responds with a smile. "Trusted sources are hard to come by, and people love the appeal of a juicy story, true or not."

"Wise words, if I ever heard them," Payton says, an appreciative grin stretching his face. "You picked a smart one, Hayes."

"She is, but I'd like to think she picked me. However, the jury's still out on that particular choice."

Paige laughs and swats my arm. "My picker is perfect, I'll have you know."

Payton tips his head in a familiar way that I know means he's taking her measure and he likes what he sees. I wrap an arm around Paige's shoulders and pull her against me possessively. She curls into my side and sighs.

"Zander should be here, somewhere. I know he's looking for the kind of trouble that will take some of the heat off y'all with the press, if you know what I mean." Payton raises an eyebrow at me. We both know our brother is reckless enough to do just that.

"He better keep his fucking shit together if he knows what's good for him," I growl, thinking of the impending roll-out of phase two and the offers we are about to shower on some unsuspecting hoteliers in a bid to create the largest privately held boutique hotel chain in the country. The recent coverage of my own life is just enough below the radar to not affect business deals, but Zander has a habit of making bigger and more noteworthy splashes that haven't been good for business in the past.

A sobering thought bubbles in my awareness. What if William Fairchild refuses to sell *because* of my involvement with his daughter and the mess of a marriage bargain he's made with the Daniels? Is he nearly as calculating as his wife? If that's the case, I need to work on a plan B, stat.

As if conjured by us speaking about him, Zander appears, a tall brunette tightly encased in a silver dress clinging to him.

"Speak of the devil," I murmur under my breath.

"I thought that was you," Paige quips next to me. Payton hears her and chokes out a laugh.

I look down at her and laugh with him. She beams and nuzzles her nose against my neck in a way that has me wanting to turn my back on everything at this party and take her straight home.

"The mysterious woman who's captured our brother's frozen heart!" Zander booms, drunker than Cooter Brown already.

"You must be Zander, the baby of the family," Paige replies, expertly hitting Zander where he's most self-conscious. She holds out a hand to him and I have visions in my head of diamond rings that would look lovely on her slender fingers.

He opens and closes his mouth, his usually quick retorts mysteriously absent as he appraises Paige. He takes her hand and shakes it firmly, his expression finally landing on respect.

"Paige Fairchild as I live and breathe. Do Mommy and Daddy know you're here with an old man?" Zander smiles as he ruthlessly digs into our age gap.

"They certainly do, and I'm glad I was able to meet you. It was nice of your mother to let you stay out so late."

She mimes looking for a watch on her bare wrist.

"It must be so tough to have a curfew while your big brothers get to play all night."

She's barely containing her grin and I'm floored at her sarcastic ease around people as ruthless in the boardroom as my brothers.

Payton hoots and slaps Zander on the back as his lip hitches up.

"How's that burn feel, Zand? Better be careful, she's feisty."

Paige turns her attention to the bored brunette next to Zander with a warm smile.

"Hi, I'm Paige. Your dress is beautiful."

She shows Zander's arm candy all the respect due to royalty and I'm reminded of her good-to-the-bone nature. She truly is too pure for me, as I had already written off Zander's date.

"Svetlana," the arm candy replies with a thick accent as she weakly shakes the tips of Paige's fingers when she holds out her hand.

I lift an eyebrow at Zander and he shrugs as if to say he'll take them impressively dull as long as they look a certain way.

"Looks like a good turnout," Payton observes, glancing around. "People really like the booze. Glad you picked this one up."

"Payton, Hayes was telling me about your fondness for the water and mentioned you have boats. Where's your closest docked?" Paige asks, turning the conversation around when it easily could have become a boring business recap.

"So my brother talks about his family, but refuses to share any details about you? Where are your priorities, Hayes?" He jokingly punches my arm, but it's enough to make me spill bourbon right on Paige's dress.

"Watch it!" I snap, mad that his immaturity caused me to ruin something as beautiful as her dress. I drop to my knees to dab at the liquor with a cocktail napkin.

"It's just the train. Not like I'll see it," she says, waving off my efforts to staunch the stain on the glittery fabric.

Bits of the black napkin are sticking to the sequins and rough glitter, my attempt to clean making the situation worse. She was right when she said there is no such thing as comfortable evening wear. This shit is ridiculous and she's a saint for having worn it.

I stand and look around as I dust off my hands. My brothers are both staring at me, with looks of shock on their faces. I scowl.

"What?"

"I shit you not, I think that is the first time Hayes Olsen has dropped to his knees to clean up a mess in his whole goddamn life. What, no order to get someone to clean it for you, bro?"

Zander's teasing is marked by true astonishment. I think he's right though, and that thought both infuriates and humbles me.

"Paige, can you please keep putting up with this man's madness? I think you're the best damn thing to happen to his attitude that I can personally account for," Payton says, placing a hand on her shoulder.

I narrow my eyes at him until he removes his touch from her skin.

Zander makes his way closer, intent on adding his two cents. "We might even see the unrelenting lion ease up at work if you stick around. Let me tell you, that would be a nice change for those of us who have to work closely with his sourpuss attitude."

"You're both idiots," I say, my tone not carrying as much bite as it could. They may be idiots, but they're my idiots, so I'm stuck with them.

Twenty

Hayes

Paige tries to cover a big yawn a little after midnight. We've been making the rounds at the party for hours, taking congratulations and questions from anyone who manages to grab our attention for more than a passing moment. She's been a perfect date, completely at ease making conversation with strangers and finding common ground with business associates and industry professionals alike. She's completely blown my low expectations for her addition to my responsibilities as the business owner out of the water. I think I've even enjoyed myself, all because she was willing to share the brunt of the social obligation with me. But now my focus is on her, and I need to take that yawn seriously.

"Tired, angel?"

"I can rally. Don't you worry about me." She rests her head on my shoulder and squeezes my arm.

I kiss her forehead while she's close.

"I want you to enjoy this party and the company you've pushed to be even better because you believed in their products. I love hearing the gratitude each member of the company expresses for what you've done. This wouldn't be possible without you, so soak it in."

My chest expands with pride as she speaks. I've never needed anyone's affirmation for my work before, but hearing her now does something to me that breaks down any barriers I may have had left where she is concerned.

"I believe we've more than fulfilled our obligations for this party and can make an exit whenever you're ready," I tell her, running my finger along her arm.

Her soft skin rises in goosebumps, her responsiveness to my touch giving me all sorts of ideas that require the loss of this dress.

"Fuck it, let's get out of here," I say, my mind made up.

She gives me a knowing grin and nods. "I'm ready. *So* ready." Her husky voice makes my dick throb on the spot.

I tuck her against me and make the agonizingly slow trek through the crowded venue with impatience. Even the valet takes too long, my unrest manifesting in my fingers drumming along Paige's shoulder as we wait.

She covers my tapping fingers with her little hand, stilling my movements.

"It's just time, Hayes. We have plenty of it, so stop trying to rush. It's making you agitated. Slow your thoughts and let the delay be more of our foreplay."

I look down at her to see a smile raising one side of her mouth.

"How are you the expert now? You just completely changed my whole outlook."

"I've been waiting my whole life for this. For you. I'm enjoying the anticipation."

This woman. I face her, running my hands up her bare arms until I cup her face. I lean in slowly, working through my desire to rush in and claim her, and slant my mouth over hers. Her hands grip my wrists as she opens to my tongue, taking me in and claiming every part of my soul with a kiss.

Someone clears their throat. "Sir?"

I slowly end our kiss, pulling away with my eyes still locked on Paige's face.

"I'm a little busy."

"Your car is here, but please take your time."

I look over at the valet, a kid in his early twenties who probably just drove the most expensive car he's ever seen tonight, and nod.

"Thank you."

I tip him and help Paige into the car before taking my spot behind the wheel.

It's a maddening feeling to drive the speed limit when the roads are wide open and begging me to speed home where I can have Paige all to myself in whatever way she allows. Paige trails her hand along my thigh, edging closer and closer to my dick that begs to be released. I do what she suggested, savoring every moment, every touch, and fight to keep my impatience at bay because she's right. This is the most intense foreplay to be performed by two people barely touching each other. I'm completely tuned into her by the time we get home, hearing each hitch of her breath when my hand skims under the slit of her dress and rests heavy and warm on her thigh.

Our kisses begin before we even leave the garage, her shoes dangling off her fingers and dropping in the hallway as soon as we make it inside. Cerberus greets us at the door, but he only gets a cursory pet from us both and a command to stay before we've mounted the stairs. It takes no time at all to get to the bedroom, the bed looking like an inviting altar where I will finally be able to worship Paige as she deserves. Our hands are rushing now, skimming over each other, and we kiss like our lives depend on the connection. I'm hunting for a zipper on the back of Paige's dress when she presses her hand to my chest and breaks our kiss.

"It's a corset. You'll have to unlace me," she says, her eyes flickering with heat.

She slowly turns her back to me, her hands lifting her hair and pulling it all over one shoulder to expose her back. I'm shucking off my jacket and working on my shirt buttons when she looks over her bare shoulder at me.

"Undress me, please."

"Fuck yes."

My impatience for my own clothes finally breaks me and I yank my shirt apart, buttons flying everywhere. I discard the shirt and slow my breathing as I take the two steps that bring me flush against her back. Her head dips forward, exposing more of her slender neck as my hands caress her arms. I pause with my hands on her shoulders and lower my lips to the spot where her neck meets her shoulders and press a soft kiss to her skin.

She trembles and sighs. "That feels amazing."

I brush my fingers down her back, taking my time as she shivers, finally discovering the red laces that are tucked in the back of her dress. I fish them out, letting the long tails trail against her skin before I untie them with deliberate slowness in every movement. I make every movement precise and unhurried despite my desire to have her under me already. She makes me want to change everything about myself, slow every one of my hasty actions, so I can do justice to the moment.

I loosen the corset of her dress, my cock thick and hard from the desire just this simple act brings out. I trace my finger across the red indents the corset made against her fair skin and imagine the marks we will make together. I pepper the skin of her neck with kisses as

I push the straps off her shoulders, the dress slipping down her body and pooling around her feet.

"No panties? Naughty girl," I growl, dragging my teeth across her shoulder and sliding my hands down to her hips. I trace my fingers across her thighs, sweeping them through her silky wetness before I move my hands.

"I couldn't. The lines." Her breathy response is shaky, her own need growing stronger.

"You should have told me. I like the idea of having your arousal dripping down your thighs."

"We never would have left the house if you knew." She gives me a sultry laugh at the thought.

The chuckle dies on her lips as I pull her naked body against my front and grind my dick into her ass.

"Oh, we would have left. Eventually. We might even have missed the press."

Her hands reach back and between us, fumbling for my belt.

"Let me take these off you."

I allow her to turn in my arms. She slides her hand up my chest to my neck, brushing my throat with her thumb, and places a lingering kiss on my pec before she drops to her knees in front of me.

"Jesus," I groan when she looks up at me while at eye level with my cock.

She smiles and closes her eyes, rubbing her face gently against my crotch, and I nearly lose it right then. I fight the urge to roughly undo my belt and push my pants down just low enough to feed my cock through her red lips. Instead, I take a deep breath and let her take her slow and methodical approach until she's tugging my pants down my legs. I step out of my shoes, my pants and socks following. Finally, I'm standing in my boxer briefs while she's still on her knees.

"You want my cock free?" My voice is primal, the words too strong for her innocence, but her eyes shine and she nods eagerly. I pull the waistband of my boxers down, my dick springing forward, thick and hard.

"Oh, my God."

Awe laces her words as she tentatively reaches toward me, one finger gently stroking my shaft and making it jump.

"You're huge, Hayes."

While her words puff my ego, I know there's hesitance in them.

"We'll fit, I promise. Your body is made for mine. We'll go slow."

Her eyes roll up to look at me again and I'm lost to the image of her on her knees like this.

"Can I taste you?"

I tip my head back and groan. "God, yes."

Her pink tongue darts out as her lips part and she eagerly licks at the pre-cum beading on the head.

I groan and force myself to stay still instead of gripping the base of my shaft and directing my cock between her lips. The warmth of her mouth and feel of her lips as she slowly slides the tip of the head in nearly brings me to my knees.

Her lips naturally close below the head and she swallows, the suction forcing my legs to shake. When she lets my dick pop from her lips, a trail of pre-cum still connecting us, I gently haul her up off her knees.

"That feels too fucking good to let you play for too long."

I pull her against me, my cock pressing between us.

"I want to eat your sweet little pussy until you're screaming. Do you want my mouth on you?"

She nods as a blush tints her cheeks from my filthy words. "I want you so bad I'm dripping."

I scrape my lip with my teeth and groan at her words.

"That's just what I want, baby."

I walk her backward until the bed hits her legs and she sits. I place my palm between her perfect tits and gently push her until she's flat on the bed.

"Open your legs for me." The words are soft but commanding.

She does it, and if she's read my unspoken directions, her hand glides down slowly to swirl the tip of her finger in her own wetness. Her inner thighs are glistening with her need, and I'm not a man who will refuse this woman what she wants. I kneel in front of her and say a silent prayer that I can maintain the slow and deliberate movements without losing my control. I press a fingertip against her center, her greedy pussy instantly drawing me in. I use the wetness to part her lips, painting everywhere I want to lick, then follow with my tongue.

"Oh, God." She sighs as my tongue breaches her opening and I coat my mouth with her.

The taste is exquisite, once again sweet and mild, the perfect combination to get me high on her. I press my finger into her dark heat and am rewarded with a moan as her muscles clench around me.

"More."

Fuck. I withdraw and return with two fingers, her body lubing the way and not resisting this time. I pump my fingers slowly as her hips begin to rock against my hand. I trace my tongue through her lips, nipping and sucking before I return to her clit. I keep a steady rhythm going with my fingers and tongue and within minutes she's shaking, her body tensing and ready to make that leap into the pleasure that's building.

"I want you to come for me," I command. My mouth drops back against her and I suck her clit with precision focus.

"Yes, Hayes!" She clenches the duvet in her fists as her hips buck against me and her pussy squeezes my fingers. Warmth floods down my hand as I stroke her.

"That's my good girl," I soothe, my fingers gently massaging the inside of her.

Her head thrashes from side to side. "I need you, all of you, please. I want you inside of me."

"Damn, baby."

I pull my fingers out and stand. I gather her in my arms and kiss her flushed cheeks, her ruby lips and murmur into her hair.

"If that's what you want, that's what you get."

I move her to the pillows and pull out a drawer on the nightstand to retrieve a condom. She rolls her head to watch me rip the foil open, pinch the tip, and roll it down my straining cock.

I climb onto the bed and pause. "We have to go slow, especially at first. Try to relax, even when it hurts," I coax, my fingers playing in her slick heat as her hips roll against my hand.

"God, I need you so bad. I'm ready. I want you, now. Please, Hayes."

She's growing more demanding, her passion stoking the fire in her that cries out her desires.

I fit myself between her legs, dragging my cock up to her clit and back down to notch the head against her opening. She presses against me, impatient with need, and gasps as the tip slides in and stretches her tight pussy where I meet resistance.

"Breathe," I say, both to her and for myself because I nearly pass out with the delicious tug her body is putting on me to bury myself to the hilt.

I circle her clit with a finger softly, giving her more than just my dick stretching her.

"It's so big."

She closes her eyes tightly and I can feel her forcing her body to relax around me. When the pressure eases, I pull out a little and push farther in, feeling her membrane snap and the way clear. I freeze, watching the surprise and bite of pain pass over her face, waiting for her to tell me to stop. She takes a few deep breaths and nods, her hands pulling at my shoulders, forcing me closer. I repeat the motions, giving her a little more of me with each exquisitely slow plunge inside of her body and she's responding. Her breaths are less strained, more pleasurable gasps as the resistance fades and she grows accustomed to my size.

"That feels so good," she moans, shivering with the pleasure from my fingers on her clit and the feel of us together. She hooks a leg around my hips and pulls me toward her with a force I hadn't anticipated.

I press all the way inside until our bodies are flush, my fingers circling her clit, and she cries out in ecstasy. An orgasm cracks her open, her muscles squeezing me tight in rhythmic waves. I drop to my elbows over her, my eyes screwed up tightly, and take in measured breaths to keep from losing it right along with her.

I feel her lips against my face as her arms wrap around my neck and open my eyes to see her pull back with a lazy smile.

"I want that again. More of you."

A feral need to possess her, to mark her as mine, rears up in me and I answer it. I lift off her and pump my hips, my movements more forceful, faster, full of heat and desire. She gasps and tips her head back, her round tits bouncing with each thrust that rocks her whole body. I strum her clit, then press and circle as I roll my hips with hers. Her fingernails dig into my back where she grips me fiercely, the pain blending into the pleasure deliciously. She's meeting me with every thrust, her hips rising and pulling back in a desperate need to meet my intensity and soothe her own demons.

"It's right there, oh God. Hayes!"

"Fuck, Paige!" I answer. Her body pulses and clenches around me. I manage one, then two more strokes before I roar, straining against her, and coming as her pussy throbs in time with my cock. Our ragged breaths ease slowly as I drop to cover her body with mine. I bury my face in her neck, breathing in her scent and imprinting this moment on my brain for the rest of my life.

"That was amazing," she gushes.

Her arms lazily wrap around my shoulders and hold me close to her body.

"It's you who's amazing, angel."

I bury my face against her neck again and inhale slowly. She shivers at my exhale and sighs, the sound soothing every last nerve in my body.

Twenty-One

The Atlanta Haute List

U nderworld Spirits The Specter Of Hedonistic Libations For Atlanta's Elite

Atlanta just welcomed a new liquor darling with the public launch of billionaire Hayes Olsen's newest business acquisition, Underworld Spirits. The black-tie affair was filled with the movers and shakers of the South, including all three of the enviable and delicious Olsen brothers.

Our favorite brothers looked every inch the billionaires they are with all eyes on them throughout the party. Payton was without a date, so we middle-brother lovers can rejoice that he's still on the eligible bachelor list. Youngest brother Zander was seen with model Svetlana Konstantina, but we know not to attach their names quite yet. The adventurous Z-man moves through models faster than we can type the gossip.

Hayes was seen once again with new love interest, and recent society darling, Paige Fairchild on his arm. The two make the perfect pairing of wealth and elegance and seem to be madly infatuated with each other, if not more, given their very public displays of a hot burning affection. While we at the Atlanta Haute List wish them the very best, we can't help but wonder if it will last. Hayes has been notoriously private about his love life but has been linked to a few women over the years who seem to have all been fleeting affairs. Will the young Fairchild be the woman to turn the bachelor around? Hit Like and Subscribe for all the Haute Gossip as we continue to follow the pretty new couple and all things haute in Atlanta.

Twenty-Two

Paige

I wake up wrapped in Hayes's arms, his sleeping form covering me completely in a safe and secure wonderland of carnal bliss. My body aches, but in a luscious way I've never known. I smile, knowing it's the echo of Hayes making love to me resonating through my body hours later. Despite the ache, I want him again. He's awakened a hunger in me, and the only way to feed it is by joining our bodies again.

I can feel his hard length pressed thick and warm against my backside and it stokes the need to be filled by him again. I gently sway my hips against him, my bottom sliding against his… I feel a blush creep up my cheeks and I hate the bit of innocence that lingers. I am a woman who has been with a man, and I am capable of using dirty words.

Just say it, Paige.

Cock. His beautiful cock. I don't even have to say the word out loud to know I like the taste of it in my mouth almost as much as I like Hayes's cock in my mouth. Yes, his long, thick, perfectly formed cock that fit so perfectly inside of me that I know he was made especially for my body. I whimper with the visceral memory of being filled by him.

Hayes stirs and kisses my hair. "What's the matter, angel?"

I roll my hips as the need increases, my body humming and longing for him.

"I need you again. Please," I beg, the desire unfolding and taking me over.

Hayes unwraps his body from mine and rolls to the side of the bed. I hear the foil rip and then he's back and pressing against my backside, one arm slipping beneath me.

"Hold on."

He waits for me to grip the sheet before he angles his cock against me from behind and pushes in. The instant stretch forces a gasp from my throat, but it feels better than the first time, and I'm quickly pressing my hips back against him to be closer.

"Mmm yes," I moan in a hoarse whisper.

I press my face against the bed and ride out the coveted fullness with the smooth press of Hayes at my back. I didn't know you could have sex while spooning, but this is incredible and so intimate for not being able to look into his eyes. I still feel him from my head down to my feet that tangle with his.

His hand circles my hip and presses between my legs to caress my center. Electric sparks surge through me, snapping nerve endings and creating a heady euphoria of feeling. I'm wild with desire, my body moving faster against Hayes as it builds. The noises coming from me are foreign, every oh and yes from a sex-crazed woman. I struggle to breathe at the precipice, his fingers pressing firmly and circling like that elusive release. He moves slightly, the angle of him in my body intensifies, and I'm jolted straight off the cliff. I scream his name and claw at the bed, feeling him tense and explode right along with me. Our breaths become ragged shrapnel, sweat mingling and slicking against our skin.

"Fucking hell."

I'm not even sure which of us says it, because it's exactly what I was thinking.

I rouse him from sleep two more times throughout the early morning hours.

I beg for him again when he brings me breakfast in bed.

I'm insatiable now that I know what I've been missing, and my body seems to want to make up for lost time. Each time he rises to the challenge, and each time it gets better.

When we collapse on the bed after what he cheek-ily called an afternoon delight, though it wasn't even noon, he rolls me on top of him and strokes my hair as we breathe.

"You've ruined me. There is not a single woman who could come close to how perfect you are."

"You better not be looking for anyone else," I joke, my cheek pressed against his chest.

He smooths my hair away from my face and tucks it behind my ear.

"Is that you taking this to the next level?"

I turn my head so I can see his face.

"I'm not sure what that means, exactly. How do relationships level up? Is it like a video game? If it is, I think you're a maxed-out character and you're power-leveling me with all this sweet lovin'." I wiggle my eyebrows at him and smile.

He laughs, the sound booming and shaking me on top of him. "I like your analogy, though I hadn't pegged you as a gamer girl."

"Alex was a gamer, so I had to learn a thing or two in my time." I grow quiet and trace a pattern on his chest before speaking again. "I'll have to get used to the idea that you might have to find someone else eventually, when I go home and my mama inevitably chains me to her side and makes me a business deal bride." I pout, still unhappy with my parents.

He drags me farther up his body and kisses me. It stills the unpleasant thoughts from swirling through my head the same way my finger moved through the light dusting of hair on his chest.

"I know how we can make it so your parents won't have a say in who you marry or for what reason. You wouldn't have to marry Garrison, that walking piece of garbage."

I sigh deeply, the name alone stealing my post-coital mellowness and sinking me into the pit of helplessness that surrounds my uncertain future.

"Garrison said it was a done deal whether I liked it or not. Mama pretty much said the same thing. I'm just delaying the inevitable by hiding out here and refusing to be a part of it. What happens when I have to show my face in Savannah again? The problem will still be there waiting for me."

"They can't arrange a marriage for you if you're already married."

My eyes widen as I inhale sharply. "Are you...?"

"Marry me and I'll make it all go away."

I blink slowly, wondering if I'm dreaming or suffering orgasm-induced delusions. "You've known me for a week. We barely know each other. Things could change so fast and you'd be legally stuck with me." I bite my lip as my mind races.

"I'm willing to take that risk."

He rolls me to my side so we're facing each other.

"I love everything about you. You are sweetness and steel, a stronger, more resilient woman than anyone could imagine. You're smart, funny, poised, and we just work."

I tuck my head under his chin so I can think without meeting his eyes. He loves everything about me, but does he even love *me*?

I've always dreamed of a relationship built on love and support. My mama and daddy may have had an arranged marriage, but they really are a good team and I know they love each other, despite the beginning of their relationship. I think part of why I hated the idea of being married off for business is that love would be removed from the equation entirely, leaving only calculation and heartlessness. Not to mention, a man who tried to prey on me as my partner. Gross.

Marry me.

Could Hayes and I have developed the support and love a marriage needs to be long-lasting and happy? I told him once that I am a true-blue kind of woman. I want to marry for life and be unwavering in my commitment. I don't take the idea of marriage lightly. Probably why I was willing to give up everything to avoid the arrangement my parents made for me.

I'll make it all go away.

Could this really be the answer I need? Hayes is certainly right about one thing. Mama and Daddy can't marry me off if I'm already married. Marrying him would completely erase the problem at home, so I would be doing more than just running from it. I would be taking it into my own hands and solving it by any means necessary. As for love, well, I know he has already made his way into my heart and claimed me. I just hope the same is true for him.

Granted, Hayes isn't the worst option when I imagine what I would want in a husband. He's a freaking billionaire, a talented businessman, a kind and generous person, and he wants *me* without the strings of a business deal attached. I could do far worse.

I laugh to myself and Hayes pulls away so he can see me.

"What's so funny?"

"You're kind of like top-shelf marriage material. No, you're the reserve stuff that has to be held onto for years before you break it out."

He gives me a grumpy look.

"Are you calling me old, Miss Fairchild?"

"Not old, *perfectly aged*," I clarify. I lean in and kiss the tight line of his mouth. "So, how do we do this?"

"Is that you saying yes?"

"You didn't exactly get down on one knee and ask me, so it's a fitting answer." I raise an eyebrow at him.

Maybe the romantic in me is a little disappointed at the pragmatic proposal of his. It's not what I had in mind when I imagined the love of my life asking me to be his wife, but it will have to do. We can get to the love of our lives part later, right?

Hayes runs a hand through his hair and looks up for a moment. His eyes brighten and he kisses my nose.

"Stay put. I'll be right back." He jumps out of bed, pulls his pants on, and walks out of the bedroom.

"Well, that was weird," I say out loud to the empty room.

If he's going to leave me here, he's going to get a prize when he comes back. I roll out of bed and walk naked to the closet.

A few minutes later I hear the click of Cerberus's nails on the bedroom floor. I walk out of the closet in the red lace baby-doll nightgown I bought the first day I was with Hayes.

"Hey, buddy, where's your daddy?" I ask as he walks around the bed and sits.

He's wearing a sheet of paper hanging around his neck by a red ribbon. I walk over and squat in front of the big, proud dog, lifting the paper to read it.

Bring me up from the depths of hell, my angel, make me pure and light.

Our souls are entwined forever, my heart lost to you at first sight.

Grant me my ardent wish, the most beautiful life.

Marry me, Paige, please say yes, be my wife.

"Oh," I warble, the tears springing to my eyes as I read his handwritten poem. I throw my arms around Cerberus's neck and bury my face in his sleek fur.

"Damn it. I knew I should have signed it so you would know it was me, not the dog, asking you."

I look up and run my fingers under my eyes to remove the tears.

"He had such a good delivery, you can't fault me for thinking it was all his idea."

Hayes meets me on my knees with Cerberus beside us and takes my hands, his green eyes burning with intention.

"It's definitely me asking. I know it's crazy and fast, and there are so many reasons not to, but this feels right. Do you think you could grow to love me? To not just be my bride, but my partner in everything? I want to rule beside you, take over empires with you, fight for you. Do you think you could spend your life with me?"

My jaw has come unhinged, dropping lower with each romantic pledge. This ruthless businessman just went all emotional on me. How did I manage to find this perfect man?

"When you put it that way, it's pretty hard to say no."

"Say the words, Paige."

"We really are crazy."

He raises an eyebrow at me.

"Yes—on one condition."

His chest inflates only to freeze with the breath in his lungs. "Continue."

"We'll never treat our relationship as a business deal. Deals can be undone and businesses can fail. I don't want to fail with you."

"Never."

"Then, yes, I'll marry you."

Hayes smiles and pulls me to his chest, his lips crashing against mine and claiming another little piece of my heart.

Twenty-Three

Hayes

The lights of Las Vegas grow smaller as the jet climbs into the night sky, but they were never bright enough to outshine my new *wife*. Paige is curled in my lap, my hand stroking her thigh, alternating pulling her left hand up to admire her new diamond rings, and proclaiming just how insane we are. Cerberus is sprawled at our feet, his duties as best dog now fulfilled even though he's still wearing his bow tie collar.

"Mama and Daddy are going to kill me."

I kiss Paige's silky, raven-dark hair.

"They'll have to go through me first. Let me tell you, that would require a Herculean effort."

"Really, though."

She rests her head on my shoulder and threads her fingers into my hair to gently scratch my scalp. I shiver in response before she continues.

"I'm their only child, my mama's only daughter and I just took away her chance to plan a wedding. Do you know how angry she's going to be? She'll be mad as a Hydra getting its heads cut off."

I smile at her Hercules reference to match mine. She really is perfect.

"If the only thing she's mad about is not planning your wedding, we'll be just fine," I assure her. "She can plan the five-year anniversary vow renewal. Or we can renew our vows every year. Whatever makes you happy."

I feel her smile against me.

"She'll have plenty to be mad about besides that. I just cost her a manufacturing deal. I could be the reason the Thackery Agriculture Company meets its demise after more than a century in operation. Not only have I single-handedly stolen the wedding planning she's dreamed of my whole life, I've also crushed her own family legacy. I'm heartless."

I pull her closer to me.

"You have the biggest heart of anyone I know. You also know your own mind, not content to be sold off to suit her business aspirations."

"How do I tell them?" She shifts restlessly in my lap and twists my own gold wedding band on my left hand where it rests on her leg.

"We'll do it together. We can go to Savannah tomorrow and plan to see them Tuesday."

I have some business to conduct with my new father-in-law that could be done in person so making an appearance in Savannah kills two birds with one stone.

An unfamiliar stab of guilt pierces my chest as I think of the plans set to take place this week. Olympus International is beginning phase two tomorrow, our teams are poised and ready to deploy lucrative offers to each of the hoteliers targeted for acquisition. The Xenios Group will be in a nice long meeting with my team while I keep to the background. My brothers and I stay out of the negotiations until absolutely necessary, keeping the family anonymous and some distance from our company with its many branches.

I look down at Paige, *my wife*, and wonder if she'll ever understand that my motivations for marrying her have nothing to do with buying out her legacy. I shut my eyes and hope like hell I'm not about to sabotage my own happiness. She will eventually see I'm doing this for her.

"Are you a part of the mile-high club?"

My eyes pop open and I move so I can see the devilish grin Paige is giving me.

"Why do you ask?" I slip my fingertips under the hem of her dress where it rests just above her knee and grip her thigh.

"I think I'd like to join. I was hoping to find an existing member to grant me membership to this exclusive club. I am the wife of a billionaire now. I might as well have all the perks."

"*You* are a billionaire now, Mrs. Olsen. What's mine is yours."

Her eyes widen. "There wasn't a prenup, but I will absolutely sign anything you want me to in order to protect your fortune. I'm not in it for money, Hayes. I'm in it for you."

"That's exactly why there wasn't a prenup." I slide my hand up higher to grip her hip and she gasps with the pressure. "We're not going to fail, so there wasn't a need. I want you to be completely provided for in any untimely event that could befall us."

Her legs spread apart. "Well, it sounds like you have everything covered. How about you make love to your new wife and admit me to the club."

I gather her in my arms and stand. "Cerberus, stay."

I cross to the private bedroom at the rear of the cabin. "What my wife wants, she gets."

Paige sighs as I lay her out on the bed.

"That's a word I like a whole lot more with you than I did when I was fighting the other option."

I shrug off my shirt and make quick work of my pants. "You'll never have to fight alone, and you're free of that scoundrel."

She giggles at my wording, but the laughter stops when I grip her ankle and tug her toward me.

"Show me that juicy pussy."

She drags her teeth across her bottom lip and pulls the skirt of her soft cream-colored dress up her thighs. She is the goddess of anticipation, knowing just how to drag a moment out to completely savor it, but it jacks up my libido, and my impatience to have her gets the better of me.

Just as her dress skims over her hips, I dive in, pulling her lacy panties to the side so I can sink my mouth in her silky warmth. Her hands bury into my hair and hold me close as I devour her. She moans as I delve two fingers into her folds and push into her center, her hips rocking against me. I give her everything she loves with my own ferocity and when she comes, it's with my name on her lips.

I pull away from her slick pussy and move up her body, kissing her while her taste is still on my lips. I undress her relaxed body and return to my pants for a condom, turning once it's on to catch her dip her fingers in her pussy, and then bring them to her mouth. My grip on the base of my cock tightens as her pink tongue licks a finger and then plunges it into her mouth.

"Jesus, Paige, I'm going to blow just watching you taste yourself."

"I wanted to know what you were tasting. I think I prefer your cock, though."

She skims her slick fingers down to her breasts and rolls her nipples, her back arching.

"I need you. Please, Hayes."

I'm back on the bed in an instant, but I surprise her when I lie on my back next to her and drag her body to cover mine.

"Ride me, angel. I want to see you on top, taking everything you want."

She slowly lifts her body and scoots so she's sitting on my thighs, my dick hard and ready in front of her. She eyes my length with trepidation, visually measuring the cock I want to bury as deep as I can into her perfect pussy, bottom out, and push in even more.

"How do I do this, exactly?"

I take her hand and move it to the base of my dick, wrapping her fingers around the shaft so she lifts it straight up.

"Climb on."

I keep my hand around hers as she shifts, rising on her knees and moving forward so my dick is notched against her opening. She presses down tentatively, her body yielding to my cock and taking me in.

"Oh, God," she moans as she takes me to the hilt. "How are you bigger this way? I feel you everywhere."

"Rock your hips," I instruct, my hands finding the delicious spot where her legs crease at her hips and start the motion. "Up and down is fine, but I think you'll like this better because of where it hits you."

Her eyes flutter closed. "Oh, wow, okay, that's good."

She takes over the rocking, starting slowly, but discovering the rhythm that suits her quickly and in no time, my angel rides me like a pro. Her hands press into my chest, giving her more purchase to drag her body back and forth on mine as her nails embed in my skin.

I hold her tightly, increasing the friction and the motion she's enjoying. Just watching her face as she gets closer to her release could make me come, but I hold back.

"Oh, Hayes," she says, her head tipping forward to spill hair around her face as her hips rock harder, dragging out the pleasure that is rising between us. "God, I love this."

The overwhelming need to be even closer to her pushes me to sit up and I grip her ass in my hands. I pull her hips back and forth again. Her arms wrap around my shoulders, nails digging into my back.

"Come with me, baby."

I pull and push her hips, my thrusts pumping into her as her body begins its trek to ecstasy. I drag my teeth across her shoulder and nip at her neck as she stops breathing and reaches the cliff.

When she tumbles head-first into her orgasm, I'm right behind her.

I keep my arms tight around her as our hot breaths mix between us, feeling closer to her right now than I have with any other person in my entire my life.

I can't lose her, no matter what. No matter my greed to have what's rightfully hers.

Twenty-Four

Paige

Returning to Savannah a little over a week after I fled my parents' marriage arrangement, as the newly minted wife of another man, no less, manages to still feel terrifying. Mama really is going to kill me, or I'll finally give her that heart attack she's been threatening for years on my account.

We take the Maybach back to The Abyss, and I feel like the wife of Batman in the sleek car as it turns heads through downtown Savannah. I'm glad the windows are tinted dark so nosy neighbors and Mama's acquaintances can't glimpse us as the occupants of the extravagant car. I'm sure she would be blowing up my phone faster than the ride through town after the rumor mill alerted her to the return of her prodigal daughter. I'm not quite ready to face her with my news, and her eagle eyes would spot the delicate rings on my left hand immediately.

I look down and admire the rings we picked out together. His yellow gold band matches the setting on my ring, a beautiful oval diamond flanked by two round diamonds, and a third trillion cut diamond flowing out on either side. The diamond wedding band nestles up to the engagement ring and gives some weight to the rings on my finger. He offered me my pick of the entire jewelry store we visited in Atlanta before flying to Vegas, showing me huge emerald-cut stones and blinged-out settings, but my traditional heart went with this one.

"You like your rings?"

"Very much. They're perfect."

"Just like you."

I give him an appreciative smile as he pulls into the garage at The Abyss.

"Is it weird having an apartment at a nightclub?

"It's actually quite convenient. I own the building and the club only needs the first two floors. The third with that huge rooftop was just right for a place for me to stay when I'm in town for business."

He parks the Maybach and I see my pretty AC Cobra still parked and undisturbed a few spots away. It reminds me of the many Saturdays I spent helping Daddy restore his prized classic cars and the feeling of elation I had when he gave me my own for my birthday. It feels like a year ago that I fled Sunday dinner and found myself running away with Hayes, despite it only being eight days that have passed.

He opens my door and helps me out of the car, our bags already in his hand.

"What made you decide to put in the greenhouse? Elysium is incredible, but it's not exactly run of the mill for a nightclub."

"Exactly. Having the garden made this place more exclusive and far more special than any other nightclub in Georgia."

"But why did you pick Savannah? This club seems more fit for the Atlanta crowd than a touristy, slower-paced small city."

I hit the button for the elevator for him since his hands are full. I have to fish out the special keycard to get rooftop access from Hayes's pants pocket. I'm tempted to keep my hand in there and fish for something else, but my lady bits are a little sore, so I shouldn't start something that'll lead to more sex.

"My brothers and I have smaller corporations under the Olympus International umbrella that lean toward our interests. I like good alcohol, a decadent nightclub people are vying to get into, and expensive cars. Savannah had the history and architecture I wanted for a project like this, and it's become somewhat of an attraction in its own right. Besides, it's nice to take a short flight and get the hell away from my brothers and the stifling scrutiny of Atlanta."

"The Atlanta Haute List sure seems to like you." I smirk and exit the elevator ahead of Hayes.

"That fucking gossip site is the bane of my existence. They seem to have a special fixation on my family and are always looking for dirt on us. Usually, Zander is the subject of their interest, but you and I have made their radar and are at the top of their current list, unfortunately."

I unlock the door to his flat and hold it open so he can put the bags down inside.

"Have they written more about us?" My heart races thinking of the things Mama has probably read about us.

He stops me from entering the flat by circling my waist with his arms and hauls me back against his chest before I can step inside.

"Don't you dare walk through that door. I'm carrying my bride inside."

I pop my hand on my hip and laugh at his insistence.

"You already did that when we got back to Atlanta."

"Every threshold to a home I will share with you requires my due diligence to ensure a happy marriage. Don't question my Southern breeding and the traditions I cherry-pick as my own, dear wife."

He lifts an eyebrow at me and barely contains the smile that wants to burst forth.

I laugh and hold my arms out for him.

"As long as you admit that you pick and choose what traditions you follow, I'm fine with it."

He scoops me up and carries me inside, kicking the door closed behind us, and walking across the flat to set me down on the bed, crawling up beside me.

"There's something about you that makes me feel a little more traditional. I've never cared much for the way things were done, always looking for the way that worked in my favor instead. You make me want to be so much better than that."

"You're far more romantic than you give yourself credit for, you know that?"

"Absolutely not. All lies," he jokes, his face screwed up in a comically bad pout.

"One, you've gone out of your way to accommodate me when you didn't have to, including housing, feeding, clothing, cuddling, and bedding me."

I wiggle my eyebrows at him and he cracks a smile.

"Two, you wrote the most beautiful marriage proposal poem any Southern belle has ever received."

I flutter my eyelashes and sigh, getting a chuckle this time.

"Three, you insist on following traditions to ensure a happy marriage." I tick off each point on my fingers as he grudgingly nods his agreement.

"You, my love, are a bona fide, heart on your sleeve, lover of grand gestures, sappy, romantic."

"Your love, huh?"

"Of course you fixate on that." I laugh and push my hand into his unyielding chest.

"Yeah, I do. You're mine, you know."

He grasps my hand and holds it against his body.

"Your what?"

"You know I'm desperately in love with you, right?"

"It's like pizza," I say, and he gives me a confused look. "You would have told me because I'm not a mind reader."

His look of understanding precedes his noise of approval.

"Well, because neither of us is a mind reader, I want to make it known to you and this empty apartment that I am desperately in love with my wife and will kiss the ground she walks on from now until eternity because she is the very model of grace and perfection."

I smile widely, but my hands are sweaty and there's something so foreign about proclaiming this to one another for the very first time. I fall back on humor, like he has, to ease some of the nerves. "I guess you wiggled your way into my little old heart, too."

I place my hand on his face and dip my head to rest against his as I find a way to strip myself even more bare than I've been with him before. It'a about time he knew exactly how I feel. We are married after all.

"I love you, Hayes, and I look forward to watching this fresh new love grow into a wrinkled, lived-in, and weathered love that is talked about for ages to come."

The nerves that twist my stomach into knots from admitting my feelings are more excited to admit this than terrified of what it means. *Mostly.*

He rolls on top of me and kisses me far gentler than I expect, lazily exploring my mouth and trailing sweet kisses down my neck until I'm moaning. I'm rethinking my no sex because I'm sore stance when his phone rings and disrupts the moment.

"Fuck," he grunts, rolling to his side and pulling out his phone. "It's work. I'm so sorry, angel. I have to take this."

"Don't apologize. It is Monday and a workday, after all. Go get your work done."

"How are you so understanding?" He kisses me again and leaves the apartment for his office next door as he answers the call.

This is exactly what I expected life to be like with Hayes. He is a consummate workaholic, and I watched Daddy leave family dinners and downtime for work emergencies far too many times while growing up to not be understanding of my own husband doing it now.

"So this is the life of a billionaire businessman's wife," I say to the empty room.

I miss Cerberus, my demon spawn shadow who would have listened to me bemoan my new reality of Hayes being dedicated to his work first and foremost and me having nothing to do. The big dog stays in Atlanta with a trainer when Hayes goes out of town and can't take him. The rooftop flat *is* a bit small for a one-hundred-pound canine, so I can understand Hayes's reticence to bring him with us, but it doesn't stop me from missing the dog anyway. My thoughts drift to a solution to this problem, and I start daydreaming about finding a home here in town with a nice big backyard for him to enjoy so he can come with us. That would be so wonderful and would give me a permanent place in my hometown to enjoy.

So what will I do with myself now, and how will I manage The Mansion when it looks like we may be spending a significant portion of our time in Atlanta? The general manager of a hotel is not exactly a position that lends itself to a remote work environment. I'll have to figure that out before the new year when I'm set to take on my new position. That is, if my parents don't completely revoke my trust, disinherit me, and pretend I don't exist when they find out what I've done. That would solve the problem of splitting my time in two cities, not that I like the prospect one bit.

But...I would still have the work with Underworld Spirits that Hayes has promised me to look forward to. It's a good backup plan for me should the worst-case scenario play out. The feeling of floating on clouds with Hayes deflates as I think of my parents and their inevitable response to my hasty marriage and my end to their plans. They won't be happy, especially Mama. I've made a habit of making her incredibly displeased recently, which is a first. I guess it took her crossing that final line to set me on a new path that deviated from the good, obedient daughter role I had played for so long. Will I be able to keep this up once faced with her wrath? I sure hope so, or I'll be in for a world of hurt and disappointment.

Twenty-Five

Hayes

"Their immediate response was a fat hell no. Even though we've been working through all of our bargaining chips, they're not even interested in entertaining the offer. We went in above market value and it would be more than generous, but they don't care." Diego Vallarta, the senior vice president of finance at Olympus, sounds perplexed as he updates me on the Xenios takeover and it's not what I want to hear.

"Could be a tactic to get us to raise our offer."

These multimillion-dollar acquisitions can sometimes take months to hammer out details and get each side what they want. There are concessions each side has to make and even more that are demanded before you can find a place to settle in the negotiations. We don't have months.

"What are they holding out for?"

"Everything, as far as what they're actually saying." I hear him sigh impatiently over the line. "We expected this, Hayes."

"What can we concede that isn't going to fuck the whole thing up?" I reply, just as irritated.

"Our research shows they are particularly attached to the Savannah Mansion property. It's the family estate, where they got their start. We could remove that property from the deal and likely get them to agree a lot faster."

"Absolutely not. That's the property this entire deal hinges on. Besides, what other option would we have for Savannah at that point? We'd need to purchase another existing hotel or build one from the ground up and lose years and millions."

I run my hand over my face and tug at my hair. I'm not about to lose out on the one property that started this whole mess. I visited Savannah on a business scouting trip years ago and stayed at The Mansion. It's where the idea of branching into luxury boutique hotels first took root and transformed my ideas for the future of Olympus.

I want that fucking mansion.

"Keep at it and don't remove a single property from the table just yet. I want them all."

"You may need to step in earlier than we planned," he says hesitantly.

Fuck. "I know. I'll work on it. I'm in Savannah and will see what I can do today, if not tomorrow. Keep me updated."

I end the call and pound my fist against the desk. The last thing I want to do is go to William Fairchild with my demands at the very moment he discovers I've married his daughter and fucked up his wife's arrangements. It's only going to make him close ranks and refuse outright. From what our research into the Thackery trust and Fairchild inheritance has revealed, the marriage clause Paige referred to means she needs to be married when she eventually inherits her legacy. That doesn't look to be any time soon, given William Fairchild's health and determination to remain at the head of his company. Having married Paige now, likely decades before she inherits The Xenios Group, won't make them transfer The Mansion to me any faster. It might just make him continue refusing our offers.

I make a call to another member of my team working on contingency plans. "We need to move forward with Plan B. Make it happen now, and I don't care what you have to pay to get it. I need this to get the Xenios deal going. Use the leverage I provided and don't hold back. They need to know they have no choice but to sell, and fast, or I'll go to the press." In this case, leverage is a nice way of saying blackmail, and I don't even fucking care about the moral repercussions. It's deserved in this instance and a long fucking time coming if they give me any resistance and make me use it.

"You sure about that, Hayes? It was last-ditch when we discussed it. It's only day one of negotiations. We have time."

"We don't have the time I had hoped for and this could be a huge bargaining chip. Just fucking make it happen today."

I hate snapping at my team, but I'm nearly desperate to ensure I get the deal I want. I'm willing to resort to blackmail and force a hostile takeover for a completely unrelated deal just to have a better hand in this game. I'm hoping it will keep William Fairchild from losing his shit and shuttering all possibilities of selling when faced with losing everything. This last-ditch effort might show him he's not actually losing as much as he thinks he is. I rise from my desk with purpose, leaving the office and banging through the door to the apartment in a rush.

Paige squeaks and slips off the bed, a thud quickly following her disappearance.

Shit. I should have taken a breath and calmed down before rushing in here and freaking her out.

"Baby, are you okay?" I call as I hurry across the apartment.

"I'm fine, just surprised," she says, popping up from the far side of the bed, rubbing her knee. "You came in so fast, I didn't know what was happening."

I gather her in my arms, my hands smoothing her hair and tracing around her ear.

"I think we should invite your parents to dinner tonight. I know we said we'd tell them tomorrow, but it's probably better to get a jump on this before they learn of our marriage on their own."

She wraps her arms around my shoulders and looks up at me. "I don't think I'm brave enough just yet."

"You don't have to be. I'll be right beside you, giving you all the courage you could want."

I'm forcing her hand in this, my insistence giving her little option but to follow my lead, and I hate that I can't let her get used to the idea on her own. I take her face in my hands.

"You don't have to be afraid of them anymore or worry about what they want you to do."

It's imperative that we get this meeting over with sooner rather than later so the Fairchilds can get through the anger and animosity and move onto acceptance. I have no hope of them ever being happy about me running off and marrying their daughter without asking for their blessing or even knowledge, but grudging acceptance is as good as anything.

She gives me a rueful grin. "You better flex those muscles right along with the side of bravery you offer, because I need it all to get through a dinner with Mama when I surprise her with the fact I'm now married."

I indulge her and quickly make a spectacle of my biceps just to hear her laugh.

The look Caroline Thackery Fairchild gives me when she and William arrive at The Abyss for the quick dinner we arranged is nothing short of withering. She may be diminutive in stature, shorter even than Paige, but she comes across as a vicious and mighty warrior hell-bent on destroying me. I may have met my match for ruthlessness in Caroline.

I know exactly why Paige was worried and didn't feel brave enough to bear her intimidating mother. Lucky for her, I can be equally as protective of the woman by my side as the mama bear appraising my arm currently around her daughter's waist.

"Mr. and Mrs. Fairchild, it is my absolute pleasure to meet you," I drawl, my Southern-infused manners and a disarming smile ready despite the tension in my body.

"Hi, Mama, Daddy," Paige says, the shake noticeable in her voice.

I spread my fingers wider against her side and give her a gentle squeeze of reassurance.

"This is Hayes Olsen."

She looks up at me and I nod.

"My husband."

The color drains from Caroline's face and she stumbles against her husband. He catches her with his own stunned expression.

"Paige, what have you done?" she gasps, clinging to William.

At least I know she hasn't caught wind of any gossip blogs and the press that may have picked up on our quick Vegas trip.

"What is the meaning of this?" William snaps my way. "How dare you force a child to marry you? This is a disgusting act of coercion."

"That's rich coming from you, Daddy." Paige's voice crackles with her frustration. "Marrying Hayes was my choice. It sure beats the business deal and arranged marriage to a predator that y'all thought was so perfect for me just last week."

"We have your best interests in mind and know the alliance with the Daniels will lead to a better future for you. We would never make you marry a predator, or someone nearly twice your age," William responds, his eyes flicking to me.

The audacity of these people. I guess I have to drop this truth bomb on them right away rather than introducing the subject gradually. I let it rip.

"Garrison Daniels is a rapist."

My flat tone has all of them looking at me, mixed emotions playing on each face.

"He has assaulted no less than six women since what he did to Paige in high school. His parents discreetly paid for the silence of each of his victims when the truth was threatened, which is why he's practicing law and walking around a free man. By not reporting his heinous treatment of Paige as a teenager, and by accepting his family's hush money, you allowed a predator to remain free and hurt far more women in even more awful ways."

Caroline becomes even paler as she takes in the hard truth.

"That's impossible. We would have known." Her hand moves to clutch the pearls around her neck and she steals a glance at Paige that I think holds the tiniest hint of guilt. *She knew.*

"What is he talking about, Caroline?" William asks his wife, obvious discomfort straining his voice. If he still doesn't know, his wife is more deceitful than I imagined.

"It's nothing, William. Paige was confused about something that happened back in high school."

Paige makes a huff of frustration next to me at her mother's words. I want to throttle Caroline for down-playing what happened to her daughter and continuing to cover it up even now. Before I can tear her a new one, Paige speaks.

"Daddy, he tried to rape me." Paige's voice is small, full of shame, and breaking my damn heart. I want that piece of filth to pay.

"Oh, Paige, no, it can't be. You never told me," William says, his face a contorted mess of anger and hurt. His expression wars between fury and heartbreak and I know the exact feeling.

"What Paige says is true. Garrison Daniels is a sexual predator who tried to ruin your daughter when she was just fourteen. Your wife was aware of the situation and chose not to act when Paige wanted to report the incident."

I turn to take in Caroline, the shrewd, heartless bitch. She meets my disgusted look with her own.

"By not reporting it," I say, pointing at her, "you allowed him to continue. I have the names of his victims and the amounts the Daniels paid to each of them if you would like proof. His most recent victim was less than a year ago, so he certainly hasn't changed much, despite studying law and knowing just how in the wrong he is."

William's face is ashen as he looks between his wife and daughter. Paige tucks herself in closer to me but meets his eyes and nods and I see the truth settle on him.

It sickens me to have to share this information knowing they were prepared to give their daughter to this monster in exchange for what, a manufacturing deal with the cretins who preferred to cover up their son's proclivities? What the fuck kind of business do they run if they refused to check into the background of the people they were getting into bed with, which, for Paige, would have been literal. It's abhorrent.

Paige places a gentle hand on my chest to steal my attention that is riveted on her parents, imagining the kinds of torture that befit their negligence and greed.

"Thank you for making your point. I think they're beginning to understand just how bad that particular match was."

She steps away from my side and I reluctantly release her. I don't want her far from me, or any closer to the people who were ready to put her in the path of the same deviant that wanted to steal her innocence. She holds her hands out to her parents anyway.

"I know this is hard to hear, and we are giving you a lot to think about. Please come in so we can get you something to drink and sit down. I've missed you."

Her parents both soften at her admission and in that moment I know they truly love her, despite their flaws. William holds out his arms and Paige returns his embrace. They whisper to one another, and I'm sure he's apologizing for not having known. It's encouraging to see that they are not all expectations and ruthless negotiations that balance on their daughter's unwilling submission.

Caroline releases her pearls and takes Paige's hand, pulling her away from her father.

"You didn't have to go and marry a complete stranger to convince us you didn't want to marry Garrison. We're more reasonable than that and you know it."

Paige looks down at her feet and I'm ready to rip into Caroline on her behalf when she looks up and I catch the glint of strength in her eyes.

"Actually, I did. You wouldn't listen to me. You even sent Garrison to Atlanta to bring me home. Do you know how awful and small it made me feel to know my parents wouldn't hear me when I was speaking my truth? It was time for me to do something I wanted, finally, and I want Hayes. I love him. He makes me so happy."

Hearing her say it out loud to her parents makes it final. I'm utterly, inescapably, and deeply in love with this woman. Screw my original motivations for getting close to her. I think it's impossible not to be touched by the goodness of her heart, the kindness of her soul, and the depth of her love and not be changed by her very presence. She makes me want to be a better man simply by being herself. I want to be deserving of her.

"I could use that drink," William says, running a hand through his dark hair, so similar in color to Paige's, though she has none of the silver that streaks his temples.

I nod and lead them into the private room set up for dinner.

"Double barrel bourbon?"

"Please." William settles in next to the bar with appreciation beginning to thaw the ice of his displeasure.

I pour us both glasses and look at Caroline, still gripping Paige's hand. "Ladies?"

"Mama likes gin and tonic. I'll have the bourbon."

Caroline turns and sharply tugs her daughter's hand.

"Paige, that's simply not ladylike. You're too young for bourbon."

I bristle at her patronizing tone and would very much like to remove her hand from Paige's, maybe even separate it from her body completely.

"Mama, there is plenty I'm too young for, but a well-aged bourbon suits me just fine."

Her eyes sparkle when I catch them, knowing she meant the comment for me. The tension jacking up my shoulders eases from her smile alone. She's like a balm that soothes every irritation life could throw at me.

I return to playing bartender, passing out drinks and settling onto the black velvet wingback chair that faces a Victorian sofa upholstered in the same fabric that Caroline and William sit on. Paige perches on the arm of my chair but I can't resist the urge to pull her right into my lap, where she settles primly on my thigh instead of directly between my legs. Oh well, a guy can try, even if I just want to scandalize her parents.

"Can someone please explain to me how this *odd* pairing occurred so... quickly?" Caroline asks, her eyes, so reminiscent to Paige's, flicking up to take my measure.

My jaw tightens and I'm glad Paige speaks for us, because I would say something to purposefully shock her. *I deflowered your daughter only two nights ago. She begs for my cock now. I could ask her to crawl to me on her knees and suck me off and she would do it, willingly.*

"We met at my debutante ball. Hayes owns The Abyss and I ran into him when I needed a break from the party. I think it was fate."

Caroline's eyes narrow as she listens to Paige. "It's infatuation, not fate, you silly thing. I can't believe you ran off and got married a week after meeting him."

"Any man would be lucky to find themselves married to your daughter," I cut in, done with her barbs. "There's not a thing to dislike about Paige. She's an incredible woman. She left a mark on me from the moment we met, and when I found her fleeing your interesting arrangement, I offered her a harbor in the storm."

"Storm? Hardly, you despicable monster. She was a child overreacting and throwing a fit. You enabled her."

"I hate to disagree with you, Caroline, but Paige is an intelligent, determined adult capable of seeing through the calculated manipulation of those closest to her. What she did was act purely in self-preservation."

"I think we can agree that each story has many sides, and you both have strong feelings," Paige says, placing her arm around my shoulder and gently rubbing my neck. "Why don't we eat?"

I chuckle at Paige's mastery of maintaining the peace under tension. She will absolutely rule over the business world without anyone being the wiser to her crafts. It strikes me just how well-suited she is to take over her family's legacy and lead the Xenios Group. I feel a pang of remorse at my determination to take it from her. She'll see it's for the best, even if it's hard to part with.

Eventually.

Twenty-Six

The Atlanta Haute List

Wedding Bells Are Ringing For The Billionaire And The Belle

First comes love, then comes marriage is certainly right. Sources close to billionaire Hayes Olsen confirm, to the despair of women throughout Georgia, that he is no longer Atlanta's most eligible bachelor and is now wedded to hotel heiress Paige Fairchild. A quick day trip to Las Vegas sealed the deal between Fairchild and Olsen after a whirlwind week-long romance that was full of danger (read our recap of the carjacking he warded off a few days ago) and black-tie affairs. They stepped out publicly as a couple at the Underworld Spirits launch party just one day before their hasty marriage. The launch of Olsen's newest business venture was the most exclusive and talked about event of the year, thanks in part to the newly-in-love couple's PDA-filled appearance.

What sounds like a fairy tale come to life has transpired over the course of their short relationship and we'll be watching for any news to come from their camp to share about any possible larger wedding ceremonies or events. With the way these two move, a baby in a baby carriage may be next for these love birds! Hit Like and Subscribe for all the latest Haute Gossip so you never miss a story.

Twenty-Seven

Hayes

D riving onto The Mansion's sprawling grounds in the Maybach allows me to admire the Spanish moss-draped trees, tidy lawns bordering the drive, and beautiful gardens that instantly caught my eye when I stayed here years ago. I park the sleek car by the statement-making marble fountain in the courtyard flanked by bright hydrangeas, vibrant azaleas, heady-smelling gardenias, towering magnolias, and oaks that must be a century old.

The valet just nods in resignation as I pocket the keys to the one-off Exelero, not about to insist I let him drive the multimillion-dollar car. I survey the luxurious facade of the gorgeous property as I mount the steps to the grand entrance of the estate-turned-hotel. It really is show-stopping. The lobby is full of marble and velvet, hinting at the historic past while being fully updated for modern convenience. Part of the appeal of this property is that it's turn-key and a real focal point for our eastern contingent of boutique hotels.

"Hayes Olsen to see Mr. Fairchild," I say to the concierge.

She picks up her phone and speaks a few hushed words across the line before settling it back on the cradle.

"He's in a meeting currently. Would you mind waiting a moment? They should be breaking for lunch soon."

I nod, having anticipated this, though I hate waiting for anything or anyone. I gather the patience Paige has recently taught me and move to a plush seating area near the quiet bar full of polished furniture and dark fabrics. I check their shelves and feel a satisfied smile lift my lips when I see a few bottles of Underworld Spirits already prominently displayed on their top shelf. The roll-out is happening as we speak, the mile-long waiting list for the exclusive liquors getting the small shipments we allow.

After about fifteen minutes of studying the lobby and taking in the seamless flow of the check-in desk and the speedy staff, the concierge comes to get me.

"If you'll follow me, sir, I'll take you to Mr. Fairchild's office."

She leads me through a lavishly decorated hallway off the lobby to an executive office suite richly appointed with masculine furniture, towering bookshelves, and an air of authority. She holds the door to the office open and allows me to walk through before closing it behind me.

The office makes me feel right at home, though I could never see Paige working in a place like this, as she is light and frilly, not dark and stuffy.

"Mr. Fairchild," I say in greeting. "Thank you for taking the time to meet with me. I understand your schedule is quite busy today."

He motions to a chair across the large desk and sits back in his big leather chair with steepled fingers.

"Hayes, you can just call me William," he replies stiffly as I sit. "Interesting to see you again so soon. I was a bit surprised to hear you wanted a meeting with me."

"Yes, it's quite pressing, actually. I would never mix business with family time, so I felt it better to schedule something where we could speak man to man, rather than bog down an already heavy dinner with business."

He leans forward slowly and rests his elbows on the gleaming surface of the desk.

"You want to talk business?" He gives me an appraising look and I remain the epitome of calm and collected.

"I have a gift I'd like to give you. I think you will find it quite valuable. Consider it a wedding present, from a grateful husband to his new father-in-law."

He waves his hand jerkily in the air as he closes his eyes tightly and opens them with a look of trepidation.

"Talk straight with me, Olsen, I don't have time to beat around the bush."

"Paige told me the reason you wanted to marry her off to Garrison was to integrate the Thackery Agriculture investments and move into textiles through Daniels Industries processing plants. Well, Daniels Industries is yours. I bought the entire manufacturing outfit and subsidiaries yesterday. I thought you could run the show far better than they were, and not have the pain-in-the-ass rapist for a son-in-law or be joined as business partners with the enabling and unscrupulous people he calls parents."

"You bought them out and are giving the entire outfit to me," he articulates slowly.

"Yes, sir. I have the documents ready to sign over the entire enterprise to you today. You can run it however you'd like, keeping the staff or replacing them at your discretion. You can even rename it Fairchild Industries if you'd like. The Daniels name needs to be stamped out of Savannah completely, and what better way to do it than by replacing it with the Fairchild name as a testament to your steadfast influence and leadership."

I place my hand suggestively on the leather briefcase beside me. His eyes follow the movements and I see his throat work as he swallows. It's quite a tempting proposal for any business-minded man.

"You've proven to have sound business practices that have grown a single luxury hotel into a prosperous hotel group, so I know you'll be able to turn the Thackery Agriculture investments into the textile empire it's meant to be with this small addition to your own portfolio."

He crosses his arms and sends me a menacing look.

"Small addition? Cut the bullshit. I know you want something from me. Out with it."

I rest my elbow on the plush arm of the chair and cross my ankle over my knee as I lean back.

"Do you know much about my business dealings, William?"

"You have a nightclub in town that Paige seems to be obsessed with and some new liquor distributor." He waves his fingers dismissively at the liquor part, clearly unaware of how lucrative my new business already is.

"Those are two of my personal endeavors, yes, but it barely scratches the surface. What keeps me busy on a day-to-day basis, and the conglomerate I'm CFO of, is Olympus International. My brothers and I run the company and we want to branch off in a new direction with the acquisition of several small hotel groups, uniting all of the properties to become the largest luxury boutique hotel chain in the country."

"You shifty bastard." William's eyes narrow as he puts it all together. "You're the damn fools who want to buy out the Xenios Group. This is why you married Paige so fast. I should throw you out on your ass and have your shotgun marriage annulled right this minute."

"But you won't. I didn't marry Paige for the hotels and that's the honest truth. I really do love your daughter, whether or not you believe it. Aside from being head over heels for her, you and I both know I can give her the life she deserves. As for the business, I can take the Xenios Group to new heights, far beyond what y'all may have envisioned."

"She will never forgive you when she finds out about this manipulation. You understand that, right?"

My chest constricts at the thought, but I press on.

"She will see in time just how right this is. I don't expect her to understand right away, but I'm doing this for her."

"How can stealing the very legacy she's prepared her whole life to rule over even remotely be in her interest?"

He gives me a calculated look, but he's not outright refusing me, a good sign.

"I have my reasons and my plans, but know Paige is the driving force behind everything I do now because I want to make her happy. I would give my soul to make sure she has everything she wants, and my very life to keep her safe."

I mean every word. I just hope Paige will understand, eventually, and not hate me for what she thinks I'm doing to dismantle her legacy. She's destined for even bigger things than what the hotels would bring her, and I will make sure she finds her realm to rule over.

"God knows she will give you hell when she finds out." He shakes his head and nails me with a practiced look of parental concern.

If I were any other man, I would be quaking in my leather Prada Oxfords. Instead, it incentivizes me to win him over and get the hotels I want. *Bring it.* I level my own stare back at him. "I'm prepared for that possibility. Though I believe I can make her understand."

"Her mama may never forgive you, even with the nice *present* I'll be delivering on your behalf." He sighs deeply and leans back in his chair, giving me a measured look. "But, for some miserable reason, I actually believe you have decent intentions where Paige is concerned."

"She's my reason for breathing, now. I know what I have and I'm not about to let that go."

"You just better be prepared for the fallout when she finds out. Your cloud nine feelings will come crashing down around you both and you may lose her in your quest to take over everything you see at the very expense of the woman you claim to be doing this for."

I ignore the words that sound fit for an oracle and temper the hope that rises in my chest. "Then you'll agree to sell?" This is not a done deal, even if he does believe me where Paige is concerned.

"You've made quite a generous offer for the Xenios Group, and now this gift of the manufacturing capabilities my wife has been coveting for years. It's a hard bargain to walk away from. I'll run it by my team and we'll entertain the negotiations at the very least, but this is in no way my complete acceptance."

"I understand, and I appreciate your time. Shall we get the Daniels Industries transfer taken care of now so you can get back to your lunch?"

"You could join me for lunch and we'll get legal pulled in to make sure everything is as good as it seems."

"Smart man." I offer him a smile and my respect. Having William Fairchild for a father-in-law may not be so bad after all. My mother-in-law, on the other hand, is an entirely different story.

"Maybe you can lend me some hard-earned secrets on how to make Caroline thaw a little toward me while we're at it."

"Son, that woman is an enigma of high-strung emotions and venom wrapped in a pretty package, but good luck to you. I'll give you a few pointers I've picked up through the years and we can hope for the best on that front. She's a woman of actions, so you keep treating my baby girl with the respect and love she deserves, and Caroline may eventually thaw a little toward you."

I think that means I just earned his respect and maybe even his blessing. This impromptu meeting was worth every minute and million spent to acquire Daniels Industries just for that alone.

Twenty-Eight

Hayes

It's done. It may have taken days of hard-fought negotiations that required every ounce of control and planning Olympus International put into it, but we now own the Xenios Group. William and his team finally signed off after a late day ensuring the proper exchange for the legacy that's been in his family for over 150 years.

"You're one hell of a negotiator, Hayes." William clasps my hand firmly in his.

There is a sadness that permeates his countenance despite the incredible wealth he just gained, along with the new industry he and his wife will be able to utilize to turn another family business into an empire.

"You should see my brother. There isn't a deal he can't close."

"Well, if you'll excuse me, I need to go home to my wife and explain that, as of the new year, we will no longer have control of the Xenios Group and will be handing over The Mansion. I can feel the headache building from her shrieks and questions already."

"Maybe lead with an extended vacation you plan to take her on, then drop the bomb of the buyout to soften the blow?"

I cross my arms over my chest as I begin dreaming of the honeymoon I owe Paige. We may have opted for a quick wedding, but now that this acquisition is finished, we can do what we want. I plan to take her wherever her heart desires and spend as much time as I can worshiping her body without work commitments stealing my attention.

"Son, you best worry about your own wife and how she will react. I know my daughter. Running the hotels is in her blood. I've had my time at the helm, and left my mark, but Paige, well, she's a tender soul with one dream, and you've removed that option from her. I don't expect her to stay merciful when she finds out."

My gut twists at his words. My sweet, kind, gentle angel may very well hate me and discover the soul-clearing heat of bitterness before the night is out. I haven't worked out how to tell her, but I know I have to.

"I did what I had to. Her legacy is now part of a bigger story."

William gives me a wry look and raises an eyebrow at me.

"I damn sure hope you will be smarter than that when you tell her. You shouldn't expect her to see things the same way you do."

He slowly walks to the door of the boardroom before turning back to me.

"She likes Leopold's ice cream. Butter pecan is her favorite, and it would do you well to pick up a pint before you say a single word to her. Oh, and you better do it fast before her mama calls to tell her the bad news and poison the well against you. I can only buy you so much time by holding off until after dinner. Then you're on your own."

He pats his palm on the heavy doorframe as he exits and leaves me pondering my next steps.

Ice cream. If it helps keep her by my side, I'll buy the whole damn store.

"Well, hello stranger! You've been gone so long I assumed you'd gone back to Atlanta and forgotten your lonely wife here in Savannah."

Paige greets me from the couch where she sits cross-legged, an open book on her lap.

"Can't have you getting lonely, Mrs. Olsen."

I stow the paper bag of ice cream in the freezer and place my suit jacket and briefcase on the island. Call me a coward, but I'd rather kiss the hell out of my beautiful wife than drop bad news on her the moment I walk through the door, so that's exactly what I do. I mount the couch, take the book from her lap, and push her onto her back under me.

"You miss me, baby?"

She wraps her arms around my neck and smiles.

"Very much. I was about to hunt you down and make you come home." She raises her head and kisses my lips. "Had I known the late hours you keep in Savannah, I never would have let you leave Atlanta." She wraps her legs around my hips and brings me flush against her.

I devour her soft lips, putting the force of the feelings she's brought out of me and the exhilaration of having conquered something new into the kiss.

She opens to me, her tongue meeting mine and swirling in her curious way, always wanting more. Her hands roam my back, sliding lower until she's at my pants and circling around to pop my belt and undo the button. My girl is insatiable, and I'm more than willing to give her everything she wants.

I pull away from the kiss and sit up.

"I want you naked and on your knees by the time my pants are off."

Her eyes heat as her mouth pops open with a breathy *oh*. She's yanking the hem of her long sweater over her head and stripping the jeans from her legs before my shirt is even fully unbuttoned. She kicks her foot, stuck in the ankle of her jeans, and whimpers in frustration before she can pull her foot out. I toe off my shoes one at a time to give her the moment she needs. I push my pants down and step out of them, just as she's turning over onto her knees, her peach of an ass pointed at me tantalizingly.

I run my palm down her spine and onto the round globe of her cheek and give it a full squeeze that rewards me with a trembling sigh from Paige.

She arches her back, pressing her ass harder into my hand. Her pussy tilts back toward me, tempting me to plunge my dick in to the hilt and fuck her hard. But Paige brings out something more tender right along with the rough desires, and I bring my thumb to the glistening center of her and press into the slick heat that I love instead.

"Please, Hayes, don't play with me. I've wanted you so badly all day. I need you, now."

Paige presses her chest to the couch, stretching her arms out in front of her and angling her hips right up for me.

Fuck me. I kneel between her legs and grab the base of my cock to direct myself inside. The instant tug of her inner muscles keeps me pushing straight in until I'm seated and she's moaning with the fullness.

"How do you want it, angel?" I grit out, my control under some serious pressure with the glorious feel of her pussy dragging me under her waves.

"Hard and fast. I want you to..." She pauses, looking over her shoulder at me and biting her lip in a way that makes me throb in her tight heat. It takes her a moment and her hands gripping the edge of the couch for her to get out the request. "Fuck me."

The whispered dirty words coming out of this innocent angel's mouth are my undoing. I pull back and thrust with a roar. I grip her hips and slam into her over and over again as she moans and claws at the couch. It's the most savage I've been with her, but she's meeting me in the carnal moment, her own body rocking back into me every time I slam home.

"I want your fingers on your fucking clit, right now."

She obeys my demand, slipping her fingers under her body to strum herself, and I feel her muscles clench.

"Yes, Hayes. Just. Like. That."

She whimpers as her entire body tenses and shakes under me. She moans and gasps and I feel my control slipping right along with her pleasure.

"Goddamn," I manage, the power of her orgasm finishing me in three strokes.

I collapse, catching myself on my elbows so I don't crush her into the couch. I kiss the skin of her shoulder, working my way to her neck.

"You are absolutely divine. How do you just keep getting better?" I say with my face pressed against hers.

I feel her cheek lift with a lazy smile. "You bring it out of me."

I push off her back and pull out, the mess that follows cluing me into a big fucking oversight on my part.

"Fuck."

"What is it?" She looks back at me, eyes wide.

"We didn't use a condom. Hang on, I'll clean you up."

I leave the couch, pulling on my pants as I grab a towel from the bathroom, running the tap to get warm water before I return to her. I gently clean her up and press kisses along her spine to keep my own mistake from eating at me.

"What are you so worried about? We're married, after all. I imagine very few married couples worry about condoms. Though, I have to admit it was less messy when we used them."

I catch the smile she gives me and my worries fade a fraction.

"I assume you're not on birth control, and we haven't even talked about starting a family, so I wanted you to have full control over what and when we do. I'm sorry for taking that option from you just because I was so focused on fucking you in the moment."

I sit on the couch and pull her into my lap, pressing a kiss to her head and smoothing my hand over the dark hair that floats onto my chest.

"I begged you for it, so it's on me just as much as you. I'll make an appointment with my doctor this week and get things figured out." She pulls her head away from my chest and looks up into my face with a soft expression and rosy cheeks. "But I do want children, or at least, I want your babies. I hadn't really thought too much about when. I just know I want a family, and you make me want to bring lots of little kids into the world so I can have more pieces of you."

I smile and tighten my arms around her.

"Guess that makes two of us."

I'm surprised by the picture that grows in my head from the fear of fucking up to the future of a houseful of beautiful kids running us ragged. Unlike Paige, I hadn't even considered having a family—that is, until I married her and can now vividly imagine it.

A phone rings, but it's not my ringtone, so I pull my face from Paige's and look down at her. "Yours?"

She nods, climbing out of my lap and retrieving her phone from the island as she pulls her sweater over her head. "Hey, Mama."

Motherfucking shit. Oversight number two barrels down on me hard and this one might even be far more consequential.

"Slow down, I can't understand you. Is everything okay? Wait, what? You can't be serious. He would never. Mama, no, Daddy wouldn't."

I listen to Paige's side of the conversation, knowing exactly what she's hearing from the other line, and wait for the moment she turns on me. Her eyes cut to me a second later and there's something worse than hatred in them. Betrayal. I had her full trust and I fucked it up by not being the one to tell her about the acquisition.

"I'll call you later. Just try to rest and don't go anywhere."

She ends her call, setting her phone back on the island with shaking hands and staring at it for a moment. When she drags her gaze back to me, I'm still not ready for the look of complete and utter anguish the clear green reflects at me.

"Paige—"

She cuts me off with a hand lifted between us and three heartbroken words.

"How could you?"

Twenty-Nine

Paige

I was used.

Once again, my sole value was simply in my connections and family legacy. I'm a pawn in a bigger game that doesn't care about my heart, my feelings, or the wreckage that is left behind once my usefulness is expended. The worst part is, I willingly fell for everything Hayes offered, without once questioning his motives in helping me flee the arranged marriage of my overbearing parents' making. If he hadn't considered marrying me for the hotels before I brought the idea to his very doorstep, he certainly ran with it after.

I'm so stupid.

My head swims with the realization as I hold on to the island for support, but it's the shattering of my freely-given heart that causes the most pain. I feel it in my very bones, a splintering, sharp pang that echoes and catches as I breathe. This is heartbreak, and my naïveté brought it on myself.

"How could you?" I ask again, wishing my voice were full of rage and anger, when it's actually defeated and weak. "You bought my family's hotels, took away the only future I've known, and dismantled a family legacy over a century old in a matter of days. For what, exactly? What do you stand to make of it? What profit margin could you squeeze out of a small chain like Xenios?"

"Baby, please. Let me explain."

Hayes pinches his temples with his thumb and forefinger before he stands and moves toward me, but I back away. I don't like hearing him call me baby when I'm spiraling, my world crumbling below me.

"You never even considered telling me you had this planned? That maybe I would have liked to know your sights were set on owning more than my heart?"

I shut my eyes tight against the welling tears. I will not shed a single one for this imposter who used me just like everyone else has wanted to.

"No, that was probably your plan all along. Get the heiress to fall in love with you so you'd have an easier time convincing her daddy to go through with the deal."

I turn my back on him and wrack my brain for what I can do now. I spin and brush past him to get to my pants, his hands skimming my arms. I twist my body so he won't touch me and shove my feet into my jeans with more force than is required.

"You don't understand. I'll explain everything. You just have to listen to me."

"How long have you wanted to buy out the hotels? Did you have plans in place before you met me? How about when you took me back to Atlanta with you, did you think it was all too convenient? You owe me that bit of truth."

He freezes and considers me like I'm an unpredictable wild animal.

"I... may have had ulterior motives in the beginning." His halting cadence tells me he's considering not telling me the truth. The lines around his eyes grow deeper with the strain of his admission. *Great.* "But it wasn't about taking anything from you. I just wanted to get to know you."

"Oh, good job convincing me of your hero qualities when you're actually the villain who takes what he wants, when he wants it. I really should have taken you at your word. I'm so naive."

He told me exactly who he was from the beginning. I thought he would be different for me. I thought that I could change him in some fundamental way that would make the bad guy good. I'm a stupid idiot for being that short-sighted and delusional and it took him dismantling something I've wanted forever in such a devastating way to finally see him for what he is.

A liar and a thief.

He rakes a hand through his thick hair and scans the space before his eyes lock on the refrigerator. "I have ice cream. Let's table this discussion and maybe after you've had something to eat, and calmed down, you'll actually listen to me."

I spin on my heel as I button my pants, my eyes narrowing. He has some nerve.

"You think *ice cream* is going to fix this lie of a life I signed up for and make me understand your heartless manipulation? I may be a silly debutante, but even I'm not that stupid."

I grab my phone off the island and shove it roughly into my purse. Seeing the new phone reminds me of every lie he told me about protecting me, about wanting to be better *for me*.

"You promised, Hayes. This wasn't supposed to be a business deal." I hate how my voice breaks, betraying the tears that want to force their way out and down my face.

"This isn't how I meant this to go, Paige! You just have to calm down and listen to reason for a few fucking minutes."

The look on Hayes's face is one I have seen a million times before on Mama's, making me feel like a scolded child. Instead of calming me, his words unlock something in me, an unhinged, feral desire to scream and rage after years of being the calm and obedient little girl.

"Calm down? Listen to reason? How dare you, Hayes!" A foreign growl of frustration rips from my throat as my mind whirls with the insanity of the situation.

Hayes runs his hands through his hair and blows out an exasperated breath.

"I didn't want you to find out this way. This whole situation is getting away from us and I need you to be here in the moment, with me, so I can explain."

His beautiful green eyes are hard when they should be pleading, his words are all wrong from how messed up this is getting, and nothing he has said has convinced me that I shouldn't be as downright angry as I am, so I hold onto it. He will see what his manipulation created in me and have to lie in the bed he's made.

"Your audacity is truly monumental. What you did is unforgivable and saying you can explain is the biggest example of your legendary hubris yet."

A lifetime of making myself small to fit into the mold that was forced on me comes bubbling to the surface. The old hurts of Mama's snide remarks and slights, of never being trusted to make decisions for myself, and the barely held resentment for all of it pushes me past my breaking point. I'm not interested in bending around another person who will tell me to calm down when I have every right to be angry.

"My whole life I've been told to listen to what other people think is best without them ever considering I may have my own desires and plans. You were supposed to be different. I can't believe I thought you were."

I shake my head and pull on the boots that sit by the door.

"I was clearly mistaken. You're just like everyone else, but somehow this hurts a whole lot worse." My voice cracks as my emotions vacillate from anger to unimaginable pain. I reach for that anger again, because I do not want to be sucked into the grief that is already swirling at my ankles, ready to surge and take me down.

"Don't do this, Paige. You're making a mistake if you walk out that door," Hayes says flatly, his face so unreadable. I thought I knew every look he could give me, but I guess I was wrong, again.

I pull open the door and leave the flat, fully expecting him to follow me out, grab me into his strong arms, and maybe even grovel on his knees. Stepping into the hallway feels like I'm entering a new chapter, but I don't know the plot line. Could this be the end? My brain is still mired in anger, but my heart squeezes at the thought.

The door shuts behind me with a thud of finality and silence settles over the hallway. I walk the few halting steps to the elevator, throwing a glance over my shoulder for him while I wait for the car to arrive. I'm utterly alone, and the silence wraps around me, feeding into my insecurities, and forcing me to admit that I really don't know Hayes like I thought I did. My life doesn't feel real.

Of course it doesn't feel real.

I was just caught up in a few days of make-believe and a big, beautiful lie I bought into like the totally naive and stupid girl I am.

I hesitate when the elevator arrives, casting one last look at the flat door as I step into the black-paneled interior. I gently press the button for the garage, my heart still waiting for that movie moment where he bursts out of the apartment to stop me from leaving. My hopes that he might come after me are dashed as the elevator door shuts and begins to descend to the garage without interruption.

"Oh, God." I cover my mouth with my hand to stifle the gut-wrenching sob that doubles me over.

I'm not sure what hurts worse now, the betrayal, or him not fighting for me when it mattered most. But that's the thing, maybe it didn't matter as much to him as getting his coveted business acquisition did. After all, I'm just a part of the game, and I've been played.

I reach the garage and stumble to the Cobra, wishing it were something I could hide in. At least it's dark out and I don't have to risk running into someone I know on the worst night of my life. I start the car and let it idle. Where do I even go now?

I'm in shock and so angry at Daddy for selling my legacy, and Mama for hatching an even worse plan to marry me off for business, so I can't go to their home, no matter how easy it would be to fall under Mama's tightly guiding hand again. I won't subject myself to that again now that I've put some distance between us.

I drive the Cobra through the dark streets of Savannah, quickly numbing from head to toe in the December chill, and eventually end up at my apartment. My cold fingers fumble with the key in the lock of my door, and after dropping my keys a few times, I finally manage to get the door unlocked. It swings open and I look around the familiar space, taking in all of the surfaces and pieces of furniture that Hayes has never seen. It feels so foreign that he never even stepped foot within these walls after being so caught up in his world for mere weeks.

His world. That's right, he only wanted to be a part of mine long enough to destroy it.

Even here, in a place that should have my mark all over it, I just see what someone else wanted. Every piece of furniture, trinket, and piece of decor was influenced by Mama, if not picked outright by her. My heart cracks a bit more. I don't even have a place that feels like my own.

I unzip my boots and toss my bag in the entry, stripping out of the clothes that still smell like Hayes on my way to the bathroom. The sticky mess on my thighs is a reminder that I gave him everything, not just my trust and my heart. He took a piece of me that will never be mine again. Hayes turned my world upside down, forced his way in, and took everything he wanted, all while I thought he would cherish it.

Instead, he stabbed me in the back just when I had fallen for him completely. I may not have known it, but now I see that this is exactly why I was so closed off to anyone getting close all these years. It was far easier to guard my heart when I took everyone at face value and expected the worst of people. The one time I've opened up and let a man get close, and given him the benefit of the doubt, *this* is what happens. *Stupid, stupid, stupid girl.*

I turn the shower to scalding and stare at my vacant expression in the mirror while I wait for steam to fill the bathroom. I don't even know the person staring back at me. She's pale and listless, weak and destroyed. I step into the shower and the hot water burns color into my skin as blood rushes back into my numb fingers, but my brain and heart can't be changed by the welcomed heat. They stay cold and untouched, locked in a devastation of my own making.

When I climb into bed alone, it all hits me. The tears flow down my cheeks into my hair as heavy sobs twist my chest inside out.

My marriage is a sham.

My legacy is gone.

My parents were willing to sell off what mattered most to me, if not just sell me off completely. I don't even have the huge, silent, and comforting mass of Cerberus to cling to as I cry.

Heartbreak is the most soul-crushing feeling I have ever experienced.

And, at the very center of all of it, I miss the man who crushed my bones to dust under his shoes as he climbed the ranks of business on my back.

I hate myself most of all.

Thirty

The Atlanta Haute List

T rouble in Paradise for Billionaire and New Bride

With the wedding bells still faintly echoing, it looks like all may not be well in the marriage of billionaire Hayes Olsen and hotel heiress Paige Fairchild—or should we say *former* hotel heiress. The Xenios Group, the Fairchild family's shining star, is now owned by none other than Olympus International. In a creatively crafted press statement released by Olympus today, it was revealed that the Olsen men have an ambitious new hospitality branch that unites seven recently acquired luxury hotel groups, the Xenios Group the largest of them. This series of lofty acquisitions officially makes the newly created Olympus Hotel Group, a subsidiary of Olympus International, the largest boutique hotel chain in the U.S.

Could Olympus's steamroller move mean Olsen had ulterior motives for marrying the woman set to inherit the largest hotel group the company ruthlessly acquired? Our spidey sense is tingling on this one, and it's only looking more probable as Fairchild has been spotted looking quite miserable out and about in Savannah, sans Olsen. The once media-friendly Southern belle has refused to comment on the situation, or rumors that she's moved out of Olsen's Savannah nightclub property and returned to her own apartment. Maybe she just needed a break from the business-centric ways of her new husband who, sources have said, is keeping himself busy back in Atlanta. These two spending time apart so early in their relationship is troubling. We will keep you updated with the latest, so hit Like and Subscribe for all the Haute gossip.

Continue reading for more of the story...

Thirty-One

Hayes

"**Y**ou really fucked up this time, big brother. Your Savannah exodus and the fact Paige stayed behind is all over the Atlanta Haute List. Whatever you're trying to do here isn't staying under the radar."

I turn toward the annoyingly chipper voice and see Payton standing in the doorway to my office. It's barely nine in the morning and already he's giving me shit. My shoulders bunch into tight knots of tension and rage, and I give him a stare I'm sure he's familiar with by now.

"You've mentioned it. Do you have anything useful to say, or do you just want to fucking waste time that's better spent working on the roll-out plans?" I stand from my desk and take the few strides to face him in the doorway. I'm ready to bodily remove him from my office.

"Why the fuck are you even here?" Payton crosses his arms and returns my hard stare. "You piss and moan about work stuff that doesn't even matter when you have more important things to take care of."

"Unlike you, I actually care about what happens next with phase two, so I'm working." I grip the heavy door of my office and start to push him out when it's stopped by a more solid and imposing force than just one brother.

"Can't you see, he's hiding from his lady problems, Pay."

Fuck, now they're both starting in on me.

"I'm not hiding. I'm busy." I give up on closing the door and let it bang back into the open position as I stalk back to my chair. Payton and Zander crowd into the office after me and make themselves comfortable on the chairs opposite my desk when they should just turn the fuck around and get out of my sight before I throw my laptop at them.

"I'm no relationship expert, but even I know you need to get your ass on a plane to Savannah and win your girl back."

"Really, Zander, it's that simple?" I scoff. "You have a new woman on your arm every week and never do repeats. I think you're the last person I would take advice from and the least qualified to be dishing out any suggestions right now, anyway."

"Which is why you should really listen to this piece of sage advice that makes complete sense."

I roll my eyes at him.

"Paige seems different. *You* were different with her. She may hate your guts for buying out her company, but that doesn't mean she doesn't still love you. Let me tell you, hate fucking is even better than happy fucking, so it's worth your time and effort just to experience that side of a fight at the very least."

Payton holds out his hand to stop Zander. "Slow your roll, little bro. Hayes may have married her on a whim for his own gain, but there's no way he's in love with a girl he's known less than a month." He turns his attention back to me. "Or would you like to correct my assumption that you only married her for access to her daddy's hotels? Was she actually different and changed your view of relationships? Did you fall for her, even when you were focused on buying out the very company she was set to inherit?"

I glare at them both and stay silent. Of course I love Paige. There was very little that could have stopped that from happening after just a few days with her beautiful soul and kindhearted ways, despite my penchant for being the very opposite. A now familiar wave of dread passes through me as I think of Paige. I may have fucked this up, but she fucking left. That was a dagger to the heart of any feelings I could fall into. Now I'm trying to stay removed from any of the desires she kindled in me.

"He doesn't even have to answer. Look at that dorky expression on his face as he thinks about her now. He's head over heels, and he knows he's fucked up big time."

I turn the force of my glare on Zander and wish they would just fucking leave.

"If you care that much about her, I repeat, what the fuck are you doing here? We have everything under control and plenty of teams working on phase two. You're not needed here, but I'm sure there's a feisty girl who actually needs you right now." Payton tips his head toward the open door.

I am done with their patronizing. They don't understand the situation in the least. I slam my palm down on the desk so hard it shudders. "There's nothing to do about it. She walked out on me."

"Ah, it all makes sense now. His pride is bruised," Zander says in a mock whisper to Payton. "He's never been rejected, even when he deserved it."

Payton leans his chin onto his fist, his elbow propped on his knee. "You could have warned her, you know. Told her about your plans for the future including her hotels. Maybe she would have warmed to the idea, or not left when she found out."

I clench my fist until my knuckles crack. "Well, I didn't, so stop telling me what I should have done and get the fuck out."

"Why don't you just put her in charge of the eastern contingent of hotels? She's young, but from what I've heard, she was born and bred to run the hotels anyway, so she could be a good fit."

I snap my gaze to Zander, who leans back comfortably in the leather chair.

"Don't you think I've considered that option?" I grind out. "Paige was set to inherit the hotels, not just run them. They would have been hers, rather than a small group she oversaw for someone else. The consolation prize would be a slap in the face to her lost legacy."

"It's better than nothing. Or you could give her an entirely new legacy. You've got plenty of companies under your personal enterprise to have something that would suit her. Time to pony up the big gifts, Hater." His use of the childhood nickname ruffles the feathers he was just smoothing with the potentially plausible idea.

She could rule the Underworld Spirits brand without breaking a sweat. I don't even have to give it a second thought. I pick up my phone and dial legal. It might be an act of desperation, and who knows if she'll accept, but it may just be what she needs after what I did to her.

"Draw up contracts for the transfer of Underworld Spirits. Put it in Paige's name and give her controlling interest, too. Yes, I know that means my share would decrease. No, I don't want any stipulations for how she wants to run the business. It'll be up to her."

"And that is why I'm the CEO. I come up with brilliant ideas. You really should listen to me more," Zander quips to Payton.

"Yeah, Zand, I'll take your advice when I want an STI or a broken bone from an extreme sport." Payton rolls his eyes in an exaggerated way and I almost smile. Almost.

"One fucking time I crash from a skiing accident, and you think it happens every time. I'm all healed up and not pushing the sharp bone ends of a compound fracture out of my arm, thank you for asking."

"You refute the broken bone comment but not the STI? Telling." Payton says.

"I'm clean, so there was no need to even deem it worthy of comment."

"I started the big gesture, so you can both fuck off now." I wave my fingers along with my words and hope they just go. They can continue their bickering elsewhere for all I care. I feel the headache building and just want to make things right with Paige if she'll even let me.

"That's only the beginning, Hayes. Sure, the big gesture is nice and may soothe her hurt feelings over losing the future she was groomed for, but now you gotta figure out how to make right all the shit that likely came with it. Betrayal! Underhanded business dealings! Lies!" He animates his words with jacking off hand gestures.

"Zand is right, and I don't admit that easily, but I will when it's you who's fucked up and need to hear it."

Payton inclines his head my way and I'm back to hating my brothers. I cross my arms over my chest and glare at him. He levels me with his own surly look before he continues.

"You're in luck. We're on the case of returning your balls to Paige because she's the only one who deserves to carry them in her Chanel purse."

I bristle and I'm about to once again demand they get the fuck out when Zander speaks.

"If you want to keep that beautiful wife of yours and avoid the annulment, or worse, the divorce I'm sure her daddy is itching to file—taking half of everything you have—you better take notes." He holds up one finger. "First, you need to admit that what you did was wrong, even if you managed to get the outcome you wanted from the situation. Second, you need to apologize for putting your shit first, instead of her. Third, you need to get on your knees and eat that pussy like it's your favorite ice cream."

"Bravo, Zand. You managed to make what was a half-decent apology vulgar," Payton says as his eyes roll toward the ceiling.

"Listen, I may not do relationships, but even I know an apology is best served with a side of cunnilingus, vulgar or not." Zander brings his hand to his mouth, splitting his fingers into a V and flicking his tongue through the opening.

"You're a fucking idiot," I growl and swat at him across my desk to make him stop.

"You most definitely need to fight to get her to forgive you, but no one said you have to fight fair. Now get your ass out of this office and don't show your stupid face again until you have your bride back." Zander stands and rounds the desk, grabs the laptop out of my protesting hands, and shoves it into my briefcase.

"He has a point. Use whatever means necessary if she's really important to you. Otherwise, you might as well just let her go and move on because you got what you wanted. Either way, you need to ease the fuck up on everyone here and get on with it." Payton comes around the opposite side of the desk, palming my shoulders and forcing me out of my chair before pulling my suit jacket from the hook on the wall and folding it over my arm.

"I can't believe I'm actually listening to you two fools," I grumble, now standing between my two irritatingly stupid, but loyal, brothers.

"I already called the pilot. He's on standby to fly you to Savannah whenever you're ready."

I tilt my head and appraise Payton.

"You were that confident you could convince me that you arranged for the pilot to be on standby?" I cross my arms over my chest and wonder at the ruthless manipulation skills of my brothers. I've seen them in action many times, but I never realized they could work so well on me.

"You were getting on that plane of your own free will or with us throwing you on it, so yeah, I made the arrangements in advance."

"You shifty motherfucker."

"Oh, shut the fuck up and go get your girl already. Jesus, it's like you prefer being here, giving us shit, to fucking your hot wife. If you're that ambivalent about it, I'll take it from here."

My hand is on Zander's throat before I realize I've moved. He's pinned to the door and struggling to breathe, his hands clawing at mine.

"Don't you ever talk about fucking my wife. I don't care if it's a joke, you say one word that even insinuates you're thinking about her that way and I will end you, brother or not." My voice is a low growl of rage and Zander's eyes widen when he takes it in.

"Hayes, let him go."

Payton places his hands on my shoulders, but he doesn't force me away, likely knowing I would smash my elbow into his face if he even tried. I have murderous intent on my mind, and he'd be my next victim.

"He fucking asked for it, but you can't choke out your own brother for a misspoken and crass joke."

I release my hold on Zander and back up a step, fully expecting him to throw a punch and turn this office into the sparring ring of our youth. He rubs his neck and sends me a dark stare that crackles with electricity.

"You get one pass for being in some fucked up head-space over your girl, but if you ever touch me like that again, I'll bust that perfect nose of yours in a way no surgeon will be able to fix." He reaches out and flicks the tip of my nose with his finger. "Boop."

I knock his hand away and lunge for him, but Payton grabs me by the arms and stops me.

"That's enough, you fuckheads. Zander, get out of the fucking way and quit antagonizing him. Hayes, get your ass out of this office and try to salvage what's left of your marriage before it's too late." He shoves me past Zander and hands me my briefcase, physically separating me from going back in to knock out my asshole of a brother.

"I swear to God, if you put half of the aggression you're displaying into fighting for your wife, maybe you wouldn't be in this position." Zander's grumbling is low and fed up, but I hear him loud and clear as I spin on my heel and leave my office.

I crack my neck and shove a hand through my hair as I stalk through the building to the elevator and punch the garage button hard enough to crack it. It kills me that he's fucking right. I should have fought harder for Paige. If I transferred the energy I spent this week being irritated by my brothers to mending my relationship, I wouldn't be in this shitty place. *Unless it's too late and there's no mending what I broke.*

Fuck.

I didn't stop her from walking out on me because it hurt my ego so much that she would even consider it. It fucking hurt watching her walk away, but I couldn't comprehend her not even *wanting* to listen to me. I let her go, thinking she owed me the chance to explain myself. That she owed me the opportunity to explain, which would have been so easy.

It's taken me a few days to realize that maybe Paige was *never* beholden to my right to an explanation, though I owed it to her. It was selfish to expect her to sit quietly and let me validate my actions when every step to that point hurt her in some way. She was justified in her anger whereas I wasn't, and that's a tough pill to swallow when you're used to getting your way and having people bow and scrape to keep you happy.

It's my turn to bow and scrape. I owe that much to her. I owe her everything.

Thirty-Two

The End...?

...It's never the end when the fates are involved. Hayes and Paige's story will continue in The Bourbon Bargain! Continue to read the blurb and chapter one of The Bourbon Bargain, which is now available and free to read in Kindle Unlimited!

Thank you for reading The Bourbon Bride! If you enjoyed this book, I would be grateful if you could leave a review on the platform(s) of your choice. Reviews are so valuable to authors, and each one helps share our stories with others!

Hugs,
Adrian

Acknowledgements

To my readers—thank you for joining me on this incredibly decadent new journey! It's a far cry from drift racing books, but the heart of the story is just as strong. Your messages, comments, feedback, and help have meant the world to me over the many years it's taken me to bring this story to you. I couldn't have done it without your love and support. I can't wait to share more stories with you!

All the love and thanks to the many people who took the time to encourage, beta-read, edit, and provide feedback to help me create this novel. You're all the real MVPs!

Billy—Thank you for being my person, my partner, and the best dog daddy ever. Your support in all my endeavors, big or small, means the world to me, and your love is my everything. I love you, always.

Sharon – Girl, everything is better when you're around! I love our hikes and talks and professional life planning sessions. The reels and memes you send me daily keep me entertained and your support is unmatched. I appreciate your keen eye for proofreading and your love of my projects! Thank you for everything!

Rebecca—I am so thankful for our coffee dates and tea parties that got me back into my writing groove! It's wonderful to have a creative friend like you who inspires me in so many ways. I'm so glad we can share in the highs and lows of writing together!

Jennifer—I am so glad I have you in my life. Your unrestricted help, guidance, and love have meant the world to me as I find myself back in the book world. All the love to you!

Karin—Thank you for taking on this project with me! You let my characters and story shine, cleaning up the debris and making it as perfect as two imperfect people can be. You're the best!

The ladies in my reader group—Y'all are simply the best at motivating, encouraging, and supporting me! I am thankful you stuck with me and made me finish this book. My words and the heroes I create are for you.

Heidi Joy Trethaway—Thanks for your steadfast friendship and wonderful guidance through all things literary over the years. Whether we are talking stories, co-eating our way through Austin, or making friendship bracelets and talking about Taylor Swift, you make my life brighter!

Stephanie Higgins—there is nothing better than having a local bookish friend who is always willing to hang out, talk story structure, and get eyes on a story before anyone else. You are a delight and I am so thankful for you!

About the Author

Adrian R. Hale is an enthusiastic lover of life who embraces big dreams, for herself and in her books. She writes new adult and contemporary romance featuring strong heroes with secret cinnamon roll sides, and dream-chasing heroines, with a little angst, a lot of swoon, and all the steam lovingly sprinkled in.

Adrian loves fast cars, baking sweet treats, hiking through Texas hill country, and is affectionately known as an agent of chaos to those closest to her. A self-professed caffeine addict, she loves a good vanilla oat latte, and will never turn down a tea party, especially in celebration of little milestones. When she's not writing or reading, Adrian can be found cuddling with her five dogs and husband, watching the 2005 Pride & Prejudice, DIY renovating her home near Austin, Texas, or listening to Taylor Swift.

Website: www.adrianrhale.com
Facebook facebook.com/adrianrhaleauthor
FB Group facebook.com/groups/adrianhalereaders/
Instagram: instagram.com/adrianrhale/
TikTok: tiktok.com/@adrianrhale
Goodreads: goodreads.com/adrianrhale

Also by Adrian R. Hale

A Taste of Bliss
Drift Series
Drift Heat
Broken Drift
Southern Gods Series
The Bourbon Bride
The Bourbon Bargain
The Southern Thirst Trap
The Southern Submission